The Recipe Club

To our mothers and fathers, who taught us
how to cook and how to love.

The Recipe Club

A NOVEL ABOUT FOOD AND FRIENDSHIP

ANDREA ISRAEL & NANCY GARFINKEL

Recipes in collaboration with Melissa Clark

HARPER

NEW YORK • LONDON • TORONTO • SYDNEY

HARPER

A hardcover edition of this book was published in 2009 by
HarperCollins Publishers.

HarperCollins books may be purchased for educational, business, or
sales promotional use. For information please write: Special Markets
Department, HarperCollins Publishers, 10 East 53rd Street, New
York, NY 10022.

First published in 2009 by Polhemus Press.

FIRST HARPER PAPERBACK PUBLISHED 2010.

Library of Congress Cataloging-in-Publication Data is available
upon request.

ISBN 978-0-06-199229-2
ISBN 978-0-06-204033-6 (Walmart edition)

10 11 12 13 14   ID/RRD   10 9 8 7 6 5 4 3 2 1

"Each friend represents a world in us,
a world possibly not born until they arrive,
and it is only by this meeting
that a new world is born."

—ANAÏS NIN

...ler Cookies

...p.d butter
...up Grav. Su...
...gg (beaten)
...lla - 1 tbsp.
...cups flower)
...r

5 - 8 min. ...

...n sifted with 1/...

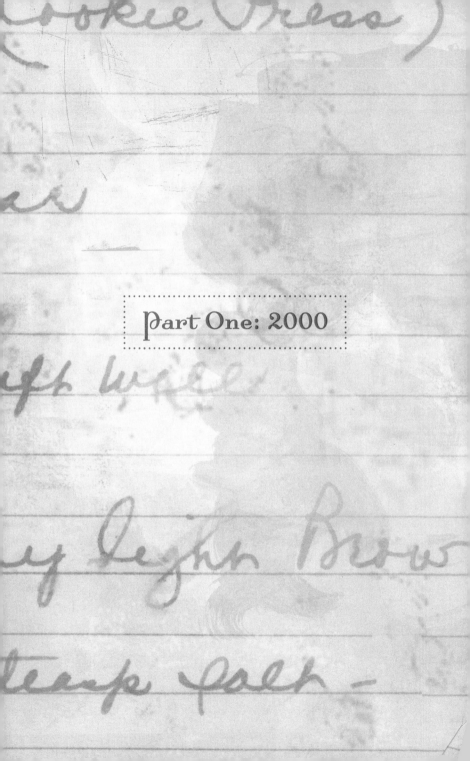

Part One: 2000

...m well
add 1/2 cup...
... 1/2 cup brow...
...pped banana...
...a in 1 tablesp...
...en 1 1/2 cups
...easp salt —

5 min. 10" x 10" p...
cream.

TO: **LSTONE@dotnet.com**
FROM: **VRUDMAN@webworld.com**
DATE: **APRIL 6, 2000**
SUBJECT: **HELLO AGAIN**

Dear Lilly,

I've started a letter just like this about a thousand times. "Dear Lilly," I'd write, as if I knew what came next. But that was as far as I got. I never knew what to say or how to say it. And I wasn't sure you'd ever want to hear my voice again.

But today I know exactly what I have to tell you, and I know you'd want this to come from me. My mother died. Last month, of cancer. Maybe your father already told you; I don't remember what he said at the funeral. It was a hard day. It's been a hard two years. And now that it's over, it feels like walking through a dream—a milky gauze of grief. And relief. And guilt at the relief.

Oh, Lilly. This is not how I hoped to find you again. But maybe it's the only way. Death always makes me want to make sense of things. I want to understand my mother's life. I want to understand my own.

Perhaps this all feels too raw, too real, too intimate. If so, I'm sorry. But I just had to take the chance that you'd still be there for me the way you once were. I can't begin to tell you how much it would mean for us to reconnect. Even after— especially after—all these many years.

Valerie

. . . .

TO: **VRUDMAN**@webworld.com
FROM: **LSTONE**@dotnet.com
DATE: **APRIL 7, 2000**
SUBJECT: **RE: HELLO AGAIN**

Dear Val,

I honestly don't know what to say. . . .

I'm so sorry about your mother. I hope you find some solace in the knowledge that she loved you and was proud of you. I hope you can carry that with you, along with her smile and that wonderful, raucous laugh that always surprised everyone.

Regards to you. And to your family.

Lilly

....

TO: **VRUDMAN**@webworld.com
FROM: **LSTONE**@dotnet.com
DATE: **APRIL 7, 2000**
SUBJECT: **A THOUSAND PARDONS!**

Forgive me for that awful version of a ten-cent drugstore sympathy card and let me start all over: Val, hearing from you has shaken me to the very core. I'm reminded of all we once had and lost. Twenty-six years of silence—and then, at long last, you appear!

When I got your e-mail I cried out loud. There you were, or the essence of you, in your brief words. So very palpable. I mean, Christ! Thanks to cyberspace, you were almost here with me in these beloved mountains.

Oh, nuts. I'm not very good at this. What I'm trying to convey, in a clumsy way, is that I've spent a lot of time and energy (not to mention thousands of bucks on therapy) convincing myself that our fight was just one of life's many painful lessons. People change, they go different ways. Even the best of friends. I told myself, so be it. "Move on . . . ," to quote Sondheim. (The very song I once used to open my act.)

But the truth is, Val, I can't tell you how many times I've whispered to myself, tonight I'll look out into the audience and she'll be there. I can't tell you how many times I've pretended that somehow, you will just turn up. That somehow we will find a way to be friends again. Look, it's all just a long-winded way of saying: yes, Val, I'm still here for you. Honestly, sweetie, you can count on that.

I know when we last spoke, so many moons ago, the problems between us—I mean *all* of us—were insurmountable (at least they seemed that way to me). Which is why I think you'll find it amazing, if not unbelievable, that at long last my father and I are becoming close. I recently moved back home to live with him. It's temporary. And though it's been good for each of us, it's also been, as you might imagine, less than easy. In fact, right now I'm taking a break at the cabin. (Yes, the family still keeps the place, complete with outhouse and NO PHONE! Can you believe it? So, to get my e-mails I have to trek all the way to Lake Placid, almost forty-five minutes from Keene Valley, to an Internet café—which I thank the techno-goddesses for.)

Anyway, at your mother's funeral, you may have noticed my father is a changed man. The infamously *stony* Isaac Stone is much more vulnerable these days. Your mother's death hit him surprisingly hard. It's the first time I've seen him weep. It must have something to do with all the losses he's facing: a recent retirement. Failing eyes. A broken heart—he's unable to let go of my mother, who's no longer with us.

Which brings me back to the real question: why didn't I just reach out to you once I heard about your mother? The truth is, I got scared. I found myself hoping, with all my heart, that you would be the brave one to break our icy silence. And I thank you for that.

I've been a coward. Maybe I just didn't know how to express the simple thing you said: I can't begin to tell you how much it would mean for us to reconnect.

I won't trouble you with the details of my life right now. In summary: deep love, despair, deeper love, deeper despair, and now . . . well, a sort of limbo place thanks to a lover who can't commit and my own confusion about intimacy. I'm trying to figure it all out, even though that's a bit like trying to lasso the moon.

My heart goes out to you. My thoughts are with you, and your family. Despite the sad reason for your e-mail, I am extremely happy to hear from you. (Do you remember what loyal correspondents we were when we were kids?)

Write again, if you have the time and the interest.

Much love,

Lilly

P.S. How is "Golden Boy" . . . Ben? Please send him my love.

....

TO: **LSTONE@dotnet.com**
FROM: **VRUDMAN@webworld.com**
DATE: **APRIL 10, 2000**
SUBJECT: **WHERE SHALL WE BEGIN?**

Dear Lilly,

I'm scattered and unfocused, broken. Losing my mother feels like an amputation. The psychic space within me that she still inhabits—will always inhabit?—has become a phantom pain. Excruciating, agonizing, relentless. And each time I realize she's gone forever—again and again, always as if it's the first time—I feel light-headed and faint. Heartsick, too, as I obsessively count and recount the many years I spent pushing her away. All in a desperate attempt to "become" the person I, in fact, already was.

Strangely enough, all this makes me realize how deeply I've missed you. I hunger for our friendship. Oh God, Lilly, we were so foolish. The only way I can make sense of what happened between us is to believe that perhaps we *needed* that terrible fight. Perhaps we were so fused at the soul as children that we had to separate in order to invent our adult selves.

And perhaps we have both needed these long, dry years to heal the deep wound of rupture?

Whatever the truth may be, I am so sorry for my part in all this, sorrier than I can ever say.

Can you believe how old we are? Oh, Lillypad, let's be friends again! How are you *really*? Please write to me. Tell me everything, and then tell me more. Whatever happens next between us, speaking to you feels like a blessing. Maybe a renewed correspondence would be uplifting for both of us. Do you want to try?

Your devoted friend, forever,

Val

....

TO: **LSTONE@dotnet.com**
FROM: **VRUDMAN@webworld.com**
DATE: **APRIL 10, 2000**
SUBJECT: **WHAT IS WRONG WITH ME?**

Lilly, I'm so ashamed of myself. I just reread your letter and then reread mine, and I realize that in my terrific preoccupation and self-absorption I didn't at all respond to what you wrote about your mother.

What do you mean, she "is no longer with us"? What's going on? I'm filled with dread at the thought of more grief. And I apologize for my selfish letter. Please forgive me.

Val

....

TO: **VRUDMAN**@webworld.com
FROM: **LSTONE**@dotnet.com
DATE: **APRIL 12, 2000**
SUBJECT: **RE: WHAT IS WRONG WITH ME**

No, "Katherine the Great," as you used to call her, didn't pass away . . . she *ran* away! Just one more act in the Stone family's ongoing saga. Even after twenty-six years, I'm sure you can remember our penchant for high drama.

If I sound glib, forgive me. It was just so damn predictable. One morning, about six months ago, my mother left my father after forty-some-odd years of marriage. She just got up from breakfast with the dishes on the table and the kettle about to boil, and walked out the door. Perhaps she'd done one too many productions of *A Doll's House.*

The sad and sorry truth: my mother never should have been married. And my father should have married someone else. She would have been much happier moving from one relationship to another. (Who does that remind you of? Yes, I am truly Katherine the Great's daughter.) And he was always looking for someone to be in awe of him, which she was not. I know I don't have to remind you of the blistering midnight battles that went on in my parents' bedroom, the ones we used to hear through the wall when you slept over.

So, my mother is finally free, living on her own, downtown. I think she's dating. Big surprise . . . what else is new? She doesn't want to talk to any of us, she said. Not until she "finds the Katherine she lost." It's like she's perpetually acting out her adolescence, even now, at seventy-three!

My father spends every day grieving. This whole thing has aged him. Since he's no longer practicing, he spends a lot of time working on his orchids. His eyes always seem to have tears. He says it's the cataracts. I think it's his broken heart.

You know, I tell myself I don't care about them splitting up. At age forty-seven, why should it matter? But at two in the morning last night I felt so very vulnerable and alone that I couldn't sleep. It was as if I was longing for something just out of my reach. And everything reminded me of my mother: her Italian shawl hanging on the back of my chair . . . the poster she did for that Shakespeare festival, on the bedroom wall, with the picture of you in the corner! (Remember how she used your face for Puck?)

The good news: I felt your presence with me and that provided great comfort.

Lilly

. . . .

TO: LSTONE@dotnet.com
FROM: VRUDMAN@webworld.com
DATE: APRIL 15, 2000
SUBJECT: THIS IS SO WEIRD!

Memory is so oddly selective. I can't remember the shape or the fabric of your mother's Italian shawl, but I can absolutely picture its blue-gray-purple-brown color. It always reminded me of firm, dirty plums. And then the frightening, strangely thrilling sound of your parents' screaming fights. (In the rooms of *my* memory, those fights stand out like some ridiculously romantic 18th-century French furniture: perverse, ornate proof that they loved each other with passionate intensity. Something I felt my parents lacked.) And of course I've always thought your mother was unbearably generous for turning me into Puck. That poster was the first thing in my life to give me a vision of my own immortality. It made me feel so pretty and so important.

The truth is, after I gasped in horror about Katherine's quicksilver escape from a kitchen filled with dirty breakfast dishes, I laughed out loud! Is it too soon to admit stuff like that to you? I hope not. You know I've always loved Katherine the Great. I know she was hard for you in lots of ways, but I always envied that your mother seemed more interested in her own life than in yours or anyone else's; I guess it was an instructive counterpoint to my mom's constant, cloistered, *cloying* overinvolvement with me and *everyone* else.

You know, the longer I write the weirder this feels. It's like the last twenty-six years have telescoped into about twenty-six minutes. But look what time has wrought. Our fathers are old and wounded. Our mothers are gone, mine to dust and yours into thin air. And it's just us left standing.

Oh, Lilly. Can we move past the past and stand *together* again?

Do you remember my mother getting into a certain mood, when she'd get that spacey look on her face and intone in a superquiet voice that was scarier than a whisper, "Don't look back, girls. It might look back at you." It always freaked us out. I never knew what it was supposed to mean. Or why she'd say such a thing to us. To me. Especially when I was so young. Now that she's gone, I can't help but wonder: was it a warning?

God, Lilly, everything always comes back to my mother. But I can't start that again, not now.

Please write to me. It would mean so much to hear from you.

Val

....

TO: **LSTONE@dotnet.com**
FROM: **VRUDMAN@webworld.com**
DATE: **APRIL 15, 2000**
SUBJECT: **I FORGOT TO TELL YOU SOMETHING...**

Lilly,

I can't believe I didn't tell you this before.

I've slowly been going through all of Mom's possessions (which has been very painful, but that's another story). Anyway, among her many things I found a gorgeous flowered hatbox—filled with your Recipe Club letters to me!

Remember? They date all the way back to the beginning, when we were about ten years old. They were just as I had left them—a little yellower and crunchier for age, but still organized (even in the infancy of my anal-compulsive style) in chronological order, wrapped neatly in blue and white satin ribbons.

Glancing at the postmarks makes me think that a bunch may have gone AWOL. Perhaps they're in a box I haven't yet uncovered.

I've been reading them, laughing and crying. I realize now that they were truly my first love letters. You, dear Lilly, were the first friend I ever loved, and who loved me back, and whom I continue to love even after all this time apart.

I just had to tell you that I found them. Just like I found you.

xxx

V.

....

JULY 22, 1963

Dear Val,

Guess what? Daddy can drive me to your house. In two weeks! I think he misses your parents as much as I miss you, and that's a lot. But Mommy won't come. She says to tell you sorry. She has a new show.

Don't worry about not knowing anybody yet. You always have me.

I wish I was your sister, too.

Here is the recipe for the chocolate icebox cake you love. You have to leave it in the fridge overnight. It serves ten, unless Ben gets to it, and then it only serves him!

Love,

....

ℛ CHOCOLATE ICEBOX CAKE ℛ

SERVES 10

|||||||||||||||||||||||||||||||||||||||||||||||||||||||||||||||||||||||||||||||||||||||||||||||||||||||||||||||||||||||||||||||||||||||||||||||||||

2 cups heavy cream	35 chocolate wafer cookies
3 tablespoons confectioners' sugar	3 tablespoons semisweet chocolate bits
1 teaspoon vanilla extract	

1. In a large bowl, beat heavy cream, sugar, and vanilla at medium speed until stiff peaks form.

2. On one side of 6 chocolate wafers, spread about 2 heaping teaspoons whipped cream. Place them on top of each other to make a stack. Top the stack with a plain wafer. Continue making stacks like this until all the wafers are used. Turn each stack on its side. Place stacks side by side to make a big log on a plate. Frost log with the remaining whipped cream. Sprinkle with the chocolate bits. Cover and refrigerate at least 5 hours or overnight.

TO: **VRUDMAN**@webworld.com
FROM: **LSTONE**@dotnet.com
DATE: **APRIL 20, 2000**
SUBJECT: **LETTERS AND MOTHERS**

Believe it or not, I have almost all of the Recipe Club letters you wrote to me, too! Mine were tossed into a cardboard box that is now mildewed and falling apart (unlike your neat and tidy system . . . therein lies the difference between you and me, right?!). But the main thing is that we both kept them. And that tells me something important: we were always holding on to our friendship, despite what happened.

It's funny to hear you say such reverential things about my mom, the horrific battles between my parents, etc. I don't think you ever realized how terribly embarrassed I was that they fought the way they did.

I remember one time when you slept over, and they started going at it after an endless night of boozing. You sat up in bed, with your legs hanging over the edge, and said, "Lilly, don't worry." That's it. Just those few words. You came over and kissed my forehead. I remember feeling so loved. And then, the next morning at breakfast, you never said a word about their bizarre behavior. You never made me feel weird. I knew that you understood what went on and you weren't judging any of us for it. You taught me the foundation of trust. Was I there for you that way, too? I fear I wasn't. (After all, I come from the King and Queen of Narcissists. Who's to say that I didn't inherit their talent for self-absorption?)

So, enough about me . . . what do you think about me? (Just kidding. . . .) In truth, a lot has happened to your old friend since our fight. I went on tour with my cabaret act. I had some success, especially in San Francisco. *The Chronicle* said I sang a stellar rendition of Harold Arlen's "Blow Ill Wind." (I will admit, it's a song made for me. Nobody does it better.) I fell in love. (And nobody does that worse.) It lasted for all of three months. Yes, *she* was a singer. (Does the gender thing still bother you? I hope not. I always thought you had trouble understanding my need to love both women and men. Especially in college, when I first fell in love. You were so jealous! Did you feel I was deserting our friendship?)

Fast-forward to the present: I've stopped singing and started catering. Food seems to always be my fallback. As for love, after various meaningless men and women, one day last year I met Bertram. We've been together, off and on, ever since. He restores furniture: hand caning for old chairs. And let me tell you, those hands can work wonders in other ways, too! The thing is, he's married. (I know, I know, what else is new?) Sometimes I think I suffer from a family curse on my mother's side. Always in search of the unobtainable. Always craving something around the corner, just out of sight.

Okay . . . so, life goes on. Let me know how you are. Hang in there.

Lilly

....

NOVEMBER 10, 1963

Dear Lilly,

Wasn't it fun to play Inventor Girls together? Daddy says next time you come we can be his assistants again. He's even going to buy us each our own white lab coat, so we won't have to share. But after you left, his Rewarming Coffee Cup set off sparks. Then all the lights went out, and not just in our apartment. My mother got so nervous she had to take a nap.

My father said it was nothing to worry about. He said you learn from all your mistakes. But all Mommy cares about is for him to invent a quiet garbage truck. He promises he will. And it will let her sleep well and make us rich.

What do you like better, banana splits or brownie sundaes? (You spell it with an "e," not like "Sunday," did you know that?) I like brownie sundaes. Ben taught me how to make them. They're not that easy, but not that hard.

Tell me if you like it.

Love,

Val Pal

....

❧ BEN'S BROWNIE SUNDAE ☙

MAKES ABOUT 16 BROWNIES

|||||||||||||||||||||||||||||||||||||||||||||||||||||||||||||||||||||||||||||||||||||||||||||||||||||||||||||||

2 (1-ounce) squares unsweetened chocolate

1 stick butter or margarine, plus additional for greasing pan

1 cup sugar

2 eggs

½ cup flour

1 teaspoon vanilla extract

½ teaspoon salt

Vanilla ice cream, for serving

Chocolate sauce, for serving

Whipped cream, for serving

Maraschino cherries, for serving

1. Preheat the oven to 375° F. Grease an 8-inch square baking pan.

2. Melt chocolate on the top of a double boiler. Remove from heat when melted and set aside. While chocolate is melting, cream together the butter and sugar until light and fluffy (it takes a long time to do it by hand, or you can use an electric mixer). Add 2 well-beaten eggs to the creamed mixture, then add the flour, vanilla, and salt. Slowly add the melted chocolate, and stir until fully mixed.

3. Fill the prepared pan with the batter and bake for 25 minutes. Cool and cut into squares.

4. Place a cooled brownie in a bowl. Top with ice cream, chocolate sauce, and whipped cream—and don't forget to put a cherry on top!

Dear Val,

Do you want to start a real Recipe Club? We could trade recipes in every letter.

I think your mom's right. If your father could invent a quiet garbage truck, then you really would be rich. Oh, and know what? I forgot to tell you we just got one of those new telephones with the buttons instead of the dial. Too bad your father didn't invent that!

That's all for now. My fingers hurt from the pencil. (Maybe your father can invent a pencil that writes its own letters!)

Love,

Lillypad

P.S. *My mother has a friend from Paris. He made this fancy meatloaf, which he called a "patay." I guess his English isn't so good.*

....

⚤ JACQUES' FANCY MEATLOAF ⚤

SERVES 6

1½	pounds ground beef	1	teaspoon dried thyme
1	cup breadcrumbs	1	teaspoon salt
3	eggs		Ground black pepper
3	tablespoons milk		
1	celery stalk, finely chopped	**FOR THE GLAZE:**	
1	garlic clove, finely chopped	3	tablespoons ketchup
1	medium onion, finely chopped	2	tablespoons Dijon mustard
		1	teaspoon Worcestershire sauce

1. Preheat the oven to 350°F. Then lightly grease a 9 x 5 x 3-inch loaf pan.

2. In a bowl, mix the meatloaf ingredients together until well combined. Press the mixture evenly into the prepared loaf pan. Bake until cooked through, 45 to 55 minutes.

3. Meanwhile, whisk together the ketchup, mustard, and Worcestershire sauce. Generously brush the top of the baked meatloaf with the glaze. Bake for 5 minutes more. Let cool slightly before slicing and serving.

NOVEMBER 19, 1963

Dear Lilly,

YES!! I would like to join the Recipe Club! And I can definitely sleep over next week. But not on a school night.

It's my turn for the Recipe Club, right? So this is Mommy's Macaroni and Cheese. The one she made last time you were here.

XXXX

Valerie

....

⊘ MOMMY'S MACARONI & CHEESE ⊗

SERVES 4 TO 6

FOR THE BREADCRUMBS:

2 to 3 slices white bread (airy, not dense), crusts removed

2 tablespoons unsalted butter

FOR THE MACARONI:

3 tablespoons unsalted butter

1 (8-ounce) package elbow macaroni

½ pound American cheese, cubed

¼ cup milk

½ teaspoon salt

¼ teaspoon ground black pepper

---

1. To make the breadcrumbs, rub the bread vigorously between your palms until coarse crumbs form. The crumbs will be unevenly shaped.

2. Melt the butter in a medium pan over medium-high heat. Add the crumbs and cook, stirring, until the crumbs are

coated with butter but not browned (the butter keeps the crumbs from burning, browns them nicely, and makes a great crunch). Transfer the crumbs to a bowl.

3. To make the macaroni, preheat the oven to 375° F. Grease a 1½-quart casserole dish with 1 tablespoon butter.

4. In a pot of boiling water, cook the macaroni according to the package directions. Drain and return to the pot.

5. Place the cheese, milk, remaining 2 tablespoons butter, salt, and pepper in the top of a double boiler or bowl set over a pot of boiling water. Cook, covered, until the cheese is melted, 3 to 5 minutes. Simmer the mixture uncovered, stirring, until smooth, about 1 minute more.

6. Add the cheese to the pot of cooked macaroni and stir to coat. Transfer the macaroni to the prepared casserole. Top with the breadcrumbs. Bake 15 to 20 minutes, until the top is golden-brown.

TO: LSTONE@dotnet.com
FROM: VRUDMAN@webworld.com
DATE: APRIL 23, 2000
SUBJECT: LIFE CERTAINLY DOES GO ON

I hope I'm not overstepping boundaries here; I just can't help but worry that Bertram is married. Relationships like that usually seem to end in a lot of agony. So I guess what I'm saying is, since it sounds like you've been down that road before, be careful.

By the way, just for the record, I was not *jealous* when you fell in love with that girl in college—I just never liked her!

What was her name again? Lakmi? Om? Tree? Branch? Oh yeah, Cloud. In any event, I will never forget how she once helped me—and hurt you.

But what did make me jealous was the way you lived your life. You always knew exactly what you wanted, and went after whatever it was. You breezed so easily past all cultural norms, as if they simply didn't matter, while all I ever wanted (and hardly ever found) was a feeling of fitting in, of belonging. (Which I guess goes a long way toward explaining the way in which I've lived *my* life.)

Let me tell you a little about it. My life, I mean.

After all that hemming and hawing, I decided to go to med school. But it was on my own terms. Instead of becoming a psychiatrist, as your father always expected, I did a double-whammy M.D./Ph.D. (sounds like me, huh?), and landed in pediatrics with a specialty in genetics. I do a satisfying combination of research and clinical work. This has definitely been the right choice for me.

Now Jeff and I are in practice together in Boston. We've been at it for about ten years. It was a big decision for us, and one that only occasionally threatens to disrupt our marital equilibrium. (Oh yeah, we got married! Right before I started med school. It was such a tiny wedding I almost forgot to go myself. We had it at my parents' house so that my mother could be there. All the Jacobses—Jeff's sister Ellen even more than Jeff—were sad I didn't change my name to theirs, but I couldn't bring myself to do it. I guess I'm a Rudman all the way to the end.) Anyway, the work partnership was a good move, and we're both pretty happy. More on all this another time. By the way, Jeff sends his best.

Lilly, being back in touch with you lifts my spirits tremendously. Let's keep talking.

Love,

Val

....

TO: **LSTONE**@dotnet.com
FROM: **VRUDMAN**@webworld.com
DATE: **APRIL 23, 2000**
SUBJECT: **I CAN'T STOP!**

It's about two seconds after I sent the last e-mail, but I guess I'm still not done talking to you!

"Was I there for you that way, too?" How can you even ask such a thing, Lillypad? Of course you were! I can still picture you breezing into the darkened living room during one of my mother's "episodes." She'd be resting (okay, make that weeping) on the sofa. And you'd trill, "Rise and shine, Kitty Cat," and open the blinds to let in some light. And like a good child, she'd always do what you told her to do: get up, straighten her hair, even laugh at your jokes. You brought life into her life. I was always so proud of you (if also terribly jealous of your magic touch). When she was miserable like that I always felt helpless and terrified. I realize now how angry I was, too, but let's not even go there.

In short, Lilly, my dearest friend, *you* taught *me* how to trust. And how to be proud of myself. And how to love without shame.

Yours forever,

Valerie

P.S. I am so thrilled that you also kept our letters!

P.P.S. The Recipe Club founder *should* be catering! You were always at your most creative behind a stove. As for your singing career, well . . . even if you've given it up, you're still getting top billing in *my* memory. (Remember that afternoon when I was in the bathroom and you stood outside the closed door, singing "Blow Ill Wind" at the top of your lungs?!!)

....

TO: **VRUDMAN@webworld.com**
FROM: **LSTONE@dotnet.net**
DATE: **APRIL 24, 2000**
SUBJECT: **FYI**

Want to know something funny? Cloud's real name was Jane Smith.

Pediatrics AND genetics . . . wow. How typically ambitious. How *very* Val. And how perfect to be doing genetics—you who always felt like an alien! Maybe one day we can trace your Martian roots. Do you provide counseling for expectant parents? These days, I think a lot about biological connections . . . nurture vs. nature . . . because of what I'm going through: I'm trying to adopt. It's a subject that haunts my daily life . . . and my dreams.

I've just started the process. My God, is it daunting! Val, you are the ONLY PERSON I've told. Bertram isn't in my life enough for me to share this with him. My father would never approve. My mother—well, even if we were in touch right now, I wouldn't say anything. (Can you imagine

Katherine the Great having to deal with being called "Grandma"?) I guess the truth is, I don't want anyone else to know. I just don't need other people's opinions. Maybe I'm also a little superstitious that it will all fall through.

I'm sharing this secret with you to celebrate our renewed friendship—testing the waters of trust, I guess. Needless to say, I'm counting on you to keep it to yourself.

Lilly

P.S. "The Recipe Club founder *should* be catering!"??? Ouch. I know you meant well, but you still have this way of sounding like you're taking my father's side against me. I could just imagine his condescending words coming out of your mouth: "Lilly, dear, it's much better that you have a steady job where you earn money. And you are *fairly* good at cooking. This performance thing is a pipe dream, don't you think?"

And then there's your other little comment: "You were always at your most creative behind a stove." Excuse me? I always thought I was at my "most creative" behind a *microphone*, not a stove.

God, it's hard for me to admit right now, when I'm in the middle of trying to live in peace with him, but my father's always been so horribly discouraging. Do you know he *never once* came to hear me perform?

I guess I haven't really made this clear, Val, but my decision *not* to sing has been very difficult. Every goddamn day I feel like I've lost a part of myself, all to win his affection. I guess it's true what they say about children of analysts: they end up the most fucked-up.

Anyway, it's all ancient history now. Water under that proverbial bridge.

....

TO: **LSTONE@dotnet.com**
FROM: **VRUDMAN@webworld.com**
DATE: **APRIL 26, 2000**
SUBJECT: **APOLOGIES...**

Lilly,

I'm so sorry! I feel awfully insensitive. I *never* meant to hurt your feelings, and I *certainly* never meant to sound like your father. Stupid me—I was just happy to hear that you were still cooking.

Let me assure you, Lilly, I am *not* taking your father's side against you. In fact, other than getting your e-mail address from him at the funeral, Isaac and I haven't spoken a word to each other in 26 years. Surely he's told you that.

You know, you call what happened with you and Isaac ancient history, but in fact it's *living* history. I know from my own experience that the past never really dies.

In fact, I had a strange experience at my mother's funeral that I wasn't going to mention for fear it would ignite old embers of anger and resentment. But now I feel I need to tell you: the second I saw Isaac—just standing there, stooped, thin, hands clasped on top of his cane, an old man by any account—I found myself falling into the black hole of my fight with you.

A better person than I would have been filled with

compassion for him. But instead I just continue to blame him for what happened. I've never forgiven him for the way he manipulated both of us, like the little puppets we were. I still hold him entirely responsible.

Looks like the water under that proverbial bridge is rising.

V.

....

TO: **LSTONE@dotnet.com**
FROM: **VRUDMAN@webworld.com**
DATE: **APRIL 26, 2000**
SUBJECT: **ME AGAIN . . .**

But on a positive note . . . think about it, Lilly, if you *are* still cooking, you *must* still be singing.

I know this because when you taught me to make spinach soufflé, you convinced me (literal dope that I was), that in order to clean spinach correctly, you HAD to sing "I'm Gonna Wash That Man Right Outta My Hair." When you taught me to make crème brûlée, you made me swear that before my first bite—even if it was in a restaurant, even if I was dining with strangers—I would sing "Brown Sugar" and make Mick Jagger lips. (Jeff made me stop ordering it in public—it was getting too embarrassing.) And remember the first dinner party we threw? By the time you were done with your solo rendition of "Food, Glorious Food," the soup was cold and all the guests were politely starving.

The list goes on and on. And now it's just the way life is— there's a song I sing for every meal I make. And with each one, I hear your impossibly high and pure Lilly voice singing right alongside mine.

Kisses,

Valerie

. . . .

TO: **VRUDMAN@webworld.com**
FROM: **LSTONE@dotnet.net**
DATE: **APRIL 27, 2000**
SUBJECT: **THANKS, BUT . . .**

I'd appreciate the kind words a lot more if they weren't sugarcoating the thing you said that was *less* than kind: "I still hold him entirely responsible."

Val, how can you nurse a grudge against my father, especially considering everything he did for you?

Look, I know I'm high-strung and a bit of a diva, but there's something I need to get off my 36 DD chest—the one you've always wished you had.

It's this: I've spent the better part of my life wild with envy that you somehow pulled off the caper of the century, getting Isaac—the cheapest man in the world—to be . . . what should I say? Not just your teacher, but your patron, giving you gifts and paying for your education. Come to think of it, he was a bit of a sugar daddy to you. And not enough of a daddy to me. But I guess we both know that already. . . .

At the risk of being dangerously blunt, *you're* the one at fault for what happened between us, not him. So Val, please don't rewrite history. And be forewarned: berating *him* won't help you bond with *me*.

Okay, enough. I'm fried. Time for a cup of ginger tea and some deep breathing. Maybe a hike up Noonmark. More later.

Lilly

. . . .

TO: **LSTONE@dotnet.com**
FROM: **VRUDMAN@webworld.com**
DATE: **APRIL 30, 2000**
SUBJECT: **RE: THANKS, BUT . . .**

I'm not sure if you want me to respond, or if that was just your way of blowing off steam, but I need to let you know kindness is not a one-way street.

Look, old wounds leave scars. So I get it, okay? I know Isaac was not the father you wished he'd been.

But Lilly, please, Isaac was not my "sugar daddy." (Ugh . . . that's a disgusting image. Shame on you.) You of all people should know that throughout my childhood he was my hero. My mentor. For years I did anything and everything he told me to do, because his love made me feel deserving, his attention made me feel special, and his expertise made me feel optimistic about my future. He opened up the world for me. He connected me to a universe of ideas—one that was exciting and inspiring—and, most important, well outside of my family's crazy, insular life.

And yet, even with all this generosity—of every kind—I *am* still angry at him. Whether or not you believe me, he *is* the reason we lost each other.

I believe we both know *that* already, too.

Valerie

....

TO: **VRUDMAN@webworld.com**
FROM: **LSTONE@dotnet.net**
DATE: **MAY 1, 2000**
SUBJECT: **ONE GIRL'S CEILING IS ANOTHER GIRL'S FLOOR**

That wonderful world he opened up for you had a "No Trespassing" sign for me. I never felt welcome. It was like the two of you lived in a weird, secret bubble together.

I've never understood it. Never have . . . never will.

Lilly

....

TO: **LSTONE@dotnet.com**
FROM: **VRUDMAN@webworld.com**
DATE: **MAY 2, 2000**
SUBJECT: **MAYBE THIS WILL HELP**

Look, Lilly, it's not surprising you don't understand. How could you? There was so much secrecy going on in my family, and Isaac played a huge role in it.

So maybe now's the time I got something off *my* chest. Maybe now's the time we finally talk about some of the things I was never allowed to say—to you, to anyone. I warn you, it's a long story—but I hope by telling it I can help you better understand your father, and clear up some fundamental *mis*understandings.

My mother had her first panic attack while she was in her twenties, just after she and Dad were married. She had a small part in an off-Broadway play (the one where she and your mother met and became friends). Apparently, just before her cue, she flipped out. (Until the day she died, she referred to her anxiety disorder as "stage fright.")

But she really started going nuts when I was five. That's when her sister and her sister's husband—Ben's parents—were killed in a car crash. (Bear with me, Lilly. I realize you know some of this, but honestly I'm uncertain about which details are old news for you. So here's the whole story.)

Shortly after the accident, Mom spiraled down into a constant state of anxiety, one that grew to define her. All I vaguely remember from those early days was that one day my mother was fun to be with, and the next she was crying and crying and crying, and had to stay home . . . *for the rest of her life.*

Enter Isaac. I don't remember the exact moment when he began regularly spending time with us. All I know is that before long he was circling like a moon orbits a planet. He had an unusually calming effect on my mother. Not that he was more caring than my ever-gentle father, but he had something . . . hard to describe. When I used to come home from school and find him there sipping tea with my mother, I always felt she was truly peaceful. Best of all, he took charge of her illness. For a long time it seemed your father held the magic key to my mother's mental health.

And yet, every day, as soon as he left, her anxiety erupted. She hid in her bed, she wept, she could barely communicate.

Then one day, when I was sixteen years old, I couldn't take it anymore. I don't know if you ever picked up on it, but I was terribly depressed. (I never really shared the worst of what was happening with anyone, not even with you.) I hated my mother with all my soul for not getting better, and hated myself for being so unforgiving.

Your father saw what was going on, and took me aside. He said I needed to understand the root of my mother's illness. He said something painful and terrible had happened to her, and if I understood it, I would be less angry and love her more. (I also think he wanted me to leave her alone, to stop provoking her with hostile questions about why she was the way she was.)

He made me swear I would never tell anyone what he was about to reveal: my mother had been driving the car in the accident that killed my aunt and uncle. He told me only my father knew, but it was best if I never discussed it with him or anyone else.

It was a heavy burden for me to carry. But the result of it was that Isaac and I became complicit in keeping my mother's secret. He promised he would always be there for me, and always help me through tough times.

Where did all this leave me? Totally emotionally dependent on Isaac. And because I felt so tethered to him, I never allowed myself to ask an obvious question: *why was he so involved with my family?*

Only now, after my mother's death, am I allowing myself to

wonder what really happened. Did my parents seek his help? Did your mother prevail upon him to take pity on her old friend? Did Isaac intervene on his own out of concern for my mother's psychiatric condition?

Or was it—as I fear—altogether more predatory on his part? Did he enjoy my—and her—dependency?

Was she a guinea pig—endless grist for the mill of his scholarly articles and books? (I mean, really, why didn't anybody put two and two together after he published *The Fear Impulse*? Wasn't she his Dora?)

Or maybe there was a mercenary aspect to the whole thing—you can't deny he profited from those shrink-circuit lectures on phobia that made his reputation and fattened his pocketbook.

Or how about this: maybe your "stony Dr. Isaac Stone" was, simply, in love with my mother.

Whatever the truth, only recently have I come to see the bigger picture: my mother was severely depressed and agoraphobic. She was never treated properly by Isaac or anyone else. And here's the worst part: *despite Isaac's promises that one day she would recover, he knew she never would.*

So do I blame him? Yes. Am I angry? Yes. Do I have a right? Yes.

And for God's sake, Lilly, look what he did to you and me! He surely gets the blame for that, too.

I don't mean to burden you with all of this. In fact, quite the opposite. I'm hoping this will lighten your load.

Valerie

....

TO: **VRUDMAN@webworld.com**
FROM: **LSTONE@dotnet.com**
DATE: **MAY 4, 2000**
SUBJECT: **YOUR EGO'S RUN AMUCK**

That's quite a little tale you've spun. And I'm sure it gives you great comfort. But if you want to lighten my load, don't dump your dirty laundry on me.

My father "in love" with your mother? Come on, get a grip!

This is unbearable . . . it's as if we're stuck right back where we were, twenty-six years ago! I don't want to go there.

But I can't stop myself.

Forgive me if I'm not being sympathetic in your time of bereavement, but you need to face facts: my father did not use or abuse your mother in any way. She was a sick woman who needed help and he was kind enough to give it to her. Instead of making my father your scapegoat, try examining your *own* father's shortcomings: he was weak and incompetent, and hid behind his so-called inventions to avoid caring for your mother. No wonder you needed someone like my father in your life. (Isn't it interesting that you barely mentioned your father in that whole long story?)

Val, for every half-baked theory you've come up with, I've got one that's well-done. So chew on this: your pining mother, "Kitty Cat," was really more of a prowling *tomcat*. In fact, if she hadn't been so needy, so clingy to my father, maybe my parents would have held on to each other a little better. (Not *all* of their marital problems can be blamed on my mother's good looks and passionate nature.)

Honestly, Val, you'd better start facing reality and stop casting blame. All of this might be hard for you to accept, but it's a lesson you should have learned long before medical school: physician, heal thyself.

Lilly

....

TO: **LSTONE@dotnet.com**
FROM: **VRUDMAN@webworld.com**
DATE: **MAY 5, 2000**
SUBJECT: **WHAT IS YOUR PROBLEM?**

Okay, let's see how you work the rules.

It's wrong for *me* to say negative things about my relationship with your father, but it's okay for *you* to call my parents names. (My mother a "prowling tomcat?" My father "weak and incompetent"? Give me a break.)

I'm a bitch to wonder aloud if Isaac had a hidden agenda, but it's okay for *you* to blame my mother, in all the pain of her mental illness, for your parents' absurd and loveless marriage?

You don't want to hear my feelings about your father? Fine, you never will again. But if you're going to tell me what I feel about my *own* father or mother, you'd better get ready to swallow a hefty dose of your own medicine: maybe you're so eager to trash *my* mother because you've always been so mad at *yours*.

She was *never* there for you! Did it ever occur to you that all your bragging about her sexual conquests—and yours—is more about feeling unworthy and unloved than it is about being a chip off the old seductress? (By the way, your mother's magic to captivate may be more the stuff of legend than of fact. Sure, she slept around a lot and let everyone know about it. But does that make her Mata Hari? Hardly. Maybe more like Monica Lewinsky.)

While we're at it, did you ever notice that you spent half our childhood being mean to me and the other half trying to win back my affection? Did you ever think that maybe, just maybe, it was payback for your jealousy of your father's friendship with me? Did you ever think about how many times you hurt *me* because you were mad at *him*?

You make me so mad, Lilly. Talk about rewriting history! Talk about creating a delusional melodrama! Talk about using my dead mother—who's barely cold in her grave!!!—as a pawn to advance a rapprochement with parents who are incapable of loving you! You're the needy one, Lilly, not me! Try understanding yourself.

Valerie

....

TO: **VRUDMAN**@webworld.com
FROM: **LSTONE**@dotnet.com
DATE: **MAY 15, 2000**
SUBJECT: **RE: WHAT IS YOUR PROBLEM?**

I've been thinking a lot since your last e-mail, and this is my conclusion: we still don't trust each other. We still don't understand each other. We still don't feel secure together. We've lost our core foundation. We're nowhere.

Lilly

TO: **LSTONE@dotnet.com**
FROM: **VRUDMAN@webworld.com**
DATE: **MAY 20, 2000**
SUBJECT: **HERE'S WHAT IT'S LIKE FOR ME**

Understand this: my mother is dead.

I breathe in the perfume that lingers on her clothing, trying to let sense memory take me deeper. I try on her dresses, flooring myself with my freakish resemblance to her—one that could have me believe she's still walking the earth and Kennedy is still president. In abject wonderment, I will myself to feel what she felt when she wore this red wool crepe sheath. To know what she saw in the mirror when she topped off the fur-trimmed burgundy coat with this matching fur-trimmed hat. To imagine—*impossibly, impossibly,* I know—just where she danced in these vampy, open-toed, way-too-high heels.

I pore over her photos and memorabilia, trying to see through her eyes the life behind the posed smiles. Snapshot, 1943: my mother and her sister, strolling up the Grand Concourse, both young, happy, and alive. Snapshot, 1951: our mothers, at Jones Beach, arm in arm, beautiful and laughing; our fathers, strong and tanned, their faces a blur.

I plead with her small handful of papers to reveal more than they say, crushed that there isn't more ink to give shape to her history. Her diary, July 11, 1953: "It's over. But never over. Not ever." *What's over?* It's her first entry in more than a year. What did she mean? Her handwriting is small, cramped, feminine, and neat. Just like her. She was pregnant with me, then, somewhere in her eighth month.

And when I finally rouse myself from the futility of all this, everything seems painfully clear. You and I have a choice: trust each other again, or go our separate ways.

Do you remember my mother telling us, "You can fool the human eye but you can't fool the eye in the sky"? I don't know why that comes to mind at this moment. But it does.

Lilly, it's hard to say this, but I don't have what it takes right now to go through more drama with you. I wanted to reach out, and part of me is thrilled to have reconnected, but getting back on track is more demanding than I can bear. I need a break from trying to understand you and us, when I'm so lost in trying to understand her and me.

You're right, you and I have lost our core foundation. I think we have to call it quits. This time, forever. We're just no good together. It hurts too much.

But know this: despite that we are painfully mismatched, always at odds, and eternally driving each other mad, our friendship has made me who I am. Crazy girl, you stir my blood like the sister I never had.

Yours always, even in silence,

Valerie

....

Part Two: 1964–1973

Dear Silly,

Guess what? I won the school-wide chess tournament! Thanks to your dad, I even beat the best sixth graders! My prize is a big book of puzzles. They're fun. To celebrate, I made this yummy pie.

Ben asked if he could join the Recipe Club, but I said no, it's just you and me. He said he thinks it's stupid to have a two-person club, but that didn't stop him from eating the pie!

Hey, did you even know your dad has been teaching me chess? We play when he comes here to visit my mom. Maybe he can teach you too. I'll ask him. It's more fun than checkers. But not as pretty as Chinese checkers because you don't use colored marbles.

Love,

Valerie

....

ℛ CHESS PIE ℛ

FOR THE CRUST:

- 1¼ cups all-purpose flour
- ½ teaspoon salt
- 10 tablespoons unsalted butter, chilled and cubed
- 3 to 5 tablespoons ice water

FOR THE FILLING:

- ½ cup unsalted butter
- ¾ cup light brown sugar
- 2 eggs
- ¼ cup heavy cream
- 1 tablespoon lemon juice
- 1 teaspoon lemon zest
- 1 teaspoon vanilla extract
- ¾ cup raisins
- ¼ cup chopped pecans

1. To make the crust, combine the flour and salt in a bowl. Cut in the butter until the mixture forms coarse crumbs. Sprinkle cold water over the butter, 1 tablespoon at a time, mixing gently between additions until the pie crust just comes together. Wrap in plastic, flatten into a disc, and chill for 1 hour.

2. Preheat the oven to 375°F. On a lightly floured surface, roll out the crust to a 13-inch round. Transfer to a 9-inch pie plate. Trim off any excess and crimp the edges. Chill for 30 minutes.

3. Prick the shell all over with a fork. Line the shell with foil and fill with pie weights. Bake for 15 minutes. Reduce the heat to 325°F, and remove the foil and weights. Continue baking until pale golden, about 10 minutes more. Transfer the pie shell to a wire rack to cool. Adjust the oven temperature to 375°F.

4. To make the filling, beat the butter and sugar together until light and fluffy. Add the eggs, 1 at a time, until fully incorporated. Beat in the cream, lemon juice and zest, and the vanilla. Beat until smooth. Fold in the raisins and chopped nuts.

> 5. Bake for 15 minutes. Reduce the heat to 325°F, and continue baking until lightly set (it should not jiggle when moved), 20 to 25 minutes more.

Dear Val,

I can't wait for you to come here for my birthday. My mother said we can go to the theater with her to see Fiddler on the Roof. *That means we'd stay up past our bedtime so you have to ask your mother first if that's okay. Okay?*

Here's a recipe for spicy chicken and rice. Mom's new friend Jorge says it comes from his mother, who still lives where he grew up in Mexico. Hot! Hot! Hot! You need lots of water when you eat this one.

Love,

....

ℛ SPICY CHICKEN & RICE ℛ

SERVES 4 TO 6

6 garlic cloves, finely chopped

1 tablespoon white vinegar

2 teaspoons salt

½ teaspoon dried oregano

½ teaspoon ground black pepper

3½ pounds bone-in, skin-on chicken thighs

1 tablespoon extra-virgin olive oil

1 medium onion, finely chopped

1 green bell pepper, cored and finely chopped

½ teaspoon red pepper flakes

6 tablespoons fresh chopped cilantro

1 (8-ounce) can tomato sauce

2 cups chicken stock

3 cups long-grain or medium-grain rice

1 cup pimento-stuffed green olives, halved

1 tablespoon capers

---

1. Preheat the oven to 350°F. In a large bowl combine the garlic, the vinegar, 1 teaspoon salt, the oregano, and black pepper. Add the chicken pieces and toss to combine. Cover and let marinate briefly while you sauté the vegetables.

2. In a large Dutch oven, over medium-high heat, warm the oil. Add the onion, bell pepper, and red pepper flakes and cook, stirring, until softened, 7 to 10 minutes. Stir in 1/4 cup cilantro and transfer the vegetables to a plate.

3. Reduce the heat to medium and add the chicken pieces in a flat layer (cook the chicken in batches, if necessary). Cook, turning once, until the chicken is slightly opaque, but not browned, 3 to 4 minutes per side. Combine all of the chicken, the vegetables, tomato sauce, stock, and the remaining 1 teaspoon salt. Cover and simmer for 20 minutes.

4. Stir in the rice, olives, and capers. Cover and transfer the pot to the oven. Cook, stirring once every 10 minutes, and adding additional water 1/4 cup at a time if the rice looks dry, until the rice is tender and the chicken is cooked through, about 30 minutes.

> 5. Transfer the meat and chicken to a platter. Sprinkle with the remaining 2 tablespoons cilantro, and serve.

AUGUST 2, 1964

Dear Val,

How's camp?

Guess what? I got purple bell-bottoms and an orange midriff shirt from my mother's new friend Angelo. Also, a beaded headband that looks really cool! Do you want to get the same pants so we can wear them out together?

This summer my father said I have to be tutored in math. I asked if he'd tutor me, like he helps you. But he said no because the stuff you do with him is advanced, and he can't spend time on stuff I should already have learned on my own in school. Why is he always so hard on me? It's not my fault I have stupid teachers. Anyway, he hired Mrs. Conklin. She's okay. She gave me this muffin recipe. We practice multiplication, division, and fractions by doubling and tripling recipes. This one is so good it should be quadrupled!

Write soon.

Love,

Lillypad

ℛ MIGHTY MATH MUFFINS ℬ

MAKES 1 DOZEN MUFFINS

|||||||||||||||||||||||||||||||||||||||||||||||||||||||||||||||||||||||||||||||||||||||||||||||||||||||||||||||||||||||||||||||||||||||||||||||||||

What's ¾ cup of sugar times 2? (1½ cups sugar)

What's ½ of ½ cup of butter? (¼ cup butter)

What's ⅙ of a dozen eggs? (2 eggs)

What's ½ of 32 ounces all-purpose flour? (16 ounces or 2 cups all-purpose flour)

If a tablespoon has 3 teaspoons, and you need 2 tablespoons baking powder minus

4 teaspoons, what do you need? (2 teaspoons baking powder)

What's a teaspoon of salt minus ¾? (¼ teaspoon salt)

What's ¼ teaspoon of lemon zest times 4? (1 teaspoon lemon zest)

What's ¼ of 16 ounces of milk? (½ cup milk)

How many cups of chopped cranberries do you need if you need 16 ounces? (2 cups frozen cranberries, chopped)

1. Preheat the oven to 350°F. Grease a 12-cup muffin tin.

2. In a bowl, cream the sugar and butter. Add the eggs, one at a time; beat after each addition.

3. In another bowl, sift together the dry ingredients and lemon zest. Add alternately with the milk to the creamed sugar mixture. Stir in the chopped cranberries.

4. Spoon the batter into the greased muffin tin, filling each cup ¾ full. Bake until golden and a toothpick inserted in the center of a muffin comes out clean, 25 to 30 minutes.

AUGUST 15, 1964

Dear Lillypad,

Do you want to come to camp with me next summer? You would love it and we could be in the same bunk, which would be like we shared a room. Maybe we can beg our parents harder to let you come next year.

I wish you could be here with me, and feel everything I do. After you get over the homesick part (which goes away after like a week), it's so great. The pine trees make the air smell delicious. Even though the lake is freezing, it makes your skin tingly and happy. You're outside all day long, and there's no waiting for elevators, and no food smell in the hallways of other people's cooking, and no feeling of being in jail when your front door closes behind you. And my mother isn't always asking me where I was, and worrying all the time.

The only time I feel a little weird is after dinner before the sun goes down. There's just something about the color of the sky or the way it gets a little chilly all of a sudden that makes me want to cry. But not from being sad, just from wanting something so much it almost hurts, but not knowing what that is. It's like being lonely, even if there are people around.

Anyway, do you think you could come next summer? We DEFINITELY *didn't beg hard enough this year, 'cause you're not here!*

Love ya,

Val Pal

P.S. *Mara, my counselor, taught us to say "Love ya." It's what the cool teenagers say. Also, when I come home I could help you with math if you want. It's really easy once you know how.*

P.P.S. *When we were on the sleepout we cooked Welsh Rabbit, which isn't really made with rabbit. I think the word "rabbit" means "cheese" in Welsh.*

....

ᘒ WELSH "RABBIT" ᘓ

SERVES 4

1¼ cups aged cheddar cheese, cubed

1 tablespoon unsalted butter

Pinch salt

¼ teaspoon mustard powder

¾ teaspoon Worcestershire sauce

Small pinch cayenne

1 egg yolk

¼ to ½ cup milk

4 slices bread, toasted

1. In the top of a double boiler or a bowl set over boiling water, combine the cheese, butter, salt, mustard powder, Worcestershire sauce, and cayenne. Cook, stirring constantly, until the cheese melts, about 5 minutes. Add the egg yolk and cook, stirring until thickened, about 1 minute more.

2. Gradually stir in the milk, adding just enough to reach the desired consistency. Serve at once, spooned on top of toasted bread.

OCTOBER 22, 1964

Dear Val,

I'm sorry your mother said no to you coming down for the night. When I asked why you couldn't be here for trick-or-treating, my father didn't answer. At first I thought your mother said no because she doesn't like me, even though I know she does. My father said it has nothing to do with me, that your mother sometimes gets a little scared of letting you go places. He said to mind my own business. But isn't it my business if we want to see each other? Sometimes grown-ups are so weird.

I'm going as an Eskimo. So the recipe I'm sending makes four meringue-covered igloos. And they're orange for Halloween. You should make this too and then we can pretend we're together.

Will you visit soon? Will our parents let us be best friends anymore? If they don't we can run away from home. That will show them.

I send you Eskimo kisses!

Love,

Lỹly

....

✺ BAKED ORANGE ALASKA ✺

SERVES 4

||||||||||||||||||||||||||||||||||||||||||||||||||||||||||||||||||||||||||||||||||||||||||||||||||||||||||||||||||||||||||||

		FOR THE MERINGUE:
4	navel oranges	2 large egg whites
1	cup vanilla ice cream	Pinch cream of tartar
1	cup orange sherbet	¼ cup sugar

1. Slice off the top quarter of each orange. Slice off the bottom of each orange, cutting just enough to stabilize the orange. Using a spoon, scoop out the pulp from inside each orange and save, if desired, for another use.

2. Filling the oranges vertically, scoop 1/2 cup vanilla ice cream into one side of the shell and 1/2 cup sherbet into the

other half. Transfer the orange shells to the freezer and chill at least 6 hours or overnight.

3. Just before serving, prepare the meringue. Start by preheating the broiler and adjusting an oven rack 4 inches from the heat. In an electric mixer, beat the egg whites until frothy. Add the cream of tartar and beat until slightly firm. Slowly mix in the sugar and beat until the meringue forms stiff, glossy peaks.

4. Top each orange with a dollop of meringue, making sure that all edges of the ice cream and sherbet are covered. Transfer the oranges to a baking sheet. Broil, watching carefully, until the meringue is just golden, 30 seconds to 1 minute.

1965

AUGUST 3, 1965

Dear Lilly,

Last week was Visiting Day. Daddy came up to visit me by himself. Mom couldn't come because she got sick again, but she cooked a lot of food including her famous roasted chicken. Daddy invented me a birthday present, which are swim goggles with windshield wipers! They're great to wipe off algae. I showed them to the girls in my bunk, and everyone wanted to try them out. It makes me realize how amazing my dad is. He is a true Inventor and Scientist. I bet one day he will do something to save the world.

Can I tell you a secret? I really miss my mother. I was so happy to leave and go to camp, to get away from her, but now I really miss her. I didn't even tell this to my father, because I didn't want him to feel bad, and also I was afraid it might make me cry and I really didn't want to end Visiting Day by crying. So I acted like I didn't care.

But all the other kids—I mean EVERYONE, *even the Junior Counselors—had their mothers there. So no matter how many letters she writes to me, and how bad my father said she felt, I still don't really understand why she couldn't come up to see me. Daddy explained that she needed to rest, but isn't that all she ever does? How tired can she really be?*

At least I am not alone in feeling bad. This year a lot of the kids are homesick. Lots more than last year. I am not sure why, but I think it's because some of the girls are acting "older," and others are still acting like last year. Some of the "older" type girls are even wearing bras. Do you? I never wanted one before but now I feel like I should have it, even though I don't need it. At all. And probably never will.

I always thought things would get better and easier when I got older, but maybe I'm wrong.

WRITE TO ME, *I mean it. That one postcard does NOT count.*

Love and xxxx's,

Val Pal

....

⟨ KITTY'S ROASTED CHICKEN ⟩

SERVES 4

||||||||||||||||||||||||||||||||||||||||||||||||||||||||||||||||||||||||||||||||||||||||||||||||||||||||||||||||||||||||||||||

1 (4½ pound) chicken, rinsed and patted dry	½ teaspoon paprika
1 tablespoon olive oil	Ground black pepper
1½ teaspoons salt	

1. Preheat the oven to 375°F.

2. Rub the chicken inside and out with the oil, salt, paprika, and pepper.

3. Transfer the chicken to a roasting pan and roast, basting every 20 minutes, until the meat is cooked through and the juices run clear when pricked with a fork, about 1½ hours. Let rest 10 minutes before carving.

Dear Lilly,

Um . . . hello? Yesterday was my birthday, remember? Now I'm 12 like you, so you can't say you're older than me anymore! I feel bad that you didn't send me birthday treats like you usually do, but at least you sent another postcard. It was pretty, too.

Did you forget it was my birthday? You must be busy doing stuff up in the Adirondacks, I guess. I hope you're having fun. Is the lake super cold? Do you still hang around with those kids in town?

My mother wrote to me that she spoke to your dad and that you're having fun, so I know you aren't dead. Are you mad at me for something? I don't know what I did. But I feel BAD that you didn't write one real letter to me this whole summer, and I don't know what I did to make you do that. TELL ME, ok? Whatever I did, I'm sorry!!!

I come home in three days. Do you want to come for a sleepover? And then we start Junior High!!!!!! I can't wait.

Love, your best friend still (I hope!),

Valerie

P.S. Our camp cook makes delicious fish sticks every Friday night. He gave me the recipe. The only problem—it was for 300 servings! But don't worry, here's where my excellent long division skills come to the rescue. This feeds four.

. . . .

⚔ FRIDAY NIGHT FISH STICKS ⚔

SERVES 4

¼	cup canola oil	½	cup all-purpose flour
1	pound flounder fillets, cut into 1 x 4-inch strips	2	eggs, whisked with 2 tablespoons water
	Salt	2	tablespoons chopped parsley, optional
	Ground black pepper		
1	cup breadcrumbs		

1. Heat the oil in a medium skillet over medium-high heat until it sizzles lightly when sprinkled with water.

2. Meanwhile, prepare the fish: season with salt and pepper. Place the breadcrumbs, flour, and eggs in separate shallow bowls. Season the breadcrumbs with a large pinch of salt, some pepper, and parsley, if using. Dip the fish strips into the flour, and tap off any excess. Next, dip the fish strips in egg, and let the excess drip back into the bowl. Coat the fish completely with breadcrumbs.

3. Fry the fish in batches, adding additional oil, if necessary, until golden-brown on both sides. Transfer to a paper-towel-lined plate to drain. Serve hot.

SEPTEMBER 3, 1965

Dear Val,

I guess I should say sorry for not writing this summer. After your sixth letter I got guilty and that only made it harder to write back. I don't want you to hate me or anything. But sometimes it feels like you want everything to stay the same all the time. My mother says your mother is that way, too.

The thing is, a lot changed for me over this summer. I met an older boy named Jim. He's 14 and a half. He was staying at a cabin near us. I liked him sort of. He had a minibike. He also smoked but his parents didn't know. We kissed once. French-kissed. The thing is, I like Jim's brother who is a year younger. He is cuter. But he didn't even know I was alive until he dared me to do something. I can't tell you what it was because I promised I never would, except maybe I will when I see you in person. Or you can guess. It has to do with how far you go with a boy.

My father is away on his latest book tour. He went off the other morning without saying much, except he left a note for my mother with a quote by Freud about betrayal. Do you know who Freud is? My father says he's a brilliant doctor who invented psychiatry. My mother says Freud is my father's word for God. All I know is whenever my parents fight, that man's name comes up. It happened this morning. The way they get so mad all the time you would think they were going to get divorced. But they never do. After the fights they go into their bedroom and stay there forever.

The thing is, I get a little scared that one day it's gonna end really bad. Like they might get divorced or something. There's a girl I know from school whose parents got divorced and now she has to travel around from apartment to apartment every week and she never knows where her headbands are. She always seems worried and her hair hardly ever looks good. I don't want to be that girl.

To tell you the truth, I'm getting sick of my parents. Everything is always about them. Where am I in this family?

It would be so great to have a brother or sister—someone I could be with and talk to during their stupid fights.

Actually, you're the only person I can tell this to. That's kind of why I'm writing.

Peace,

Lillian

P.S. *You don't have to worry all the time about the best friend stuff with us because we're getting too old for that, don't you think?*

P.P.S. *Do any of your camp friends smoke? Or, like you, are their noses stuck in their books all the time? I tried menthol cigarettes. My friend Stephana is showing me how to do smoke rings.* DON'T TELL ANYONE!!!

P.P.P.S. *My mother's new friend Berk (he's from Turkey) made dinner for us last night. You can't smoke these, but they're delicious!*

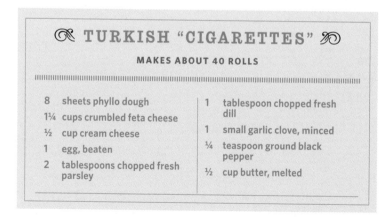

❧ TURKISH "CIGARETTES" ☙

MAKES ABOUT 40 ROLLS

8 sheets phyllo dough	1 tablespoon chopped fresh dill
1¼ cups crumbled feta cheese	1 small garlic clove, minced
½ cup cream cheese	¼ teaspoon ground black pepper
1 egg, beaten	½ cup butter, melted
2 tablespoons chopped fresh parsley	

1. Preheat the oven to 375°F. Grease a baking sheet. Arrange the phyllo on a separate baking sheet, and cover with a slightly damp towel to prevent it from drying out.

2. In a bowl, combine the feta, cream cheese, egg, parsley, dill, garlic, and black pepper; mash with a fork.

3. Lay one sheet of phyllo on a clean, flat surface. Brush the sheet with some melted butter. With the tip of a sharp knife, slice the phyllo crosswise into 5 (about 3 x 10-inch) strips. Place 1½ teaspoons of filling at one end of each strip and roll up each strip completely, sealing with additional butter if necessary. Repeat with the remaining phyllo sheets.

4. Transfer the rolls to the prepared baking sheet. Brush with additional butter and bake until brown and flaky, 15 to 18 minutes.

Note: If desired, the rolls can be frozen in an airtight container for up to a month. Transfer directly to a baking sheet, and bake according to recipe instructions.

SEPTEMBER 10, 1965

Dear Lilly,

It's not that I want things to always stay the same. I just don't want them to go away. I mean, obviously things change. Like now we're in new schools, and we have things like homeroom and different kids in every class. And I really like that, so it's not like I mind change in general.

But there is one change I don't like, and that's when your friends start acting cold just to seem cool. Your last letter gave me the feeling that you sort of want to be friends, but

*you sort of don't. So it's hard to figure out what's really
going on. Do you want to be friends with me? Or is
something the matter?*

*I can't imagine you not in my life, so I feel a little scared and
worried. But I am not mad at you, because my mother says
we're at the age where "emotions run high."*

*Oh, yeah—she also says that even old people can have best
friends. So you're just wrong about that.*

Valerie

*P.S. I don't think you need to worry about your parents
getting a divorce. A couple of weeks ago your father visited
my mother for an afternoon tea. When my father came home
that night I heard my mother say, "Isaac needs Katherine
like a drinker needs his martini." It sounds so romantic,
doesn't it?*

*P.P.S. Also, I promise I won't tell about the smoking. But did
you know that scientists have proven a link between cigarette
smoking and bad diseases? I would never smoke. Not even
to be cool to boys. Or even to you. And I am* BEGGING *you to
do the same.*

*P.P.P.S. No recipe this time. I just want to prove to you that
things don't always have to stay the same.*

. . . .

OCTOBER 28, 1965

Dear Val,

I'm sorry I've been too busy to see you because I was doing stuff with Stephana. You know what? She decided she wants to hang out with the girls in the Upper School. She won't even sleep over now at my house. Anyway, who cares about her, right? You and me always have each other. Do you want to have a sleepover with me?

Stephana and I had so much in common, but she didn't always know me the way you do. So maybe it's a good thing she's not my friend anymore. And maybe it's not a good idea to get too dependent on other people.

My mother says you should think of yourself as a hummingbird sipping nectar from each person and moving on . . . my father says "bonds of attachment are fundamentally flawed when re-created past infancy." I copied that from the jacket of one of his books. I'm not sure what any of it really means, but I do know they are having a truce right now so they were able to talk to me about me for a whole five minutes.

Guess what? I am writing a play for school about a boy hooked on drugs. It's called I'm Not Hooked. *The problem is, I don't know so much about it so I have to make a lot up. There is a kid named Danny who was supposed to have smoked grass and I was going to cast him as the lead but he asked Stephana out on a date. So forget him.*

I've been listening to a lot of music. I've been playing A Taste of Honey *over and over. At least it inspired me to make this honey cake. Tell your cousin Ben Gold this one's for him. (I'm calling him Golden Boy from now on.)*

I don't have anyone else to talk to now, so I'm glad you're around.

Lilly

....

ᘉ GOLDEN HONEY CAKE ᘉ

MAKES 1 (9-INCH) CAKE OR 1 LOAF

|||||||||||||||||||||||||||||||||||||||||||||||||||||||||||||||||||||||||||||||||||||||||||||||||||||||||||||||||||||||||||||||||||||||||||

1 cup honey	½ teaspoon baking soda
½ cup vegetable oil	¼ teaspoon ground allspice
½ cup warm, strong-brewed black tea	Grated zest of 1 orange
2 tablespoons brandy	Pinch salt
2 cups all-purpose flour	1 cup dark brown sugar
2 teaspoons baking powder	2 eggs
1 teaspoon ground cinnamon	½ cup slivered almonds, tossed lightly in 1 tablespoon flour

1. Preheat the oven to 350°F. Grease a 9-inch round cake pan or a 9 x 5 x 3-inch loaf pan and line with parchment.

2. In a large bowl combine the honey, oil, tea, and brandy. In a separate bowl, whisk together the flour, baking powder, cinnamon, baking soda, allspice, orange zest, and salt.

3. Using an electric mixer, cream the brown sugar and eggs until light and fluffy. Add the wet ingredients and mix to combine. Slowly beat in the dry ingredients. Fold in the almonds by hand.

4. Pour the batter into the prepared pan. Bake until light golden on top and a toothpick inserted in the center comes out clean, 50 to 60 minutes for the large cake, and about 5 minutes for the loaf.

NOVEMBER 9, 1965

Dear Val,

I am writing to you by candlelight. The whole city is having a blackout. What about the Bronx? Is it completely dark there, too?

My mother had to walk home from work. She met a nice man who went with her the whole way, even though he doesn't live around here. She says New York is more fun like this.

My father isn't back yet. We think maybe he got stuck in the subway if he was at your house this afternoon with your mother. We can't call because the phone lines are jammed.

Yesterday Dad said your mother still isn't feeling so good and that's why he goes to visit so much. He told us she doesn't leave your apartment! Is that true? Why? And why didn't you ever tell me this?

Love,

Lilly

. . . .

1966

Happy New Year again, Lillypad!

I had SUCH *a great time last night! We all did. It was like my mother came to life! She was* SO *funny the way she imitated Ethel Merman, wasn't she????!!!! I never saw her so happy, did you? We were all* SO *happy that your family came over.*

Do you think Ben has a crush on you? The two of you were all whispery and giggly when we were making ice cream sodas. It would be so perfect if you got married, because that would make us all related.

Isn't it weird that you and I never talk about getting married? Is that something you want one day? I don't think I'll ever find anybody who likes me enough to marry me. Or who's tall enough. Unless, of course, he likes flat-chested beanpoles with glasses.

But if I looked different—if I were different—I would definitely want to be married. I'd want a really little wedding but a gigantic cake. I would want to wear flowers in my hair instead of a veil. And my father AND *mother would walk me down the aisle. And the aisle would not be in our living room. And you would be my maid of honor. And my husband and I would live in the country but not too far from the city. We would have two children, a girl and a boy.* AND *we would also adopt two other older children who nobody else but us wants. And you would visit all the time. And we would all live happily ever after. The end.*

I was gonna call you up to say all this, but it really is more fun to write a letter, you know what I mean? Your father always tells me that I have to write things down to "harness their power." Does he tell you that too? He's giving me a lot of stuff to read.

Like he gave me a book by this guy named Theodore Roethke, who said, "All finite things reveal infinitude." Isaac and I talked about it a long time, and we both agree that means there's always hope, even when things seem stuck in their own limitations. And then he gave me this other book of poetry by Emily Dickinson, who wrote, "Surgeons must be very careful/When they take the knife!/Underneath their fine incisions/Stirs the Culprit—Life!" Isaac and I both like that poem because it's like a mix of art and science.

Lillypad, I LUV you!!! Let's spend every New Year's Eve together forever, okay?

HAPPY 1966!!! The year we're going to become teenagers!! YAY!!

Oh—I almost forgot. The recipe for the Recipe Club, in honor of last night: Confetti Spaghetti.

Val

....

ℛ CONFETTI SPAGHETTI ℬ

SERVES 6 TO 8

||||||||||||||||||||||||||||||||||||||||||||||||||||||||||||||||||||||||||||||||||||||||||||||||||||||||||||||||||||||||||||||||||||||||

1	pound spaghetti, broken into 1½-inch pieces	1	cup heavy cream
2	tablespoons olive oil	½	cup pitted black olives, thinly sliced
1	medium yellow onion, finely chopped	¼	cup pimento, thinly sliced
1	large garlic clove, finely chopped	¼	pound ham, thinly sliced
2	large carrots, peeled and grated	¾	teaspoon salt
1	medium zucchini, trimmed and grated		Black pepper
			Grated Parmesan, for serving

1. Cook the pasta according to the package directions. Drain and set aside.

2. Heat the oil in a large saucepan over medium heat. Add the onion and garlic and cook until fragrant, about 1 minute. Add the carrots and zucchini and cook, stirring occasionally until softened, about 5 minutes.

3. Stir in the cream, olives, pimento, ham, salt, and pepper. Cook until just heated through. Sprinkle with the Parmesan and serve.

JANUARY 5, 1966

Dear Val,

Gross! Ben does not have a crush on me. And we weren't whispering and giggling the way you said.

And I'll never have a wedding. Double gross!! I am never gonna get married. The reason you and I don't talk about it is that I don't believe in it. Neither does my mother, who said to tell you that women who get married are just "chattel" (whatever that means). And that she's "one of the last generations to be sucked in by the male-dominated culture" (whatever that means). And that marriage is an "antiquated institution." (Even I know what that means—if you get married and you get old, you wind up institutionalized. Triple gross.) And she warned me that if I am foolish enough to marry somebody, I'd better be ready to follow her lead and "unchain myself from the shackles of convention" (Val, do you have any idea what that means?).

Then, my mother gave me a copy of a book called The Second Sex, *by Simone de Beauvoir. I got through part of the first chapter, but there were no sex scenes. So I stopped reading it. Borrrrrring! You can have it if you want.*

Anyway, here's the most important reason I couldn't marry Ben: he's not my type. I like guys who are built. He's so skinny. And let's not even discuss the way he dresses. He needs a girl who's brainier than me. Someone serious and not so concerned with her looks. Hey—that's you! QUADRUPLE GROSS!!!!

Love,

Dear Val,

Like I told you on the phone, I wasn't laughing at you when you said you wanted to take me to the planetarium. But I want to make sure you believe me.

What really happened was that Maggie and I just got kind of goofy, the way you can be with new friends. She's the kind of person who doesn't like museums so much—she's more interested in music and stuff. But you're my smart friend, okay?

The truth is, you need lots of different kinds of friends, Val. My mom has taught me that, too. When I think about it, I realize my friends are like planets, circling around me. Each one is different, but I am always the sun. (Obviously, I don't need a trip to the planetarium to know a thing or two!)

Oh, by the way, my father reminded me I never said a "proper" thanks for the book on galaxies you gave me for Christmas. I bet he told you to get that, didn't he? He won't quit nagging about my reading. Anyway, thanks. I didn't read it, but I like that the orange planet on the cover goes good with my shag rug.

Seriously, Val, I liked it. Most of all because it came from you.

My mother's company is doing a bunch of Russian plays in sign language. She made this recipe for the cast party. Have you ever eaten duck? It's different . . . it's like exotic chicken. The meat is dark and the skin gets really crisp in the oven.

Love,

Lilly

....

⟊ WILD DUCK WITH ⟊
CHERRY ORCHARD SAUCE

SERVES 4 TO 6

FOR THE DUCK:

1 (5-pound) whole duck, rinsed and patted dry

½ garlic clove

Salt

Ground black pepper

1 onion, cut into chunks

½ lemon, cut into chunks

4 thyme sprigs

FOR THE CHERRY SAUCE:

¼ cup unsalted butter

2 small onions, sliced

1 large garlic clove, finely chopped

2 cups dry red wine

Freshly squeezed juice of 1 orange

¼ cup honey

4 cups fresh or frozen pitted cherries

¾ teaspoon salt

½ teaspoon ground black pepper

1. Preheat the oven to 500° F.

2. Rub the duck all over with the garlic. Season the duck inside and out with salt and pepper. Stuff the cavity of the duck with the onion, lemon, and thyme.

3. Transfer the duck to a roasting pan and roast for 10 minutes. Reduce the heat to 350° and continue roasting until the skin is crisp and the juices run clear when pierced with a knife, about 2 hours.

4. Meanwhile, prepare the sauce: melt the butter in a medium saucepan over medium-high heat. Add the onions and garlic and cook for 7 minutes. Add the wine, orange juice, and honey. Bring the mixture to a boil, then simmer until the sauce has reduced to 1 cup (it should coat the back of a spoon). Stir in the cherries, salt, and pepper, and cook until warmed through, about 5 minutes more. Cover and keep warm over very low heat until ready to serve.

5. Remove the duck from the oven and let rest 10 minutes before carving. Serve with the cherry sauce.

Dear Lilly,

I am so humiliated. The last thing I wanted to do was cry in front of you and all your friends. But I wasn't crying for the reason you all think. It had nothing to do with playing spin the bottle. It was because Maggie (who is the type of fake person who acts like she's nice, but she's really not) started embarrassing me in front of everybody. So what if I've never kissed a boy before? Am I supposed to start lying to the whole world about everything?

THAT's *what made me cry, not the stupid game. Is everybody still talking about what an idiot I am?*

And just for your information, I like music too. And not just classical either, although I do like it the best (especially Madame Butterfly*) and I don't care if you think it's boring. Maybe I'm not as cool as Maggie, but still.*

Sometimes I feel like you and I don't have much in common anymore. But here's a recipe anyway. For the sake of the Recipe Club. It's complicated. I hope you mess it up.

Valerie

. . . .

ℛ OPERA CAKE ℛ

1 (10-INCH) CAKE SERVES 12 TO 16

FOR THE CAKE:

Butter or shortening for greasing pan

6 egg whites

2 tablespoons granulated sugar

2¼ cups confectioners' sugar

2 cups blanched ground almonds

6 eggs

½ cup all-purpose flour

3 tablespoons unsalted butter, melted and cooled

FOR THE MOCHA BUTTERCREAM:

1¼ cups whole milk

1 teaspoon vanilla extract

¼ teaspoon salt

2 large egg yolks

¼ cup plus 2 tablespoons granulated sugar

¼ cup all-purpose flour

3 tablespoons unsalted butter, softened

1 tablespoon instant espresso powder, dissolved in ½ teaspoon boiling water

FOR THE CHOCOLATE GANACHE:

1½ cups heavy cream

12 ounces bittersweet chocolate, chopped into small pieces

FOR THE COFFEE SYRUP:

½ cup water

⅓ cup granulated sugar

1½ tablespoons instant espresso powder

2 tablespoons cognac or brandy, optional

1. To make the cake, preheat the oven to 425° F and arrange two oven racks in the center of the oven. Grease two 12 x 15-inch jelly-roll pans and line with parchment.

2. Using an electric mixer, beat the egg whites in a large bowl until they form soft peaks. Add the granulated sugar and beat until the whites form stiff, glossy peaks.

3. In a separate bowl, beat together the confectioners' sugar, almonds, and eggs until light and fluffy, 2 to 3 minutes. Fold in the flour. Fold in the whipped egg whites in several additions. Drizzle the melted butter into the mixture and fold until just combined.

4. Divide the batter between the prepared baking sheets. Use a spatula to smooth the batter into even layers. Bake the cakes until light golden and springy to the touch, 5 to 7 minutes.

5. Immediately turn the cakes out onto floured surfaces. Peel away the parchment, then turn the parchment over and use the ungreased side to cover the cakes until completely cool.

6. Meanwhile, make the buttercream: In a medium saucepan, bring 1 cup of milk, vanilla, and salt to a boil; remove from the heat.

7. In a separate bowl, whisk together the egg yolks and sugar. Whisk in the flour and the remaining ¼ cup milk. Whisking constantly, slowly add the hot milk to the yolks. Return the mixture to the saucepan and bring to a boil, whisking constantly. Simmer, whisking until thickened, about 2 minutes more.

8. Transfer the custard to a bowl and place plastic wrap directly on the surface. Let cool until lukewarm, then stir in the butter and espresso. Chill.

9. To make the ganache: bring the cream to a boil. Place the chocolate in a bowl. Pour the hot cream over the chocolate and let sit for 2 minutes. Whisk until the mixture is fully combined. Let cool at room temperature. (The ganache should thicken, but should not become firm. If the ganache hardens, reheat gently in a double boiler.)

10. To make the coffee syrup: combine ½ cup water, the sugar, the espresso powder, and (optional) cognac in a small saucepan over medium-high heat. Bring to a boil and cook until the sugar dissolves completely, about 5 minutes. Let syrup cool.

11. To assemble the cake: line a baking sheet with parchment. Cut each cake into one 10 x 15-inch piece and one 5 x 15-inch piece.

> 12. Transfer one 10 x 15-inch layer to the sheet pan. Brush this layer generously with coffee syrup, and spread the mocha buttercream evenly over it.
>
> 13. Place the two 5 x 15-inch cake layers side by side on top of the first layer, and brush them with syrup. Spread half of the ganache over them.
>
> 14. Top with the remaining cake layer, and brush with additional coffee syrup. Pour the remaining ganache over the top of the cake, using a spatula to spread it evenly over the sides.
>
> 15. Chill until set. The cake will keep, refrigerated, for up to 2 days.

FEBRUARY 16, 1966

Dear Lilly,

What do you mean you went to third base with Jerome? Where did you do it? Were you scared? Is he your friend or your boyfriend?

I don't know, Lilly, I just don't know who you are when you're with these guys. Do you feel different? Are you different? Are you the same Lilly I know, or do you start acting like a whole other person?

Maybe that's what's wrong with me. I can only be one thing: Val. I'm the same with everyone. I can't meet a boy and just talk about nothing. When I went to the debate society meeting, I dared myself to talk to this boy who is in some of my classes. At first he seemed interested. I asked the usual questions to find out who he is, what he likes. But then he didn't ask me anything back so I got nervous and started talking too much—this time about snow and crystal formation. He looked like he was about to go into a coma.

You're the type they like, I'm not.

HERE'S YOU: *telling funny stories and making boys laugh—or laughing at their jokes even when they aren't funny. Standing with one hand on your hip, tossing your hair off your shoulder . . . doing all the stuff they think a girl should do.*

HERE'S ME: *invisible. Standing with my hands stick-straight at my side, wishing I had your confidence, wishing I knew how to flirt like you. Wishing I knew how to act like a girl.*

Then I wonder, how come everybody wants a boyfriend so badly and I really don't care? I'd rather read. Or spend time with a real friend, like you.

Do you think a boyfriend could also be a friend?

The reason I ask is there's a boy in my music theory class who I'm becoming friends with. Marcus. He plays the trumpet, and listens to jazz records. He's also a really good cook (and not that many boys know how to cook). He's really nice. He is shorter than me, and has dark, curly hair and is very quiet and serious. He's scared he will need braces, and if he does he might not be able to play trumpet. He's really good at sight-reading music, but bad at music history. And yesterday, he lent me a record AND gave me a recipe! Here it is.

Love,

Val

. . . .

☙ JAZZY JELLY ROLLS WITH ❧ HOMEMADE RASPBERRY JAM

MAKES 8 TO 10 SERVINGS

5 eggs

⅔ cup plus 5 tablespoons granulated sugar

1½ teaspoons vanilla extract

1¼ cups cake flour, plus additional for dusting

Pinch salt

¼ cup unsalted butter, melted

¾ cup raspberry jam

Confectioners' sugar, for dusting

1. Preheat the oven to 350° F. Grease a 10 x 15-inch jelly-roll pan. Line the pan with parchment paper.

2. In the top of a double boiler or bowl set over a pot of simmering water, whisk together the eggs, ⅔ cup granulated sugar, and vanilla until warm to the touch, but not hot. Transfer the mixture to a bowl and beat on high with an electric mixer until the batter forms thick "ribbons," about 10 minutes.

3. Sift together the flour, the remaining 5 tablespoons granulated sugar, and salt. Fold the dry ingredients into the batter in three additions. In a separate bowl, fold 1½ cups of the batter into the melted butter to lighten. Fold the butter mixture into the bowl with the remaining batter.

4. Pour the batter into the pan, using a spatula to spread it evenly to all the corners. Bake until the cake is pale golden and just springs back when touched, 8 to 10 minutes.

5. Sift confectioners' sugar over a dish towel. Invert the hot cake onto the towel, and remove the parchment. Spread the cake with jam and roll tightly lengthwise, using the towel as your guide. Cover with the towel and let cool completely. Dust with additional confectioners' sugar before serving.

Dear Val,

My mother and father just had another fight.

We were at the dinner table. He was showing us the galleys of his new book. He looked up and noticed she was wearing a bracelet. He asked where she got it. You could see from the look on his face that he was already hurt. She shrugged and told him it was a gift from the "smashing new choreographer" of her show. No other explanation. As if that was enough. But it wasn't. He got really mad. He said with all her experience, it was probably her teaching him the moves.

I didn't like hearing that. I don't want to know about their business. But it's really hard not to listen when it's right in front of you.

They started screaming. It was like I didn't exist. She threw his book on the floor. He threw the bowl of potatoes against the wall. Splat! Potatoes everywhere. I yelled for my parents to stop and that's when they realized I was still there. I ran into my room and slammed the door. I wanted to cry but the truth is there's no point crying about something that's never going to change.

An hour later my parents came into my room. They apologized. For two seconds I thought everything was better. But then my mom said she had a great idea. From now on I should call them both by their first names: Katherine instead of Mom, Isaac instead of Dad. My father turned purple in the face. He said that's just wrong. He says children should respect their parents and not talk to them like they're friends. It started all over again. They argued through the night.

This morning my father said if I call him Isaac he won't talk to me. So he's Dad and she's Katherine.

You can call me by my new name: Sad. But at least something came out of this mess—a recipe for "smashing" smashed potatoes. But use a potato masher, not a wall.

Daughter of Katherine

⟪ "SMASHING" SMASHED POTATOES ⟫

SERVES 2

2	teaspoons salt, plus additional, if necessary	5	tablespoons unsalted butter
2	large potatoes, peeled and cubed	¼	cup finely chopped chives
1	cup sour cream		Black pepper, to taste

1. Fill a medium pot with water; add 1 teaspoon salt and the potatoes. Bring to a boil and cook until fork-tender, about 20 minutes. Drain.

2. Using a potato masher or fork, break up the potatoes. Add the remaining 1 teaspoon salt, sour cream, butter, chives, and pepper, and mash to the desired consistency. Taste and adjust the seasoning, if necessary. Serve immediately.

Dear Val,

It's the middle of the night and I can't sleep. I feel like I'm going to explode. There's a secret I need to tell you. But you have to promise it's just between you and me.

Here it is. They are going to break up. I heard my father say it last night when they thought I was asleep. He said she's not a wife to him so he doesn't have to be a husband to her anymore.

What should I do? Where will I go if they leave?

I'm terrified.

P.S. *Call me the minute you get this. Although by then I might already be living in an orphanage.*

....

APRIL 12, 1966

Dear Val,

I'm late for my audition, so no time to write, but I wanted to get this recipe to you. I am trying out for Peas in the Pod, which is a professional children's theater. My mother is friends with the director. My father isn't so thrilled with the idea. He's probably afraid I'm turning into my mother. But they are getting along better now (you were right about that!) so he's not making too much of a stink.

The coolest part: if I get in I will be allowed to leave school early two days a week!

Love,

Lillypad

....

ॐ PEAS OUT OF THE POD ॐ

SERVES 2 TO 4

|||||||||||||||||||||||||||||||||||||||||||||||||||||||||||||||||||||||||||||||||||||||||||||||||||||||||||||||

2   cups fresh or frozen peas
3   tablespoons chicken stock
1 ½ tablespoons unsalted
    butter

2   tablespoons chopped fresh
    mint
½   teaspoon salt
    Ground black pepper

In a saucepan bring the peas, stock, and butter to a simmer. Simmer until the peas are tender, about 5 minutes. Stir in the mint. Season with salt and pepper.

APRIL 30, 1966

Dear Lillypad,

Congratulations! Soon you'll be a star, I'm sure. Good thing I'm saving all your letters, so when you become a famous actress I will have a million of your autographs.

That's it. I really have nothing to say but I was in the mood to talk to you, and stupid Ben's been on the phone ALL NIGHT, *talking to this girl he likes.*

Sometimes this house is too crowded for all of us. Now the kitchen table has turned into my father's workshop. This means we have to eat on folding tables near the couch, which would be great except my mother won't let us have TV *dinners, even though she wants us to pretend we're like the perfect* TV *family. She doesn't seem to get that we're more like the Addams Family than Ozzie and Harriet.*

And poor Ben is stuck having to live with all of us.

Did I tell you my father's building something called a "handheld calculator" for people like you who have trouble in math? He's obsessed. He works through the night, then goes to work early to prepare for his students. He's so tired my mother worries about him all the time. But then she's the one to go take a nap.

I sometimes wonder how he keeps believing in the things he invents when he never really sells them. I hope one day I will be as optimistic as he is.

Love,

Valsky

P.S. *We had Or'Derves (French for appetizers) at my cousin Steven's Bar Mitzvah. My favorite was the Pigs in Blankets, which you can make with Bisquick.*

....

✂ COZY PIGS IN BLANKETS ✂

MAKES ABOUT 3 DOZEN

||||||||||||||||||||||||||||||||||||||||||||||||||||||||||||||||||||||||||||||||||||||||||||||||||||||||||||||||||||||||||||||||||||||||||||||||||||||

2 cups Bisquick baking mix	1 (12-ounce) package all-beef (Kosher) cocktail franks
½ cup cold water	Ketchup or mustard for dipping

1. Preheat the oven to 375° F, and grease a large baking sheet.

2. Stir together the Bisquick and water in a bowl to form a soft dough. Gently smooth the dough into a ball on a floured board. Knead lightly several times.

3. Roll dough out into a 12-inch square. Cut the dough into 1-inch-wide strips and roll a strip around each cocktail frank, sealing the dough together with your fingers. Arrange the pigs in blankets seam side down on the prepared baking sheet.

4. Bake in the upper third of the oven until pale golden, about 15 minutes. Serve hot, with ketchup or mustard for dipping.

SEPTEMBER 28, 1966

Dear Val,

Daddy left us. We woke up this morning and there was a note from him on the table. It was to me, not Katherine.

I don't know what to do. He said he is staying at a hotel and that he will call us.

I know they've been fighting about each other, about my mother's friends, about my father's work. But there's a little voice inside me that says it's my fault, too. I get my father so frustrated because I don't like so many of the things he likes. And at times I think my mother wishes she never had me. I'm in her way.

If I hadn't been born things would be better for both of them.

I'm writing this to you because it's too hard to talk about. I can't tell anyone at school except maybe Maggie, but we aren't talking so much anymore.

Love,

....

Dear Lilly,

I KNOW your dad will come home soon.

And it's not your fault! Not at all!

He loves you more than anything in the world, even if he sometimes IS mad at your mom. Anyway, where would he go? He can't stay in that hotel forever. He was here a long time yesterday afternoon, and even stayed to eat dinner with us, but he's gotta go back home soon, right? So try to be patient and don't worry too much. Even though he acts all Isaac-y, I can tell inside he feels really sad and lonely.

And don't say that about your mother not wanting to have you. You know in your heart that she really loves you, too.

I feel so bad we had to hang up so fast before we finished talking about all this, but like I told you, now we have that new ten-minute telephone rule. Sometimes my father is really cheap. He says it's just because we can't afford big phone bills, but it feels cheap to me. I asked if we were poor, and he said we're middle class. So what's the big deal with talking on the phone?

Now my mother is yelling at me to turn off the light and go to sleep. Not that she cares if I'm tired tomorrow—she's just worried about paying the stupid electric bill. Money is always such a thing around here. I wish we were rich.

If you're worried again, let me know. And even if you're not, I will call you—a hundred million times, ten minutes each time.

Lots of love, from your pal,

Val

....

DECEMBER 23, 1966

Dear Val,

I'm hoping my father will come home for good. He says maybe. When I told Mom (who says I can call her Mom again if I want to) that the whole time he's been away he's been spending lots of time with you and your family, she surprised me by saying he had to be there because your mother counts on it. And he's "addicted to adoration." But she kind of rolled her eyes when she said it, so I don't know if she was being sarcastic. Do all parents speak a different language than the rest of the universe?

When I told her I was kind of mad that you've been seeing him more than me, she said, "Your father is incapable of giving his heart. But don't worry, one day you'll find someone who can." She was trying to make me feel better, but the weird thing is that it made me feel worse.

The carpenter on my mother's show is named Dag. He gave us a recipe for Swedish Crescent Cookies. They are made with nuts, so tell Golden Boy he will love them. You have to roll them carefully in the sugar or they can become too sweet.

I haven't heard from you in a while. Write back.

Love,

⊘ SWEDISH CRESCENT COOKIES ⊘

MAKES ABOUT 3 DOZEN

1 cup unsalted butter (2 sticks), softened	2½ cups all-purpose flour
½ cup confectioners' sugar, plus additional for coating	1¾ cups finely chopped walnuts
1 egg yolk	Butter or shortening for greasing baking sheets

1. In a bowl, beat the butter and ½ cup sugar together until light and fluffy. Beat in the egg yolk. Add the flour and nuts gradually.

2. Form the dough into a ball and flatten into a disc. Cover and chill for 2 hours.

> 3. When you are ready to bake the cookies, preheat the oven to 375° F. Grease baking sheets. Removing about 1 heaping tablespoon of dough at a time, shape the dough into crescent shapes. Arrange about 1½ inches apart on the prepared baking sheets. Bake until the cookies are lightly golden around the edges, 15 to 20 minutes. While still hot, coat the cookies generously with confectioners' sugar. Transfer to a wire rack to cool.

DECEMBER 28, 1966

Dear Lilly,

I'm so glad your dad finally came home!!! Maybe now he won't have to be here so much. No offense. It's just that he was here more than ever, and he kept bossing me around, telling me not to ask my mother questions because they upset her. All I asked was why she never leaves the house, and why she cries all the time. EVERYTHING *makes her cry lately.*

I can't help it, I want to know what's wrong with her. Isaac keeps telling me it's wrong to be mad at her. Is it? Because no matter what he says, I am. And for so much. For not going shopping with me, or coming to my piano recitals, or going to open school week, or to your house for Christmas, etc., etc., etc. My father never complains that she never goes out with him, not even to do grocery shopping. It's like everyone pretends that she's normal, when she's really nuts. NUTS! *There, finally said it.* NUTSNUTSNUTS!!!!!

Do you think I'm being really horrible by saying that? My cousin Ben says stop complaining—a bad mother is better than no mother at all. But to tell you the truth, he's a little weird, too. He's like Superman or something—with a double life, like a shadow or a ghost. Here but not here. I mean, you can feel he's a million miles away even when he's right next to you. And a lot of the time he's literally just "out," and nobody even makes him say where he was when he comes home. I guess you need to be a boy to have freedom in this house, since my mother gives me the third degree if I'm in the bathroom too long.

Meanwhile, my stupid father just acts as if everything is normal, when it's obviously not. Whenever I try talking to him about anything, he just smiles and nods and kisses the top of my head. But he's not even listening. It's like he lives in another universe.

Or maybe it's just me. Maybe they're all normal and I'm the freak?

And now I feel bad and guilty for being mean and writing all this stuff to you. PLEASE KEEP THIS LETTER SECRET!!!! SWEAR YOU WILL!!! If anybody else ever saw this, I would die.

Love,

Valerie

P.S. I'm growing a hundred feet a day. I'm like a thousand feet taller than last time we saw each other. I'm going to be a freaky giant if this keeps up. I pray every night that I will shrink. I wish I was someone else.

P.P.S. I almost forgot—my turn for a recipe. Since I feel like the Not-So-Jolly Green Giant, this is one is in honor of me—and my crazy mother.

. . . .

✺ GREEN SALAD WITH GIANT ✺ CROUTONS AND NUTS

SERVES 4 TO 6

6	tablespoons extra-virgin olive oil	8	cups mixed salad greens
2	teaspoons dried oregano	1½	tablespoons red wine vinegar
1	(6-ounce) piece French bread, cut into ½-inch cubes (about 4 cups)	½	teaspoon salt
			Ground black pepper
¼	cup grated Parmesan (1 ounce)	½	cup toasted sliced almonds

1. In a large skillet over medium-high heat, warm 3 tablespoons olive oil. Add the oregano and cook for 30 seconds. Add the bread cubes and toss to coat with the oil. Toast, tossing occasionally, until light golden, about 5 minutes. Sprinkle the croutons with cheese and toast until the cheese melts and turns golden, about 2 minutes more.

2. In a large bowl, toss the salad greens with the remaining 3 tablespoons oil, the vinegar, the salt, and pepper. Add the croutons and almonds, and toss once more to combine.

1967

JANUARY 1, 1967

Dear Val,

Happy New Year!

It was weird not seeing you, but my father said since he's just come back we needed to be alone together.

Last night he made something called "glug" to celebrate my mother promising not to see Dag anymore. (Of course he made a batch with no alcohol for me, but I snuck some Aquavit into mine). We raised our glasses and Dad toasted the end of my mother's "smorgasbord of men."

Does he really believe that's the end of it? It's obvious everybody falls in love with her. The other day we were walking down the street together and she was wearing new leather kinky boots with a black miniskirt and a white maxi-coat that's split up the middle so her legs showed. Two men were staring at her so hard they almost walked into a wall.

But it's not just the way she dresses. It's just . . . her. The way she is. She's so powerful, it's almost scary. No other mothers look like her. I would never say this to her face because it would make her even more conceited, but I hope I'm just like her one day.

When we got home she offered to help me get ready for the school Winter Dance. I couldn't believe it! Do you know how many times I've begged her to do this with me? She figured out that if I wore my pink midriff with my vinyl miniskirt and go-go boots, I would be great. I figured out that if I borrowed her sequined choker, I would be more than great—I would be perfect.

We were both right. My science teacher, Mr. Felder, said I looked amazing and asked me to dance. He asked most of the girls, but he couldn't keep his eyes off me even when he was with them. What a lech!

Drink up!

Love,

Lilly

....

Ꮭ HAPPY NEW YEAR'S GLUG Ꮭ

SERVES 4 TO 6

¼	cup honey	2	whole cloves
1	cinnamon stick	1	(750ml bottle) red wine
2	cardamom pods, lightly crushed	1	(3-inch) strip orange peel

1. In a medium saucepan, combine 1 cup water with the honey, cinnamon, cardamom, and cloves. Bring the mixture to a boil; reduce the heat and simmer for 3 minutes.

2. Add the red wine and orange peel and simmer for 5 minutes more. Serve immediately, or keep warm over low heat.

Hi Lillypad,

I hope you're fine.

I can't write a long letter 'cause I'm late, late, late for music school.

I'm supposed to play in a piano recital next month, but I wish I didn't have to. I hate all that stuff of going on stage and having everybody stare. You are so amazing to me that you like it—and you're so great at it, too. You have real stage presence, Lillypad. I much prefer just playing alone, or with you. Next time you're here I'll play and you can sing!

Okay, here's my recipe. It's fast and good.

Love and kisses,

Val

. . . .

❦ BETTER-LATE-THAN-NEVER ❧ ZUCCHINI QUICKBREAD

MAKES 2 LOAVES

Butter or shortening for greasing pans

3 cups all-purpose flour

1 teaspoon salt

1 teaspoon baking soda

¼ teaspoon baking powder

1 tablespoon ground cinnamon

3 eggs

2 cups sugar

1 cup vegetable oil

2 cups peeled, grated raw zucchini

1 tablespoon vanilla extract

½ cup chopped nuts

½ cup raisins

1. Preheat the oven to 350° F. Grease two 9 x 5 x 3-inch loaf pans.

2. In a large bowl, combine the flour, salt, baking soda, baking powder, and cinnamon.

3. In a separate bowl, whisk the eggs until light and foamy. Mix in the sugar, oil, zucchini, and vanilla. Slowly add the dry ingredients, stirring until just incorporated. Fold in the nuts and raisins.

4. Bake until golden-brown on top and a toothpick inserted in the center comes out clean, about 1 hour. Let cool 5 minutes in the pan, then turn out onto a wire rack and let cool completely.

Hi Lilly,

Last night my mother was in the mood for Chinese food, so
she sent me and Ben to get it. But she said we could eat in
the restaurant first before bringing home the food. So just
the two of us had dinner at Fong's Village. For a minute I
pretended we were on a date when people looked at us
sitting there.

We actually had fun! We rated each other's friends. When
we got to you, he said, "Lilly? Oh, on a scale of one to ten,
your friend Lilly is a definite thirty-four!" When I looked
shocked, he gave one of his stupid laughs. But I could see
he meant it in a really nice way. He definitely goes ga-ga
for you. Obviously!!! (And so do I, of course!!)

I can't really answer your questions about how I act and feel
about all that making out and feeling up stuff, except that
even talking about it in a letter makes me uncomfortable.
(Which I know you know, but you always seem to forget so
I have to tell you again. Or do you just pretend to forget?)

Reminder number 62 zillion: I still never even kissed a boy
yet. I haven't even hugged anyone, except to close-dance a
couple of times. And the only "date" I've been on has been a
fake date with my fake brother.

Do you think they let Jewish girls join convents?

Love,

Sister Val

....

☙ GA-GA-GAI PAN ❧

SERVES 2 TO 4

FOR THE MARINADE:

- 1 tablespoon finely chopped, peeled gingerroot
- 2 teaspoons sesame oil
- 2 teaspoons oyster sauce
- 1 teaspoon soy sauce
- ½ pound skinless, boneless duck breast, sliced crosswise into ¼-inch strips

FOR THE SAUCE:

- ¼ cup chicken stock
- 2 teaspoons oyster sauce
- 2 teaspoons cornstarch
- 1½ teaspoons soy sauce
- 1 teaspoon sesame oil
- ½ teaspoon lemon juice

Pinch sugar

Pinch salt

Ground black pepper

FOR THE STIR-FRY:

- ¼ cup vegetable oil
- 1 tablespoons minced, peeled gingerroot
- 1 garlic clove, minced
- 5 ounces sliced mushrooms (about 2 cups)
- 6 ounces snow peas, trimmed (about 2 cups)
- ¼ cup bamboo shoots, drained
- ¼ cup water chestnuts, drained

Cooked rice, for serving

1. Whisk together the marinade ingredients in a bowl. Add the duck pieces and toss to coat. Cover with plastic and refrigerate for 30 minutes.

2. In a separate bowl, whisk together the sauce ingredients.

3. In a wok, heat 2 tablespoons vegetable oil until it just begins to smoke. Add the ginger and garlic and cook 30 seconds. Add the mushrooms and cook, tossing, for 30 seconds. Add the snow peas, bamboo shoots, and water chestnuts. Cook, tossing occasionally, for 2 minutes. Transfer the vegetables to a plate.

4. Heat the remaining 2 tablespoons oil in the wok until it just begins to smoke. Add the duck breast and the marinade. Cook, tossing, until just cooked through, about 2 minutes. Add the vegetables and cook for 1 minute more. Add the sauce and cook until the mixture thickens, 30 seconds to 1 minute more. Serve hot, over rice.

Hi Lillypad,

This year Visiting Day fell on my birthday, which was great. Except, of course, my mother didn't come . . . again. The bad part is that I never stop wishing she would.

Anyway, I got the BEST birthday present! My bunk had a cookout with a boys' bunk, and when it got dark, this boy named Peter Strauss gave me a caramel almond kiss from his care package—and then he REALLY kissed me!!! My heart was beating so fast I thought I would die. We made out for a really looooooong time, so long that my lips went numb. But his lips were really soft. He smelled like the campfire and pine needles.

Then . . . you will die! . . . we French-kissed! Ooh-la-la, chérie!! He started it, and at first I got nervous and pulled away. I was scared a little because I didn't know what I was doing, but then it just happened so naturally, like I had always been doing it.

The sweetest part was that in between kissing me he kept whispering into my ear, which gave me chills up and down my whole body. He said really nice things—like I was pretty and smelled good, and that my skin was soft. He said he'd been wanting to kiss me all summer, but I was such a woman and he was such a boy, so he was afraid. Can you believe it? Me a woman? And then he said he really liked me.

Afterwards we went back to the cookout area and he carved a stick for me to toast marshmallows. I wanted to save the stick, but it was too gooey, so I threw it in the flames and made a wish.

Lilly, I think my wish came true! I feel normal for the first time ever.

Love,

Val

P.S. *Peter's mom made the caramel candies, and he got the recipe from her! You'll faint from how great they are. And they're romantic, too, except when they get stuck in your teeth, so we'll definitely both want to serve them at our weddings. Or at least at my wedding, since you're never going to tie the knot.*

....

❦ FIRST-KISS CARAMEL ❧ ALMOND KISSES

MAKES ABOUT 64 KISSES

Butter or shortening for greasing pan

1 cup granulated sugar

1 cup light corn syrup

1 cup condensed milk

½ cup unsalted butter

3 ounces unsweetened chocolate, chopped

1¾ cups heavy cream, warm

56 almonds

1. Grease an 8-inch square baking pan.

2. Combine the sugar, the corn syrup, the condensed milk, and butter in a saucepan over medium-high heat. Bring to a boil. Stir in the chocolate, and cook, stirring occasionally, until the mixture registers 240° F on a candy thermometer. Slowly stir in the heavy cream and cook, stirring constantly, until the thermometer registers 246° F.

SEPTEMBER 14, 1967

Dear Val,

Does Golden Boy still have that girlfriend Ava? I'm not asking for me. It's for Maggie, who thinks he's cute (ugh!— no offense). We saw him outside of Pino's Pizza with a bunch of his friends. (Too bad Ben's allowed to come down on the subway by himself but you can't. Why can't he bring you with him? Have you ever asked?)

Here's a riddle: How do you know when it's time to go to the dentist? Tooth-hurty. Dumb, right?

My father is off lecturing at a meeting of psychiatrists in Florida. Hey, did you read that horrible article about him in the newspaper yesterday? Some doctor accused him of making up statistics. It was an extra big deal because it's the third time someone wrote mean things about him. My mother thinks they just want to hurt his reputation. She says they're jealous because he's a true pioneer and they're just sheep. It's a relief to hear her defending him for a change, instead of just criticizing him.

The good that's come out of all this bad press is that my parents are getting along better than ever. Thank God. I couldn't stand one more minute of their war games.

Anyway, my father sent a crate of oranges. I used them to make these sugary candied orange peels. They need to soak overnight, but it's worth it—they're great with a cup of hot chocolate.

Love,

....

❧ CANDIED ORANGE PEELS ☙

MAKES ABOUT 2 CUPS

6 oranges	2½ cups sugar
1 tablespoon salt	

1. Cut each orange in half, and cut each half into thirds. Using a paring knife, slice the peel away from the fruit (remove as much of the bitter white pith as possible from the peel). Slice the peels lengthwise into ¼-inch-wide strips.

2. Fill a bowl with 4 cups water and the salt. Add the peels. Cover with a plate that sits directly on top of the peels; weigh the plate down with a heavy can to keep the peels immersed in the water. Let stand overnight.

3. The next day, drain the orange peels and rinse thoroughly with cold water. Place the peels in a pot and cover with water. Bring the peels to a boil; drain. Repeat 3 times to help remove the bitterness from the peel.

4. Combine the peels with 2 cups sugar and ½ cup water. Heat, stirring, until sugar has melted completely and peels turn translucent. Most of the syrup should be absorbed. Drain.

5. Spread the remaining ½ cup sugar out on a large plate. Toss the orange peels in the sugar, then lay the peels out on a wire rack to dry completely.

NOVEMBER 19, 1967

Gobble-gobble, Lilly!

I'm so excited you're coming here for Thanksgiving! We started planning our menu already, and we're making something special for each person in your family:

– Lilly's Luscious Limas with creamed corn.

– "Katherine's Karrots," with brown sugar, parsnips, and dill butter.

– "Isaac's Ice Cream Pie," with a ginger-cookie crust (this year we're making it equal parts chocolate, strawberry, and vanilla, with toasted coconut mixed into it).

xxxxxxxxx and love,

Me

P.S. *My dad invented something just for you! It's a microphone that you don't need a separate amplifier for. (He said I could tell you in advance so you could get excited.) So now you can sing like a professional when we perform our show-tune duet after dinner!! I've been practicing piano a lot, especially* OUR *song, "There's a Place for Us" (is it still your favorite?).*

❧ LILLY'S LUSCIOUS LIMAS ❧

SERVES 4 TO 6

2	tablespoons unsalted butter	½	cup heavy cream
1	small yellow onion, sliced	2	tablespoons finely chopped chives
1½	cups frozen lima beans		Salt
1	cup fresh or frozen corn kernels		Ground black pepper

1. Melt the butter in a medium saucepan over medium-high heat. Add the onion and cook, stirring occasionally, until the onions are softened, 5 to 7 minutes.

2. Add the lima beans and corn; cook for 3 minutes more.

3. Stir in the cream and cook until just heated through, about 2 minutes. Stir in the chives, season to taste with salt and pepper, and serve.

❧ KATHERINE'S KARROTS ❧

SERVES 6

3	tablespoons unsalted butter	1	pound parsnips, peeled and cut into ½-inch-thick rounds
3	tablespoons light brown sugar	½	teaspoon salt
1	pound carrots, peeled and cut into ½-inch-thick rounds	1½	tablespoons fresh chopped dill
			Ground black pepper

1. In a medium skillet over medium heat, melt butter and sugar. Reduce the heat to low and add carrots, parsnips, and salt. Cook covered, until just tender, 15 to 20 minutes.

2. Stir in the dill and pepper. Cook, uncovered, until the mixture is bubbling and syrupy, about 2 minutes more.

ISAAC'S ICE CREAM PIE

1 (9-INCH) PIE SERVES 8

2   cups toasted coconut

1½ cups finely crushed gingersnaps

6   tablespoons unsalted butter, melted

3   tablespoons confectioners' sugar

1   (2-ounce) chunk semisweet chocolate

1   pint chocolate ice cream, slightly softened

1   pint strawberry ice cream, slightly softened

1   pint vanilla ice cream, slightly softened

1. To toast the coconut: spread the coconut flakes out on a baking sheet. Toast, tossing frequently, in a 325° F oven until golden, about 10 minutes.

2. To make the crust: preheat the oven to 300° F. Toss the gingersnaps, butter, and sugar together. Press the mixture into the bottom and sides of a 9-inch pie plate. Bake the crust until firm and slightly colored around the edges, 15 to 20 minutes. Let cool.

3. Shave the chocolate over the bottom of the crust. Sprinkle ¼ cup of the coconut over the chocolate. Using a spatula, smooth the chocolate ice cream evenly over the coconut. Repeat the layering using strawberry and vanilla ice cream; finish with a layer of coconut.

4. Cover and freeze until set, about 30 minutes. Slice and serve frozen.

DECEMBER 1, 1967

Dear Val,

Thanksgiving was cool. The meal was perfect and everybody got along so well, it was great.

And man, you and I blew them away! You really are a great accompanist—and your dad's mike had me sounding like Aretha.

So why did you need to go all psycho by acting like you were hiding something when we went into your room? Big deal, who cares if my father gave you a million boring books . . . and who cares if he wrote inside the front cover of them? Why were you acting like it was some huge secret? I really don't care. (You know I don't read that type of book anyway—in fact, I don't really like to read. And I don't care about Madame Curie or any of the others you like. I'm more interested in music and theater.) That's probably why he gave those books to you, not me. Because he knew I wouldn't want them. Maybe he even wanted me to have them but changed his mind. I bet that's what happened.

Besides which, Maggie and I got into Peas in the Pod for next year! We're just two Broadway babes on the rise! Hooray!

Love,

Lilly

P.S. Oh yeah, I forgot the whole reason I'm writing. I had this at Maggie's house. We love cooking together. Does that bother you?

....

❧ BROADWAY BABY BACK RIBS ❧

SERVES 4 TO 6

||||||||||||||||||||||||||||||||||||||||||||||||||||||||||||||||||||||||||||||||||||||||||||||||||||||||||||||||||||||||||

2 racks (2½ pounds total) baby back ribs	¼ cup freshly squeezed lemon juice
Salt	¼ cup Worcestershire sauce
Ground black pepper	¼ cup Dijon mustard
FOR THE BARBECUE SAUCE:	1 red onion, finely chopped
2 cups ketchup	4 garlic cloves, finely chopped
¾ cider vinegar	2 tablespoons smoked paprika
¼ cup dark brown sugar	1 tablespoon honey
¼ cup chili powder	2 cups water

1. Preheat the oven to 350° F. Season the ribs with salt and pepper. Place the ribs meat side up on a baking sheet. Bake for 30 minutes.

2. Meanwhile, combine all of the sauce ingredients with 2 cups of water in a medium pot. Simmer until thickened, about 30 minutes. Strain.

3. Brush ¼ cup sauce over each rack. Bake for 20 minutes. Brush another ¼ cup sauce over the ribs and bake 20 minutes more. Brush each rack with another ¼ cup sauce and bake until tender, about 30 minutes more. Slice each rack into thirds and moisten with additional, warm barbecue sauce.

1968

Dear Lilly,

I am FURIOUS!!!!!

Tonight was Open School Night. My mother SWORE TO ME she would "get over this stage fright, once and for all!!" SHE SWORE!!!! I really wanted her to meet Mr. Curtis, my math teacher who I love. Now he'll probably think she's dead or something. And he'll pity me.

Oh, Lilly, she SWORE she would go! I was SO SO SO happy, watching her get dressed. She looked so beautiful—she had on makeup, jewelry, and a new dress my father bought for her that fit her perfectly and made her look like Sophia Loren. I was so proud.

My father was there with me, sitting on the edge of their bed. We were all nervous, but very happy. And then, just as they got to the front door of the apartment, she turned all pale and sweaty, started shaking and crying, and ran back into her room. She still hasn't come out.

Maybe Mr. Curtis will be right. I HOPE she dies.

Val

....

MARCH 24, 1968

Dear Val,

You don't have to worry. Nobody thinks badly about you because of your mother. Anyway, I really like her. I like how she laughs at my jokes and things when I'm at your house. And it's okay if she doesn't come to stuff. What's the difference? You know she loves you more than she loves anybody.

Let me explain something about your mother's condition. My father says medicine doesn't work for her, so it's not really her fault. So my advice: stop spinning your wheels. Don't be so flipped out by her and then you might feel better, too.

Oh, and when she gets all crazy and stuff, my father says that's because she doesn't sleep enough. Noise bothers her, you know? Like when we were running down the hallway screaming that time? Or those garbage trucks she's always complaining about?

The main thing is, it's not your fault, okay?

Plus she is a good cook. So be glad you inherited that from her!

Love,

Lilly

P.S. Don't blame yourself for not knowing this stuff. Because my father's a psychiatrist, I have a lot of psychological insight. Maybe if you make this for your mother she will get a little better.

....

A NOVEL ABOUT FOOD AND FRIENDSHIP   109

𝒢 GET-OUT-OF-BED BREAD 𝒟 PUDDING WITH CINNAMON ICE CREAM

SERVES 8 TO 10

FOR THE ICE CREAM:

1 pint vanilla ice cream, softened

1 teaspoon ground cinnamon

FOR THE BREAD PUDDING:

  Butter or shortening for greasing baking dish

12 (½-inch-thick) slices French bread

3 tablespoons unsalted butter

6 whole eggs

3 egg yolks

1 cup sugar

⅛ teaspoon salt

4 cups whole milk

1 cup heavy cream

1 teaspoon vanilla extract

½ teaspoon ground cinnamon

¼ teaspoon ground nutmeg

1. Spoon the vanilla ice cream into a bowl. Stir in the cinnamon until well combined. Cover with plastic and transfer to the freezer until ready to serve.

2. To make the bread pudding, preheat the oven to 350° F. Grease a 2-quart baking dish. Spread one side of each bread slice with butter. Arrange the bread in the baking dish, butter side up.

3. In a medium bowl, beat the eggs, yolks, sugar, and salt until combined.

4. In a saucepan over medium-high heat, bring the milk and cream to a boil. Whisk the milk mixture slowly into the egg mixture. Strain. Whisk in the vanilla, cinnamon, and nutmeg.

5. Pour the custard over the bread slices.

6. Place the baking pan in a larger roasting pan. Fill the roasting pan with boiling water halfway up the side of the

baking pan. Bake until the custard is set, but still slightly jiggly, 40 to 45 minutes.

7. Let cool 10 minutes before slicing.

JUNE 14, 1968

Hey, Val!

I think I'm in love. I'm serious! His name is Luciano Magestro, but we call him Luke, and he's almost three years older. He has a little beard growing under his chin that makes him look like an artist. He has the most beautiful hands you've ever seen. He plays the guitar. He played "Hey Jude" and I thought I was going to die. Really. He asked me to come hear his gig at a coffeehouse up near Columbia University. I don't know if I can go, but I want to more than anything in life. I might have to tell my father I'm visiting you. Would that be okay? He never lets me do anything these days. He even told me to quit Peas in the Pod. (He finally admitted he doesn't want me going down my mother's path.)

My mother went to a folk festival in Portland. She just took off yesterday with Serge, who is the new artistic director of her show. My father's stomping around the house like an angry dinosaur.

Luke's Nonna cooked this amazing soup for us, and she said I could have the recipe if I marry him. Obviously she was just joking. But afterwards, when we were alone, Luke said marriage is a state of mind. I think he was hinting that he wants us to get closer—things are heating up between us, and it's not just because of the soup.

Got to run. I'm late for rehearsal for Sweet Peas, as we call ourselves. We will be doing a show based on Aesop's Fables. It's good. I play a donkey. Thanks for coming to the last show. It was fun to know you and your dad were out there in the audience even if I couldn't see you. And I loved the rose you gave me. That was sweet.

Love,

Lilly

....

❧ ITALIAN WEDDING SOUP ❧

SERVES 8

FOR THE MEATBALLS:

5 ounces ground beef
5 ounces ground pork
5 ounces ground veal
½ cup grated Parmesan cheese
⅓ cup chopped parsley
1 slice day-old bread, torn into small pieces
1 small onion, grated
1 egg
1 teaspoon minced garlic
1 teaspoon salt
Ground black pepper

FOR THE SOUP:

12 cups chicken broth
1 pound escarole, chopped into bite-size pieces
2 eggs
2 tablespoons grated Parmesan cheese, plus additional for garnish
Salt
Ground black pepper

---

1. To make the meatballs, combine all of the ingredients in a large bowl. Shape into ½-inch balls, and transfer to a baking sheet. Cover until ready to use.

2. To make the soup, bring the chicken broth to a boil in a large pot. Add the meatballs and escarole, and simmer for 10 minutes.

3. Whisk together the eggs and cheese. Stirring the soup in a circular motion, gradually drizzle in the egg mixture. Stir gently with a fork to form thin strands, about 1 minute.

4. Season the soup with salt and pepper. Serve, garnished with additional cheese.

SEPTEMBER 30, 1968

Dear Old Friend Lilly,

I don't know what I'll say in this letter. Maybe I won't say anything. I'm very depressed. All I want to do is sleep or cry—and the only thing that keeps me from giving in is that more than anything, I don't want to become my mother.

So instead of sleeping my day away, I write. Poems, stray thoughts in my journal, and, of course, letters. Sometimes I mail them, like this one to you, and sometimes they're just letters to myself. Sometimes it's stuff that I don't even know I'm going to write—like it's coming from someone else's mind but it's in my handwriting.

It's hard to stay focused. What helps is to think about all that's good in the world. Like friendship. Science. Literature.

My English teacher this year and I always argue over poetry. He thinks it must have certain form and restrictions, and it must be uniform throughout. He's so wrong! Did you ever hear of Ferlinghetti? He wrote, "The penny candy store beyond the El/is where I first/fell in love/with unreality. . . ."

To me that's so deep. I mean, to mix the familiar with the profound. And to see that underneath the most common "real" thing is its opposite. Who really knows what reality is?

My mother was up all night again because of the garbage trucks. She gets so obsessed with the noise they make. And she acts paranoid, like they're doing it just to bug her. I don't even hear them. And then she guilt-trips my father about it, as though he has the power to silence them.

Sigh.

Love,

V.

....

OCTOBER 20, 1968

Dear Val,

I wonder how often people fight about something that's really just a way of fighting about themselves? I never want to do that ever. My parents do it all the time.

Now my father's slamming the door to his orchid room, where he spends half his life taking care of those stupid flowers. I think he likes plants better than people.

Luke bought me an incense holder and some apple incense. It's really cool. I told him I love him. But here's the problem—he didn't say it back. Not only that, but he says it would be wrong for us to make love. He says I'm too young. It's like the good Italian boy takes over whenever we start fooling around. And it's driving me nuts. I thought girls were supposed to act like this, not guys.

You know what? I would let him do anything almost. Really. I mean, who cares about virginity? What's the big deal if you lose it? Especially if it's with someone you love. He's probably just afraid of falling in love with me—and losing his heart. I'm sure that's what's holding him back.

Well, I've got a foolproof plan. My parents will both be out on Saturday night for my mother's opening, so the house will be empty. I'll make him a romantic, candlelit dinner. And just at the end of it, I'll seduce him. First with my famous chocolate chip cannolis—one bite and he'll think I'm Italian—and then with ME! Nobody can refuse the Lillian Stone magic. Look out, Lucky Luke, I'm ready, whether you think so or not!

By the way, I'm glad you liked him, Valsky. Luke liked you, too.

Love,

Lilly

P.S. I saw Ben yesterday with that girl with the stringy blond hair and buggy eyes. Tell him to get some handcuffs—she had all eight of her arms wrapped around him like a hungry octopus. Is that his new girlfriend? She seems kind of short for him, and they really don't look good together. Also, I've heard she's kind of a tramp. Think you should warn him?

☙ CHOCOLATE CHIP CANNOLIS ☙

MAKES 8 CANNOLIS

1½ cups ricotta cheese	8 store-bought cannoli shells
¾ cup confectioners' sugar	¼ cup chopped toasted pistachios
Finely grated zest of ½ orange	
¼ cup bittersweet chocolate chips, finely chopped	

1. In a bowl, combine the ricotta, sugar, orange zest, and chocolate chips.

2. Just before serving, fill each shell with some of the ricotta mixture.

3. Dip each end of the cannolis in the chopped pistachios.

OCTOBER 27, 1968

Dear Val,

Look, no matter what you say, and I appreciate that you're trying to make me feel better, last night with Luke was a total disaster.

Just the same, it helped to talk to you. Except that when I hung up I felt even more alone.

So, how do you fix a broken heart? Maybe with ricotta cheese. That's why I just spent the whole afternoon making lasagna. Believe it or not, my father even helped. And you know the only thing he knows how to cook is martinis.

He called what we made "Lovelorn Lasagna." I guess he figured out something was wrong even though I didn't exactly tell him about me and Luke breaking up. He probably guessed because of how I was sighing and singing sad songs in a fake Italian accent.

At first my father tried to be helpful in his usual unhelpful way. You'd think I was some textbook case he was studying. He said something like, "Classic melancholia is often sublimated rage. What are you really angry about?"

He stared at me, waiting for an answer. I had no idea what he was talking about, and at the same time I hated that he was kind of right. I am angry. Of course at Luke. But it's more than that. I feel trapped. Why can't anybody see I'm not a child anymore? I got so furious I threw down the oven mitt and started to cry.

Then my father did something so unlike him—completely honest and real. He said, "Sometimes people we love can't love us in ways that we wish to be loved. Not because we aren't worthy of that love, but for other reasons, beyond our control." He put his arms around me. I wanted to stay there forever.

Your sad and lovesick friend,

Lilly

. . . .

⚭ LOVELORN LASAGNA ⚭

SERVES 8 TO 10

FOR THE SAUCE:

3   tablespoons unsalted butter

3   tablespoons extra-virgin olive oil

1   medium onion, finely chopped

2   garlic cloves, finely chopped

1   teaspoon dried oregano

1   pound ground beef

1   pound Italian sausage, removed from its casing and crumbled

3   tablespoons tomato paste

2   (28-ounce) cans whole peeled tomatoes

1   cup beef stock

2½   teaspoons salt

½   teaspoon black pepper

1   bay leaf

FOR THE LASAGNA:

2   tablespoons extra-virgin olive oil

¾   pound lasagna noodles

12   ounces fresh ricotta cheese (3 cups)

6   ounces grated mozzarella cheese (1½ cups)

6   ounces grated Parmesan cheese (1½ cups)

1. To make the sauce, heat the butter and oil in a medium pot over medium heat. Cook the onion, garlic, and oregano until the onions are translucent, about 5 minutes. Add the beef and sausage, and cook, breaking the meat up with a fork, until well-browned, about 10 minutes. Add the tomato paste and cook 1 minute. Add the tomatoes, stock, salt, pepper, and bay leaf. Simmer, uncovered, until thickened, for 1 hour.

2. Meanwhile, add the oil to a large pot of salted water. Bring the water to a boil. Add the noodles, and cook until al dente, 8 to 10 minutes, or according to package directions; drain.

3. Preheat the oven to 350° F. Ladle some of the sauce on the bottom of a 9 x 13-inch baking pan. Arrange a layer of pasta over the sauce. Top with a layer of the ricotta, a layer of the mozzarella, and a layer of the Parmesan. Repeat until all of the ingredients have been used, finishing with a generous layer of mozzarella and Parmesan.

4. Bake, uncovered, until golden and bubbling, 45 minutes to 1 hour. Let cool 5 minutes before slicing.

1969

L—

Isn't it kind of peculiar how everyone uses New Year's Eve as an excuse for getting drunk and saying, "This year will be different." Because everything stays the same. All the people who say "We shall overcome" don't even know what tyranny is all about. We're always living in fear and threat of wars and hatred.

It's because people can't communicate! Except for you, my dearest darlingest Silly, there's nobody I can really tell everything to. I feel free telling you everything. Oh, wait a second. Be right back. . . .

It's twenty minutes later. My mother just told me to shut off the oven. When I passed by her bedroom on the way back I saw she was lying on the bed crying. My father was trying to make her feel better by brushing her hair. But it didn't help. Nothing helps.

I'm going insane living in this crazy house. I can't wait to go to college. Maybe I should try graduating early. I have enough AP credits, but knowing HER, *she'll keep me chained to the radiator in my room until I'm 35 and dead.*

But I still love you, if no one else. . . .

Valerie

P.S. *You know what was in the oven? My mother's phenomenal pot roast. (Not her head, don't worry.) She may be crazy, but she sure can cook. Whenever I eat this, I remember that I love her.*

....

❧ KITTY'S PHENOMENAL ❧
POT ROAST WITH OVEN-ROASTED POTATOES

SERVES 4 TO 6

1	3-pound brisket, rinsed and patted dry	2	medium carrots, peeled and cubed
1	garlic clove, finely chopped	2	medium onions, halved and sliced
	Salt	3	tablespoons chicken fat, melted
	Ground black pepper		
2	medium baking potatoes, peeled and cubed	2	bay leaves

1. Preheat the oven to 350° F. Rub the brisket all over with the chopped garlic. Season generously with salt and pepper.

2. Toss the potatoes, carrots, and onion with the chicken fat. Season generously with salt and pepper. Spread the vegetables and bay leaves in a 9 x 12-inch baking pan. Place the brisket on top of the vegetables. Cover with foil.

3. Bake, covered, basting every 20 minutes with the pan juices, until the meat is fork-tender and cooked to the desired doneness, 2 to 3 hours.

4. Let the meat rest, covered, 10 minutes before slicing.

FEBRUARY 14, 1969

Dear Val,

Happy Valentine's Day! Val-entines . . . it's your day!!! Get it?

I'm very excited because Luke broke up with his girlfriend! I found out because I was in Pino's after school and ran into Ben with two of his friends. We were all laughing our heads off, harmonizing our own version of "Sittin' on the Dock of the Bay," while we waited for our pie-ie-ies to roll in. Funny, right? Guess you had to be there.

Anyway, I looked up and there was Luke. It seemed like he'd been watching us for some time, staring with a jealous look on his face. When I saw that, my heart started to pound. I was in a panic, and I knew I had to think of something fast. So I threw my arms around Ben and whispered for him to play along. I promised if he gave an Oscar-worthy performance I'd pay for his pizza. I gotta tell you, that cousin of yours sure knows how fake it. You would have thought he was Mick Jagger and I was Marianne (Un)Faithfull.

Luke sat alone at a booth, facing away, but I could see him stealing glances in the mirror. I have to admit, I loved the feeling I got when I knew that it bothered him to see me with Ben. When I thought that Luke couldn't take it anymore, I went over to his booth to say a casual hello. I acted like nothing weird had happened between us. He did the same. He was very friendly and warm, and said I looked older. He said it in a way that I know means he digs me again because his eyes kept going up and down my body. You know how guys do that? (I know you don't usually like it, but this time even you would have.)

Of course, Ben didn't understand the joke was over. He followed me to Luke's booth, and threw his arm around me, caveman style. God help the woman he ends up with. He almost ruined everything. Good thing he knew the Twiggy lookalike who walked in. She managed to distract him long enough for me to have some time with Luke.

And here's the fabulous part: he asked me out again! For a minute I was going to play hard to get, but I figured I made him suffer enough. We're meeting tomorrow. I can hardly wait.

Okay, here's a recipe for chocolate-dipped heart cookies. Everybody should have some love today!

Your pal,

Lilly

P.S. *Did you get your eyeglasses, four-eyes?*

....

❧ CHOCOLATE-DIPPED ❧ HEART COOKIES

MAKES ABOUT 4½ DOZEN COOKIES

1	cup unsalted butter	2 teaspoons baking powder
1	cup sugar	¾ teaspoon salt
2	eggs	12 ounces semisweet chocolate, chopped (about 3 cups)
1½	teaspoons vanilla extract	
3	cups all-purpose flour	

1. Combine the butter and sugar in a large bowl. Using an electric mixer, beat until light and fluffy. Add the eggs, 1 at a time. Add the vanilla.

2. In a separate bowl, whisk together the flour, baking powder, and salt. Beat the dry ingredients slowly into the butter mixture. Form the dough into a ball, and wrap tightly with plastic wrap. Chill for 3 hours.

3. When you are ready to bake the cookies, preheat the oven to 325° F. On a floured surface, roll the dough ¼-inch thick. Cut out the dough using a 2- to 3-inch heart-shaped cookie cutter. Place the cookies 1½ inches apart on baking sheets and bake until lightly colored on the bottom, 12 to 13 minutes. Transfer the cookies to a wire rack to cool.

4. While the cookies bake, melt the chocolate in the top of a double boiler, or in a bowl set over a pot of simmering water. Let cool until lukewarm.

5. Dip one vertical half of each heart-shaped cookie into the chocolate. Return the cookies to the wire rack to set completely before serving.

FEBRUARY 21, 1969

Dear Lilly,

I couldn't ask you ANYTHING *on the phone because there's not a minute of privacy in this apartment. My mother is underfoot like a house cat. And she's always listening, listening, listening to every telephone conversation I have. It's like I live at* FBI *headquarters.*

My father MADE *me go to a school dance tonight. You know how I've always said that the best part of being dead was that there were no more school dances? Now I know I'm right.*

It was so awful. I was standing in a crowd of other girls I know, and the boys came up to inspect us like we were fruit to be picked. I only got asked to slow-dance once, by a kid who looks like Ichabod Crane with zits. We stepped on each other's feet so hard that I was actually relieved to sit by myself the rest of the night.

How could it be almost two years since that summer with Peter? Was it a dream? Or just a one-time thing in my life? He made me feel so beautiful and important, even though I know it was just a kid thing and just a kiss and just a stupid summer romance and just a moment in time, that kind of connection is something I long for.

But Lilly, I have to confess something terrible. I'm envious of you and Luke. I'm not jealous, because I am happy for you. It's just that I'm so aware that my life is empty in that way. I feel lonely. And there's nothing to do about it.

But I hope you don't think it's jealousy that makes me say what I told you on the phone: I think you should go slowly with Luke. I really don't think you should sleep together. Yet. Give it some time to see if you really trust him.

Anyway, back to my horrible school-dance nightmare. By the time I left, someone had splashed sticky ginger ale punch on my lap, and I overheard two girls saying they were glad they weren't me.

When I got home I was so miserable I decided to try your method of cooking to cheer myself up. It worked! I made one of the first recipes my mother ever taught me.

Write soon if you can. I really do miss and love you.

Val

....

❧ THANK GOD FOR ❧ BUTTERSCOTCH PUDDING

SERVES 5

2½ cups whole milk

3 tablespoons unsalted butter

¾ cup dark brown sugar

½ cup heavy cream

¼ cup cornstarch

4 egg yolks

1 tablespoon vanilla extract

1. In a medium saucepan over medium-high heat, combine the milk, butter, and sugar. Bring to a simmer.

2. Meanwhile, in a medium bowl, whisk together the cream and cornstarch. Let rest 1 minute. Whisk in the yolks and vanilla. Slowly add the hot milk mixture, whisking constantly, until incorporated.

3. Return the pudding to the saucepan and cook over medium-low heat, whisking constantly, for 10 minutes. Strain into a bowl and let cool 5 minutes.

4. Divide the pudding among 5 (6-ounce) ramekins. Cover each ramekin with plastic wrap and chill at least 3 hours before serving.

MARCH 1, 1969

Lilly,

I keep calling, but you still aren't home. There's so much I want to say, and nobody to say it to.

I just finished Catcher in the Rye *for the third time. (Did you ever read the copy I sent home with your father?) Holden*

Caulfield searches for a world that doesn't exist, just like I do. He doesn't really connect with anybody, but yet he loves them. Just like me. Have you ever felt like this? Please read it.

I had an epiphany of sorts. You know how I always say boys don't like me? Well, it's not exactly true. Some do, but they're not the ones I want. They're all too serious, too intense, too awkward, too unpopular. In other words, too much like me.

So what does this mean? Am I rejecting them because I hate myself? Am I simply rejecting them before they have a chance to reject me? Or is it just like the old saying, that opposites attract? What prevents me from having a popular, handsome, confident boyfriend? Will I ever be capable of having true intimacy with another person? (I can just hear you asking another question: will I ever loosen up enough to just have fun, not worry, and stop asking questions and analyzing things all the time?)

Years from now, will any of this matter? Isn't it true that the work a person devotes her life to means as much as love? In fact, isn't work a form of love? If so, my life will be okay. Because I know for sure that the work I do when I grow up will be important and will help people, and that's an amazing thing.

Anyway, speaking of amazing things, how's Luke—or should I say, Luke AND Tomaz? I guess I'm glad you like him (them) the way you do. On the other hand, aren't you being just a drop flighty or disloyal to Luke? I mean, you don't like it when a boy lies to you about being with other girls, do you?

Oh, never mind. We've just established that I know nothing about this, and that I am fated to be president of the Platonic Friendship Club. Ignore me.

I should go. Tons of homework tonight, but I'm distracting myself with a highly scientific, statistical study of the types of girls that boys like.

Valerie

....

⟨ CATCHER IN THE RYE BREAD ⟩

MAKES 2 MEDIUM LOAVES

2	cups rye flour	1	tablespoon honey
2	cups whole wheat flour	⅓	teaspoon dry yeast
2	cups bread flour	1	egg yolk, stirred with 1 teaspoon water
2	teaspoons salt		
3	tablespoons vegetable oil	2	tablespoons caraway seeds

1. The night before baking the bread, mix together the flours and salt in a large bowl. Add the oil and rub the mixture together with your hands, breaking up any large clumps.

2. Stir the honey into ½ cup warm water. Add the yeast and let dissolve for 10 minutes. Add to the flour mixture and stir to combine. Mixing the dough with your hands, add 2 cups water, a little at a time. Knead the dough for 5 minutes, until it pulls away from the bowl. Transfer to a floured surface and knead for 5 minutes more. Transfer the dough to a well-oiled bowl and cover with a very damp towel. Let rise overnight.

3. The next morning, transfer the risen dough to a floured surface and knead for 5 minutes. Divide the dough into two balls and shape each ball into a loaf. Arrange the loaves on a large baking sheet. Cover with a damp towel and let rise for 2 hours.

4. Preheat the oven to 375° F. Brush each loaf with the egg yolk mixture and sprinkle with the caraway seeds. Bake the loaves for 45 minutes to 1 hour until they are golden on top and make a hollow sound when rapped with your knuckles. Let cool completely before slicing.

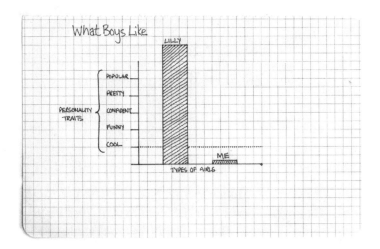

23 MARCH 1969

lilly . . .

i am very sad sitting here with drizzling clouds surrounding me and i really don't know how to stop the skies and the gods from crying when all i wish to be is two years old again so i can climb on daddy's shoulders and mommy will go outside with us and we will all lay together on a blanket in the grass and feel sunlight on our faces and all around us is laughter and love. . . .

*and i know the only choice is to start out on new roads all
by myself and try to find the place which once welcomed me
and caressed me . . . a new home i can only find within
myself . . . and i want to touch that place and thank it and
take from it the wondrous strength of becoming myself,
painful though the journey may be. . . .*

i wish you peace, my friend, peace. . . .

V.

p.s. – i still miss you, and wish you'd write. . . .

....

MAY 4, 1969

Hellooooooo Val!

*See me . . . feel me . . . touch me. Do you like The Who? Do
you like* Tommy? *Everybody is listening to it. I don't know. I
think it's kind of stupid. But maybe I like it okay, too.*

*So, did you get accepted for that junior counselor job? I
don't really understand why you want to do that, but I guess
it's your thing.*

*It's definite now: end of July I'm going to England. I just got
a letter that the exchange program wants me to come. A
month in Cambridge to study drawing. Then a cruise around
the Mediterranean.*

*I can't wait to get out of here. Time feels as if it's slowed to a
crawl. A minute feels like an hour.*

*Except when I'm with Luke. That's the only thing I don't
want to leave. I can't stand the idea of not feeling his arms*

around me when we walk down the street. And I really get a rush when other girls watch us go past. Knowing they want what I've got.

At night I try to imagine what it will be like to go so far from home, where I won't know anyone. Will I have anyone to talk to? What if I hate it? I can't exactly walk home across an ocean. It's weird, but the truth is, because of camp, you've had more experience being away from home than me, even though I'm much more sophisticated in every other way.

Today's recipe: scones, in honor of my trip.

Hope you cheered up by now. You can be such a downer!

Love,

Lilly

....

❧ CURRANT AND GINGER SCONES ❧

MAKES 8 SCONES

1¾ cups all-purpose flour	2 eggs
2½ teaspoons baking powder	⅓ cup heavy cream, plus additional for brushing
1 tablespoon sugar, plus additional for sprinkling	¼ cup chopped crystallized ginger
½ teaspoon salt	¼ cup currants
¼ cup (½ stick) unsalted butter, chilled and cubed	

1. Preheat the oven to 425° F. In a bowl, whisk together the flour, baking powder, sugar, and salt. Cut in the butter until the mixture forms coarse crumbs.

2. In a separate bowl, whisk together the eggs and cream. Stir into the dry ingredients until the mixture just comes together to form a sticky batter. Fold in the ginger and currants.

3. Turn the dough out onto a floured surface and pat into a ball, adding flour as necessary until it's not sticky. Transfer to a baking sheet lined with parchment paper. Pat dough into a ½-inch-thick disc. Score the dough into 8 equal wedges, cutting almost, but not completely, through the dough.

4. Brush the top of the dough with cream and sprinkle evenly with sugar. Bake until golden, 20 to 25 minutes. Let cool 5 minutes before serving.

MAY 8, 1969

Dear Lilly,

You're right. I think lately I have been pretty depressed . . . sorry if my letters are bumming you out. I will try to be happier. I am trying, actually. For my sake.

Hey—speaking of cheering up, I got a great new recipe for salmon croquettes! They're delicious with our Recipe Club Macaroni and Cheese on the side. And they're great at room temperature, too—try making a sandwich on Catcher in the Rye bread spread with mayo and mustard.

Meanwhile, back in the real world, school's sort of almost over, and not a minute too soon. I am so bored I could scream. The only interesting things I learned this year I learned from Isaac. What's the point of going to school? Isaac says he'll teach me anatomy and advanced bio in the fall. I just hope he won't make me meet with him as often as he did this year. As much as I love what he teaches, sometimes our sessions leave me feeling suffocated. (Am I being too critical of him? It's just that he's so demanding and I'm not sure what exactly he expects. It's like he's always testing me, and I'm afraid of failing. Is that how you feel with him too? Sometimes?)

Love,

ValPal

P.S. *I definitely got the junior counselor job. I don't know what you don't understand—or why you even have to be so critical of it. Can't we like different things and not judge each other?*

. . . .

◈ CHEERFUL SALMON CROQUETTES ◈

MAKES 2 DOZEN CROQUETTES

2	cups canned salmon	½	teaspoon salt, plus additional for sprinkling
1⅔	cups breadcrumbs	¼	teaspoon paprika
¼	cup scallions, sliced		Ground black pepper
4	eggs	½	cup all-purpose flour
3	tablespoons chopped fresh parsley		Vegetable oil, for frying
2	tablespoons mustard		

1. In a medium bowl, combine the salmon, ⅔ cup breadcrumbs scallions, 2 eggs, parsley, mustard, ½ teaspoon salt, paprika, and black pepper; mix well.

---

2. Crack the remaining 2 eggs into a shallow bowl and whisk lightly. Place the flour and the remaining 1 cup breadcrumbs in separate shallow bowls. Form 1½ tablespoons of the salmon mixture into a small patty. Dip the patty into the flour, tapping off any excess. Dip into the egg, letting the excess egg drip back into the bowl. Coat well with the breadcrumbs. Repeat with the remaining salmon.

3. Heat ¼ inch oil in a large skillet over medium-high heat. Fry the patties in batches until golden-brown on both sides, 2 to 3 minutes per side. Transfer the patties to a paper-towel-lined plate to drain. Sprinkle with salt and serve hot.

JULY 10, 1969

Dear Lilly,

This is the most wonderful summer of my entire life, and I just wanted to share a little with you. I'll make it short, though, because rest hour is almost over.

Working here is the most profoundly stirring thing I've ever done, even though the camp administration is a bit of a mess. Down syndrome kids and autistic kids and physically handicapped kids are all together in one big group, as though they're all the same. (I think the administration's attitude is that one "defect" is like any other. Yuck.)

The good news is that I really love the work. I just love work, period, when it feels meaningful. There's one girl here, Tatiana. She's nine. She was born with CP, *so she moves with great difficulty. Well, yesterday we had a dance therapy session, and by the end of it, Tatiana was Queen of the Ball! She was spinning and twirling, and had the most beautiful smile on her face. She looked so proud and I could see that she felt free.*

I love that there's no name calling or shame here in our little society—it's quite a relief from the rest of the world! Speaking of the rest of the world, I hope you've gotten over your nervousness about traveling this summer. The question is not if you're ready for England, but is England ready for you! Try not to seduce too many Dukes, Counts, Lords, or Princes.

Loads of love and kisses, and an armload of sunshine your way,

Valerie

....

JULY 20, 1969

Dear Val,

One small step for man . . . one giant step for mankind . . . one huge step for girlkind! I FINALLY WENT ALL THE WAY with Luke while the astronauts walked on the moon!

But now I'm not so sure I like him that much anymore. Did I ever mention he kisses a little funny, too?

Love,

Lilly

P.S. *I leave tomorrow for England.*

....

ᏧᎳ HOMEMADE MOON PIE COOKIES ᏧᎳ

MAKES ABOUT 12 PIES

FOR THE CHOCOLATE
COOKIES:

Butter or shortening for
greasing baking sheets

1¼ cups granulated sugar

⅔ cup vegetable shortening

2 large eggs

2 teaspoons vanilla extract

2¼ cups all-purpose flour

½ cup unsweetened cocoa
powder

2 teaspoons cream of tartar

1 teaspoon baking soda

1 teaspoon salt

1 cup milk

FOR THE FILLING:

½ cup (1 stick) unsalted butter,
softened

1 cup confectioners' sugar

2 cups Marshmallow Fluff

1 teaspoon vanilla extract

1. Preheat the oven to 350° F. Grease 2 large baking sheets.

2. To make the cookies, cream the sugar and shortening in
the bowl of an electric mixer. Beat in the eggs and vanilla.
In a separate bowl, whisk together the flour, cocoa powder,
cream of tartar, baking soda, and salt. Add the flour mixture
to the wet ingredients, alternating with the milk, until fully
combined. For each cookie, spoon 2 tablespoons of batter,
2 inches apart (they will spread), onto the prepared baking
sheets. Bake until darker around the edges and firm to the
touch, 8 to 10 minutes. Transfer the cookies to a wire rack to
cool. Repeat with the remaining batter.

3. To make the filling, beat the butter and sugar. Beat in the
Marshmallow Fluff and vanilla until smooth.

4. When cookies have cooled, sandwich about 1 tablespoon
filling between 2 cookies. Repeat with remaining cookies.

5. Serve, or store in an airtight container in the refrigerator
for up to 2 days.

JULY 24, 1969

L—

I just got your letter and OH MY GOD*!!!—I can't believe it!
And I can't believe you're in England and we can't talk
details on the phone! You'd better write back and tell me
everything, and I mean* EVERYTHING*!!!*

*In fact, to make sure you don't leave anything out, I am
enclosing a sex questionnaire (Alfred Kinsey, eat your heart
out). You can mail your answers back to me in a plain brown
wrapper. (Let's just hope the camp director doesn't throw me
into jail for soliciting pornography.)*

What did it feel like?

Did you like it?

Where were you when you did it?

Was it romantic?

**If he kisses funny, how come you've been making out with
him all this time? And how come you actually went all
the way?**

**What did you call it to each other? Making love? Having
sex? Screwing? F***ing? (I can't even write that word.)
Getting laid? Getting it on?**

**Did you talk about doing it first, or did you just get carried
away with passion?**

Did you use birth control? (You'd better say yes to that.)

Did you get totally naked or did you leave some clothes on?

Did you know what to do, or did he have to show you?

(Actually, now that I think about it, did HE *know what to do, or was it his first time, too?)*

Do you feel different now, and if so, how?

Do you look different?

Could I tell you did it just by looking at you?

And most of all, Lilly, has this changed you forever? Can we still be friends?

You'd better answer, and I mean soon.

I can't believe I have to airmail this to you! I've never sent a letter overseas before. So glamorous!

Love and XOXOXO,

Val

....

AUGUST 10, 1969

Dear Val,

You are such a complete mental-case moron, and you crack me up!!! So, here goes:

What did it feel like?
At first it hurt a lot. And then it hurt a little. And then it didn't really hurt at all. But overall it was good. I know that sounds weird. It's just that I really wanted to do this and so it was right.

Did you like it?
Yes . . . and no. I liked how our bodies fit together, even

though he's so much taller. I liked that I could make him feel what I wanted him to feel. I didn't so much like that I had to keep telling him what I wanted him to do. But maybe it's different if you've been together for a while. Or if you're really in love with somebody. I guess I'll just find out with the next guy.

Where were you when you did it?
Funny you should ask. Have you heard of a waterbed? Totally freaky. When Luke's band was in San Francisco last month, some hippie guy was selling them from the back of his van. Luke drove it cross-country, so it's seen more of the USA than I have. Anyway, it's a real bed, with sheets and pillowcases and everything, but when you're on it, it's like being on a rubber raft in the middle of the ocean. Nothing holds still. Then again, we were making our own waves.

Was it romantic?
More sexy and sensual than romantic, but a little of that, too. It was daytime, but we pulled the curtains closed to make it dark. And then he lit candles, so there was a lot of flickering light. Plus the TV *was on, which made it kind of surreal . . . like I was discovering my inner space while the astronauts were exploring outer space. Fortunately, he didn't plant a flag.*

If he kisses funny, how come you've been making out with him all this time? And how come you actually went all the way?
I don't know how to explain it, but I didn't really notice he's not that great a kisser until after we had sex. Maybe that's because lately, kissing has not been high on my agenda. For the last few months, carrying around my virginity has been like carrying around five extra pounds . . . I just needed to lose it.

What did you call it to each other? Making love? Having
sex? Screwing? F***ing? (I can't even write that word.)
Getting laid? Getting it on?
Houston, we have liftoff!

Did you talk about doing it first, or did you just get carried
away with passion?
Since we got back together, he's been saying he didn't want
the huge responsibility of being "my first," but I think he was
just really worried I'd fall in love with him and get all
possessive. I told him to stop flattering himself. So to answer
your question, you might say that I talked him into it—but I
can't say I heard any complaints.

Did you use birth control? (You'd better say yes to that.)
Yes, Mother.

Did you get totally naked or did you leave some clothes on?
Um . . . naked as a jaybird. Or newborn baby. Or Liberated
Woman!

Did you know what to do, or did he have to show you?
(Actually, now that I think about it, did HE know what to do,
or was it his first time, too?)
Are you kidding me? I was born knowing how to do this.
I'm a natural. But despite his claims of great experience,
he's the one who could use some practice.

Do you feel different now, and if so, how?
I feel like I've crossed a threshold of some kind. Like I'm in
on the big secret.

Do you look different?
I grew three inches and my boobs went up two bra sizes.
Immediately. Before I even put my clothes back on.

Could I tell you did it just by looking at you?
Depends where you look.

And most of all, Lilly, has this changed you forever? Can
we still be friends?
Yes, this has definitely changed me forever. But one thing
will never change: you will always be the only best friend
dopey enough to send a stupid questionnaire like this. And
I love you for it.

Lilly

P.S. *England is jolly good. Still researching whether the men*
here kiss with a stiff upper lip.

....

AUGUST 23, 1969

Dear Lilly,

I gotta tell you, when I read your answers to my questions,
I felt so many things. Awe at your confidence. Envy at your
lack of inhibition. Embarrassment to have to ask such naïve
questions. Curiosity to know more. (Not just the sex stuff,
either—a waterbed? I can't even imagine it. If I ever went on
one, I'd probably get seasick.)

Oddly enough, I also have these weird feelings, like I'm all
alone and I'm losing you. It's upsetting. I feel like you're
moving far away from me. Not just the three thousand miles
across the ocean, but in terms of maturity. I can't help
feeling like I may never grow up.

Lilly, have a wonderful, amazing, exciting summer. But

don't travel so far from me that you forget how to come home.

Love always,

Valerie

....

Dear Val,

Cambridge is really beautiful, but I miss everyone. I've never been this far away before. But I also feel, for the first time, like I can be my own person.

Right now I'm sitting under a weeping willow on the bank of the river with Cassandra. She's a good friend I made on this trip. She draws really well. She's the best in the class. The thing I like most about her is that she really listens. Whatever I tell her, she totally understands. She has these gray-green eyes that just look right into your heart. You would like her, I think. She and I speak the same language, if you know what I mean. If she was a boy I would say that I would fall in love with her. Is that a weird thing to say? Anyway, I haven't thought about Luke once.

Cassandra and I found an amazing bakery called FitzMitchell's. They make shortbread and other "bickies," which is what they call cookies here. I got a recipe for us.

Next week we go on the cruise. I'll write you from the boat, too.

Love,

Lilly

✂ FITZMITCHELL'S SHORTBREAD ✂

MAKES ABOUT 2 DOZEN SHORTBREAD

||||||||||||||||||||||||||||||||||||||||||||||||||||||||||||||||||||||||||||||||||||||||||||||||||||||||

2 cups all-purpose flour	2 sticks unsalted butter, softened and cut into cubes
¾ cup confectioners' sugar	2 teaspoons vanilla extract
¾ teaspoon salt	

1. Preheat the oven to 325° F.

2. In a large bowl, whisk together the flour, sugar, and salt; add the butter and vanilla. Using an electric mixer, blend the mixture until it begins to come together. Form the dough into a ball.

3. Press the dough in an even layer into an 8 x 8-inch baking pan. Prick the shortbread all over with a fork. Bake until light golden, about 35 minutes. Slice into "fingers" while still warm.

AUGUST 30, 1969

Dear Val,

Greetings from Tunisia!

The cruise is fun. Our room is pretty tiny. We have bunk beds and Cassandra sleeps below me.

The ship is Greek but it has an Italian crew. All the guys who work on it are constantly flirting with us. Last night two sailors took me and Cassandra to the top deck and one of them kept pressing up against me and pointing to the stars.

Then, when he was kissing my neck, I looked over to Cassandra, who was making out with her sailor, and I kind of wondered what it felt like to be kissing her. Not that I wanted to, but I was thinking how it should be important to connect to the person that you kiss . . . or if you do more than kiss, it's even more important to feel something for him, right?

But on the other hand, how do you even find the right person? How do you know that the person you fall in love with today will be right for you in ten years—or ten days, for that matter? How do you choose one person and know for sure you haven't made a terrible mistake because someone even better is around the corner?

Why am I even worrying about all this now? Maybe because being this far from home gives you room to room-inate. (Now I sound JUST LIKE YOU!!! That was such a Val-y thing to say!! Are you laughing? Laugh louder, I can't hear you.)

They served scampi on the boat last night. Every meal we've had is Italian (which reminds me, I need to break up with Luke when I get back). I had to kiss the chef to get the recipe, so I hope you like it.

I'll be home soon. I miss you, Valerie Rudman.

Lilly

....

✺ STARRY NIGHT SCAMPI ✺

SERVES 4

|||||||||||||||||||||||||||||||||||||||||||||||||||||||||||||||||||||||||||||||||||||||||||||||||||||||||||||||||||||||||||

5   tablespoons extra-virgin olive oil

3   garlic cloves, minced

½   cup dry white wine

1   sprig rosemary

¾   teaspoon salt, or to taste

⅛   teaspoon crushed red pepper flakes, or to taste

    Ground black pepper

1½ pounds large or extra-large shrimp, shelled

⅓   cup chopped fresh basil or parsley

2   tablespoons capers, drained

    Freshly squeezed juice of half a lemon

    Crusty bread, for serving

1. Heat the olive oil in a large skillet. Add the garlic and sauté until fragrant, about 1 minute. Add the wine, rosemary, salt, red pepper flakes, and plenty of black pepper, and bring to a simmer. Let the wine reduce by half, about 2 minutes.

2. Add the shrimp and sauté until they just turn pink, 2 to 4 minutes, depending upon their size. Discard the rosemary. Stir in the basil, capers, and lemon juice, and serve accompanied by crusty bread.

SEPTEMBER 4, 1969

Hey, Val,

I can't believe the whole summer went by already. I called home to see who would pick me up at the airport and my father said to take a cab. Welcome home.

I was kind of hoping I would come back to find things have changed. But no such luck. Just as I arrived, my mother

*was splitting for Woodstock with some musician guy. My
father didn't want her to leave. But did he say so directly?
No. In his typical way, he said, "Katherine, don't you see
this adolescent behavior is just an inadequate coping
mechanism? Don't you see how you're constantly
transferring your Oedipal anger onto me?" My mother
blew up and stormed out with her usual parting shot:
"Why don't you kiss Freud's ass!" She barely said hello
or good-bye to me.*

*It's a weird feeling when you return from a long trip, where
you had all these amazing life-changing experiences, only to
find out everyone back home has been frozen in time. It's
like my parents don't even see how I've changed. They've
barely asked anything about the trip. Not that I should have
expected them to. But I guess in some way I'm still holding
on to old fantasies that one day I'll wake up and my "real"
parents—the ones I haven't met yet, the ones who are kind
and loving and actually act their age—will be here to take
me away from all this.*

*Lesson to be learned: no matter how much I grow up, my
parents never will.*

*No recipes this time, unless you want me to include bad
airplane food in our club! (Joking.)*

Love,

Lilly

*P.S. Let's get together the minute you get home from camp,
okay?*

....

Dear Val,

A terrible thing happened. There was a girl in my history class who got killed in a car accident. They said we didn't have to go to class yesterday if we wanted to attend her memorial service. Me and Maggie were the only ones who didn't go because it seemed wrong. I mean, school just started, so we didn't really know her. And most of the kids who went just did it to get out of class. That made me sick. It seemed so phony. And there's another reason they went. They all want to feel important because they know a dead person.

I've never known anyone who died before. (Unless you count Ben's parents, who I never met, but he told me about them.) And I keep wondering what was taken away from her. What was she going to be? What did she want to see and do? Who would she have married? And then I think, what if I was going to die tomorrow? What if you died? What if our parents die?

Anyway, this whole thing made me want to tell you that I think about you a lot, even when I don't write or call so much. We will always be friends, right? And we'll live forever, right? I mean, not forever, but however long we're supposed to, which is a long, long, long time.

Love,

Lilly

....

Dearest Lilly,

Death is so weird. For a while afterwards everybody acts like it will change them and make them appreciate everything— friends, family, each new day. But then, little by little, life just resumes being normal again. You forget the dead person, or if you don't exactly forget them, you just put them into deep mental storage, like you're putting away furs for the summer.

This is what I learned when Ben's mom and dad were killed in that car crash, even though I was only a little kid. After Aunt Sonya and Uncle Jake died, for a while I thought WE would all die from the sadness. But we didn't. Not even Ben. (Of course, all this holds true for everyone in the world except my mother. She really DID change forever after the accident, and not for the better, either. My mom and Aunt Sunny were inseparable. Storybook sisters, like you and I would be if we were sisters.)

All I really know is that hearing terrible news about a kid our age dying makes me—more than ever—want to do something important with my life. By the way, I really respect your not pretending to be best friends with the girl who died. And you're right about one other thing, too: we will always be friends. And we'll live as long and as hard as we possibly can. I really love you, Lilly. No matter what.

Valerie

....

1970

JANUARY 4, 1970

Hi, Lilly.

*I feel like it's the end of an era or something. There's part of
me that understands why you wanted to spend New Year's
Eve with your new boyfriend at that party in the Village. But
there's another part, and honestly it's bigger, that feels really
hurt that you didn't want to continue our tradition. And that
you didn't want to spend time with me.*

*It's hard to believe it's a whole new decade. Hope we see
each other sometime before 1980.*

Take care,
Valerie

....

JANUARY 28, 1970

Hi Lilly,
Just a quick note to say thanks for your letter.

*I guess you really mean you're sorry if you're actually
inviting me to go on a double date with you and Conrad!
What can you tell me about his friend Kip? Is he cute? Is he
nice? I'm excited! Is he taller than me? Where are we going?
Will I like him? Tell me everything. Tell me what to wear.*

*So yeah, okay, I forgive you. And no, I won't hold a grudge.
(You know I never do. But you wait—one day I'll learn how
to. So watch out.)*

And to show you how happy I am that the two of us will be going on a double date, here's the time-honored recipe for the amazing Rudman blintzes that you've been begging for. I know you can never decide which you love better, the cheese or the potato. So make both.

Thanks again for the letter, crazy girl. I can't wait to see you on Saturday night!

Love,

Me

....

⟨ DOUBLE DATE BLINTZES ⟩

MAKES ABOUT 12 BLINTZES

FOR THE CRÊPES:

1   cup milk

4   eggs, lightly beaten

1   cup all-purpose flour

1   teaspoon salt

    Melted butter, for frying

FOR THE CHEESE FILLING:

¾   pound cottage cheese, drained

1   egg yolk

½   tablespoon melted butter

1½   teaspoons sugar

    Pinch ground cinnamon

½   teaspoon salt

FOR THE POTATO FILLING:

1¼   cups mashed potato

1   egg, lightly beaten

1   tablespoon melted butter

½   teaspoon salt

    Pinch ground nutmeg

    Ground black pepper

---

1. To make the crêpes for the blintzes, whisk all of the ingredients, except the melted butter, until smooth. Let the batter rest 30 minutes.

2. Heat 2 tablespoons butter in a large skillet over medium-high heat. Working in batches, pour ¼ to ⅓ cup batter into the pan, tilting to spread into a thin, even layer. Cook until the edges curl slightly away from the skillet and the underside is lightly browned, 1 to 2 minutes. Use a flexible spatula to flip the crêpes out of the skillet and onto a plate, cooked side up. Repeat with the remaining batter, adding additional butter to the skillet as needed. Let the crêpes cool.

3. Meanwhile, prepare the fillings: in one bowl, combine all of the cheese filling ingredients. In a separate bowl combine all of the potato filling ingredients.

4. Preheat the oven to 375° F. Place 1 crêpe cooked side up on a plate. Place 1½ tablespoons cheese filling in the center, and fold up the bottom to cover the filling. Fold in the sides, then fold down the top. Flip over and place seam side down on a baking sheet. Repeat with the remaining crêpes and filling. Fill half the crêpes with the cheese mixture, and half with the potato mixture.

5. Drizzle the blintzes with additional melted butter, then bake for 35 to 40 minutes, until golden on top.

FEBRUARY 8, 1970

Dear Lilly,

I've never been so humiliated in my entire life. No matter what you say, and how many times you say it, you're just wrong.

I HEARD KIP WITH MY OWN EARS *say to Conrad, "I know this is a blind date, but did you think I was blind?"*

They were in the kitchen when you were putting on music in the living room. And I was coming to get a glass of water. But Kip knew I was listening. And for your information, Conrad DID laugh, no matter what he tells you.

I don't blame you for what happened, but I do expect you to believe ME, not them, and to hate your stupid boyfriend JUST A LITTLE, for me.

On the other hand, I should know better by now than to go out with your friends. Whenever I do, something awful happens. My fault for always expecting the best of people, including you.

Val

....

FEBRUARY 11, 1970

Look, Val, it isn't your fault. Why don't you believe me? Maybe you need to read these words out loud to yourself: I'M NOT WEIRD. KIP IS.

It was wrong before you even got there. Conrad was all into showing off for Kip, acting like some drug king, when in reality that was the first time he bought a nickel bag in his life. And Kip is one of those guys who can't handle being around a girl smarter than he is. And on top of that, it turns out he's also got a mean streak, which I didn't know about. So when he made fun of how tall you are, it had more to do with how short he is. And when he mocked you for not getting high, it was because he can't even have a conversation when he's straight.

And it's not that I don't believe Kip said something so cruel and stupid, it's just that I don't think it's such a big deal. It's the way boys act tough together.

As for me being mad at Conrad, don't worry, we broke up. But not just because of you. After you left, Kip made a move on me and Conrad didn't seem to care. Maybe he was too stoned to notice. The hell with him.

Val, don't give up on love. One day you'll fall in love with someone so great, even I'll be jealous. And don't give up on me. One day I'll be the person you keep thinking I am.

Love,

Lilly

....

MARCH 2, 1970

Hey Sillyface,

I'm so excited I could scream! I tried calling you a hundred times but your phone is always busy, and I had to tell you immediately or I would explode.

I can graduate a year early!

Can you believe how great this is? I feel like the governor called with a reprieve! And I owe it all to Isaac's tutoring. I love him so much. You are so lucky to have him as a dad. Sometimes I feel closer to him than I do to my own father. (But don't ever tell my dad I said that—it would hurt his feelings. Even though he never says much about it, sometimes I think he's jealous of me and Isaac. Or maybe I just wish he were a little more interested in my life.)

I haven't broken the news to my mother yet—I'm afraid she'll completely freak out and forbid me from EVER graduating.

Okay, I gotta go now and clean my dorm room—oops! I mean my room.

Love and kisses,

College Girl

P.S. Hey, I almost forgot. Here's a good recipe for Cheesecake Pie, which I made tonight because I'm in such a good mood. It's creamier than a regular cheesecake, and you make it in a pie shell. I wonder what dorm food is like?

❦ CELEBRATION CHEESECAKE PIE ❧

SERVES 8

1¾ cup graham cracker crumbs

½ cup unsalted butter, melted (1 stick)

1 (8-ounce) package cream cheese, softened

2 eggs

½ cup sugar

1 cup sour cream

1 teaspoon vanilla extract

Finely grated zest of ½ lemon

1. Preheat the oven to 325° F.

2. To make the crust, combine the graham cracker crumbs and the butter in a bowl. Press the mixture into the bottom

and up the sides of a 9-inch pie plate. Chill until ready
to use.

3. To make the cheesecake: using an electric mixer, beat
the cream cheese until smooth. Scrape down the sides with
a rubber spatula and beat again. Add the eggs, 1 at a time,
scraping down the sides between additions. Slowly beat in
the sugar. Continue to beat until pale yellow and fluffy, 1 to
2 minutes more. Add the sour cream, vanilla, and lemon zest.
Beat until smooth.

4. Pour the filling into the prepared crust. Place the pie pan
inside a larger baking dish. Pour boiling water inside the
baking dish to come halfway up the sides of the pie pan. Bake
until the cheesecake is pale golden on top and still jiggles
slightly, 35 to 45 minutes.

5. Let cool to room temperature, then chill at least 2 hours
before serving.

MARCH 17, 1970

Dear Val,

A green clover cake
For you to bake
Luck o' the Irish to you!
I'm writing a poem
Since I'm bored at home
And I've got nothing to do.

Love,

Lilly

P.S. My all-knowing father says if I'm so bored I'd better do something to wake up my mind. So I turned on the television and watched the St. Patrick's Day parade. I did that to get him mad. Then he said, "Why don't you try to be more like Valerie once in a while?" He gave me a book called The Psychodynamics of Cross-Cultural Polygamy in East Asian Cultures. *Can you believe it? Even you would be bored.*

....

⟨ LUCK O' THE IRISH SODA BREAD ⟩

MAKES 1 10-INCH LOAF

3	cups all-purpose flour	1¾	cups buttermilk
¾	cup sugar	2	eggs, well-beaten
1	tablespoon baking powder	¼	cup melted butter
1½	teaspoons salt	1½	cups raisins
1	teaspoon baking soda	1	tablespoon caraway seeds

1. Preheat the oven to 350°. F. Grease a 10-inch skillet and line with parchment.

2. In a bowl, whisk together the flour, sugar, baking powder, salt, and baking soda. In a separate bowl, combine the buttermilk, eggs, and 2 tablespoons butter. Add the wet ingredients to the dry and stir until just combined. Do not overmix. Stir in the raisins and caraway seeds.

3. Pour the batter into the skillet. Brush the top of the batter with the remaining butter. Bake until golden and firm to the touch, about 1 hour.

4. Let cool 10 minutes before slicing and serving.

Hi L—

I didn't go to school for the last couple of days because I had a bad cold. Of course, that made my mother secretly happy because she had someone to hang around with all day. Lucky me. (Actually, we had fun doing crossword puzzles and watching the 4:00 movie. They showed Laura with Gene Tierney. She was so beautiful. From old pictures, I think my mother looked like her when she was younger.)

My dad will be taking me to check out colleges in a couple of weeks. Do you want to come with us? Of course, I know (because my parents don't shut up about it) that I can't afford to go to any of these "fancy private schools" unless I get a big scholarship.

The only one who doesn't seem worried is Isaac. He says he would be happy to help me out financially, whether or not I get a scholarship. Do you already know this? Anyway, my parents are arguing over this. My mother wants to accept his offer, but my father says it's his place to pay for his child's education. He says there's nothing wrong with a state school, and that he's an educator and should know. Ben is paying for art school out of the money his parents left him.

What do I think? Well, it's confusing. On the one hand I can't believe how generous Isaac is to me, and accepting his offer would give me access to a whole new universe. But if it's only going to make my father feel ashamed and hurt, then it's really not worth it. So I guess I'm glad it's not my choice, but I also feel like all these decisions are being made about me, and nobody's even asking what I think or feel or want.

Your school-dazed friend,

Val

P.S. *If only my father could invent a cure for the common cold! But till he does, try this. It's so good you'll see stars.*

....

❧ CHICKEN SOUP WITH STARS ❧

SERVES 4 TO 6

2	medium celery stalks, diced	2	cups cooked chicken, roughly chopped
2	medium carrots, diced		
1	small onion, diced	3	tablespoons chopped parsley
8	cups chicken stock	2	teaspoons salt
1½	cups pastina		Ground black pepper

1. In a medium pot, combine the celery, carrots, onion, and chicken stock. Bring to a boil; reduce to a simmer and cook for 20 minutes.

2. Add the pastina and simmer for 10 minutes. Stir in the chicken and parsley and simmer for 5 minutes more. Season the soup with salt and pepper, to taste.

APRIL 22, 1970

Dear Val,

Today my mother and I helped celebrate Earth Day. She says it's an important idea because if people get involved with healing the earth, then maybe there's hope for the world.

My father, the pessimist, says she's delusional.

Anyway, while we were cleaning up trash (gross!) in Riverside Park, I ran into Ben. He says he's moving into a loft with two other sculptors. Now THERE'S *a guy following his own heart. I asked if I could come see his new space and check out his work, and he seemed happy I took an interest.*

The funniest thing was, every time I threw something into the trash, he pulled it out and put it in a separate pile of "found objects" that he's going to "rescue and recycle" into art. We had this hysterical routine of me picking up old tires and dead shoes like they were rotting fish, and him oohing and aahing like they were crown jewels. He cracks me up.

But then he did that strange Ben thing: in the middle of what I thought was a really good time, suddenly he was gone. He left without even saying good-bye. And his pile of rescued trash vanished along with him. Why does he always slip away like that? Maybe because good-byes are too hard for him to deal with? Is he like that with everyone, or just me?

And what about that way he has of acting all fun and flirty when a girlfriend is on his arm, but being so quiet and almost sad when he's alone? What's that about? You must have noticed it. Funny that we never really talked about it.

Meanwhile, back at the ranch, here's a recipe for homemade yogurt. It's supposed to help us live forever. (But my mother says that's a bad thing, because we'll just destroy the planet a lot sooner.) Anyway, try adding fresh fruit once it's done, and enjoy!

Love,

Lilly

❧ EARTH DAY YOGURT ❧

SERVES 6

|||||||||||||||||||||||||||||||||||||||||||||||||||||||||||||||||||||||||||||||||||||||||||||||||||||||||||||

2	cups whole milk	$^1/_3$	cup full-fat yogurt
$^1/_3$	cup heavy cream		Granola for serving
$^3/_4$	cup dry milk powder		Honey for serving

1. In a medium pot, bring the milk and cream to a simmer. Whisk in the milk powder, a little at a time, until fully dissolved. Let cool until warm to the touch. Stir in the yogurt.

2. Transfer the mixture to a clean glass jar. Cover tightly with a fitted lid or plastic wrap and set in a warm place until it has thickened to a custardlike consistency, 18 to 36 hours, depending on how warm the room is. (The longer the yogurt sits, the tangier the flavor will be.)

3. Refrigerate until chilled and even thicker, at least 6 hours and up to a week.

4. Serve the yogurt topped with granola and drizzled with honey.

MAY 4, 1970

Dear Val,

Ben said you're not returning my calls because I didn't check out schools with you. Look, I'll tell the truth, okay? It's not just because I've got rehearsal for West Side Story *(I'm Anita . . . did you know? How great is that?). You said I should be more honest about how I feel with stuff. So, okay. The truth is, I'm confused about you leaving for college. There are a bunch of reasons why. One is that I'll miss you. The other is that I wish you were gone already.*

I mean, all my father can talk about is his relief that your parents finally "came to their senses" about him paying for school, and that you can go to "the college of your choice." He has your whole life planned out for you, minute by minute. (And I even wonder, do you really want this, or are you just trying to please him? My father can be very pushy.)

Anyway, it's all he talks about at the dinner table. Like he's so proud. No offense, but it makes me gag.

Then, the other night, my parents had a big fight about YOU. My father said he thinks he should have been the one to take you to visit the schools, instead of your father, because he's more "aware of your intellectual needs." My mother said that she thought he was butting in where he didn't belong and the last thing he should do is pay for your education, let alone act like your personal tour guide. I have to agree with her.

Look, the thing is, it's good you have a friendship with my dad and all, that's cool, but it just feels a little weird sometimes.

P.S. Here's another big problem if you go. What happens to the Recipe Club? You probably won't want to do it anymore. So, you know what? Let's just forget the whole thing right now. Or maybe I should start one with someone else.

....

Hey there, Lilly,

Don't be an idiot. Nobody in her right mind would start a recipe club with you. You're too crazy. You're lucky I still do it with you.

You know I'm kidding, right?

Look, the last thing I want is to have you feel bad, too. First my parents were arguing over this. Now yours. Let's not join them. It makes me feel so sad that something I'm feeling so positive and hopeful about is making everybody else miserable.

Can't we just talk about the good stuff?

There's so much to tell you: so far we've seen like a million colleges. I really loved MIT. Everyone there practically LIVES for math! And everyone looks really serious. I know I would have friends. My dream is to go there and major in math, even though there aren't that many girls.

But when I tell Isaac I want to go to MIT, he gets annoyed. He keeps telling me I should DEFINITELY get a Harvard degree like him, and do a pre-med major in biology, like he did. It makes me want to stay home and get a job cleaning birdcages at Woolworth's.

Lilly, are you starting to think about what college you want to apply to? If I go to school in the Boston area, maybe you could too. And then in a couple of years, we could move off-campus together and share an apartment! Wouldn't that be great? I can just see us fixing up some cozy little garret, cooking together in our own kitchen, having new friends over. No parents, no rules, no obligations, no worries about who might be upset or nervous or angry. I can't even imagine how sweet that sense of freedom would be.

Do you think there will ever be a time in my life when I'm not waffling back and forth about every decision, big or small?

Love,

Val

....

⊶ WORRY-FREE WAFFLES ⊷

MAKES ABOUT 6 WAFFLES

|||||||||||||||||||||||||||||||||||||||||||||||||||||||||||||||||||||||||||||||||||||||||||||||||||||||||||||||||||||||||||||||||||

1¾ cups all-purpose flour
1¾ teaspoons baking powder
    Pinch salt
1½ cups milk
2 large eggs, separated
1 teaspoon vanilla extract

¼ cup unsalted butter, melted, plus additional for brushing
1 large egg white, at room temperature
¼ cup sugar
    Maple syrup, for serving

1. Preheat a waffle iron to medium-high.

2. In a large bowl, whisk together the flour, baking powder, and salt.

3. In a medium bowl, whisk together the milk, egg yolks, vanilla, and ¼ cup melted butter. Whisk the milk mixture into the flour mixture until a batter just forms.

4. In medium bowl, whip the 3 egg whites with a handheld electric mixer, or whisk until frothy. Add the sugar to the whites and continue beating until they hold a soft peak. Using a rubber spatula, fold ¼ of the egg whites into the batter to lighten. Fold in the remaining whites.

5. Brush the waffle iron with butter. Pour in enough batter to lightly cover the surface of the iron, about ⅓ to ¾ cup, depending upon the size of the iron. Cover and cook until golden-brown and slightly crisp, about 5 minutes (a good indication that the waffles are finished is when the iron stops steaming). Repeat with the remaining batter. Serve the waffles immediately, with syrup.

MAY 18, 1970

Dear Lilly,

I haven't heard from you once in more than two weeks. Why aren't you returning any of my calls? Have you eloped with that French guy, Guy? The last I heard, Ben saw you at the movies. He said you were so busy making out, you probably saw only two out of the Five Easy Pieces.

Maybe if I send you a recipe for the Recipe Club you'll remember who I am? So here goes. Don't let the name make you think it has any hidden meaning or anything. It's a coincidence, of course.

Val

❧ BITTER GREENS WITH ❧
SOUR LEMON

SERVES 6

|||||||||||||||||||||||||||||||||||||||||||||||||||||||||||||||||||||||||||||||||||||||||||||||||||||||||||||||||||||||||||||||||||||||||||||||

3	tablespoons extra-virgin olive oil		Grated zest and freshly squeezed juice of 1 lemon,
2	pounds escarole, trimmed and rinsed	1	teaspoon salt
1	large garlic clove, finely chopped		Black pepper

1. In a large skillet, over medium heat, warm the oil. Add the escarole and garlic.

2. Cover, and reduce the heat to medium-low. Cook, tossing occasionally, until meltingly tender, about 20 minutes.

3. Season with the lemon zest and juice, the salt, and pepper to taste.

MAY 20, 1970

Dear Val,

I got your letter.

And I also just got a big talking-to from my father. I guess you told him I was at Guy's house when I was supposed to be at school. Why do you need to tell my personal stuff? What I tell you is none of his business. Got it?

Now maybe you'll understand why I don't like telling you personal things lately. You're a blabbermouth. If you want to be friends again, you have to respect that I have things going on in my life that are private. We aren't children anymore.

Lilly

....

MAY 25, 1970

Lilly,

Hi. I'm relieved we settled everything. When we're arguing with each other nothing in my life feels right.

So, for the millionth time, and just for the record, I agree: I never should have told Isaac about you and Guy. I swear to you I will never do that again.

But can I explain, a little more, about what happened? When your father asked me where you were, I didn't know what to say—you know I can't lie! I'm no good at that. It's not like I went to him and volunteered the information. He asked. In fact, he demanded that I tell him—and I felt obligated to respond truthfully.

Lilly, I don't think you understand how awkward it is to be in the position of feeling loyal to both you AND Isaac. It's hard. Both of you make demands of me, and sometimes they're conflicting.

And then there's part of me that just felt so confused and hurt that you were being so distant.

But I'll never, ever do something so stupid again.

Val

....

Oh, Lilly, I feel like my life is about to turn into someone else's—and by that I mean someone with a better life.

I've got great news: that lab assistant job came through! Thank you, Isaac!! It turns out to be not just the two-week internship I applied for, but a real job—with pay!—that lasts the whole summer. Do you have any idea how amazing this will be for my college applications???

And get this: I'll even wear a white lab coat, just like when we were my father's little "apprentices." (Remember how cute we were? I bet I'll look even cuter this time around, especially if I wear it with those strappy green sandals that you made me buy last weekend, even though they kill me. Once again, I bow to your fashion wisdom.)

So Sherlock, what else did you find out from your father about Dr. Shineman? (All Isaac told me was that he won the 1969 National Institute of Science Award in Molecular Biology.) Can you believe I'm going to be working side by side with such a luminary?

Isn't it interesting that he's such a good friend of your father's, even though he's so much younger? How old do you think he is? (I'm embarrassed to ask Isaac.) Can you find out if he's married? (I know it's a ridiculous question, but what if he isn't?) He doesn't wear any rings. (Of course, that might just mean he cheats on his wife.) He seems really nice and gentle—handsome, too, in that too-old kind of way. (Am I even his type?)

Oh, ignore me. I'm sure he's too old to have a crush on, and he'd never be attracted to me even if he were my age. So why can't I stop dreaming about him?

You must think I've lost my mind—and maybe I have! I just feel so alive. And hopeful! Ohmygod, Lilly, I'm tingling all over and on the verge of the happiest heart attack of my life.

Hey, before I go, here's a quiz. Do you remember: a) The way we used to "spy" on people using my mother's powder compact mirror? b) The time we looked in every one of Isaac's medical dictionaries to see if you could become pregnant from making out? c) Me? (Just checking.)

Love,

Dr. Valerie Rudman-Shineman, M.D., Ph.D., Nobel-Winning Scientist and Laboratory Research Assistant

P.S. *My most recent kitchen "lab experiment" was a complete success! You'll love it—it's salty and sweet and gooey at the same time.*

....

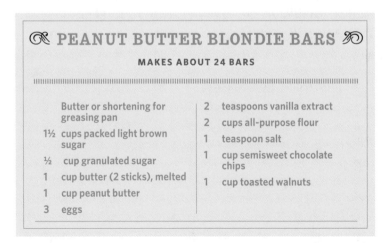

PEANUT BUTTER BLONDIE BARS

MAKES ABOUT 24 BARS

Butter or shortening for greasing pan	2 teaspoons vanilla extract
1½ cups packed light brown sugar	2 cups all-purpose flour
	1 teaspoon salt
½ cup granulated sugar	1 cup semisweet chocolate chips
1 cup butter (2 sticks), melted	1 cup toasted walnuts
1 cup peanut butter	
3 eggs	

1. Preheat the oven to 350° F. Grease a 9 x 13-inch pan.

2. In a bowl, cream together the sugars, butter, and peanut butter. Beat in the eggs, one at a time, and the vanilla. Add the flour and salt and mix to combine. Fold in the chocolate chips and the nuts.

3. Spread the dough evenly in the prepared pan. Bake until golden-brown on top and a toothpick inserted in the center comes out clean, 30 to 35 minutes. Let cool 10 minutes before cutting into bars.

JUNE 21, 1970

Dear Val,

I'm so pissed. My father won't let me work at my mother's theater this summer. When I asked why, and how come he thinks it's good for you to work in a stupid lab (no offense), all he could say was, "Some people know how to make the right choices in life, others need help to stay out of trouble." What's that all about?

Anyway, that's why I haven't written.

Here's the recipe I owe you.

Love,
Lilly

....

❦ GREEN-EYED GREEN BEANS ❧

SERVES 6

||||||||||||||||||||||||||||||||||||||||||||||||||||||||||||||||||||||||||||||||||||||||||||||||||||||

1	pound green beans, trimmed	¼	teaspoon salt
¼	cup unsalted butter		Ground black pepper, to taste
2	tablespoons all-purpose flour	3	tablespoons drained capers
1	cup chicken stock		

1. Bring a large pot of salted water to a boil. Add the green beans and cook until crisp-tender, 5 to 7 minutes. Drain.

2. In a medium skillet over low heat, melt 2 tablespoons butter. Whisk in the flour until smooth, and simmer 2 minutes. Add the chicken stock, a little at a time, and stir until smooth. Season with salt and pepper. Stir in the capers.

3. Add the green beans and cook until heated through and tender, about 2 minutes. Add the remaining 2 tablespoons butter, stir until melted, and serve.

JULY 28, 1970

Dear Lilly,

It's almost two in the morning and I can't sleep. I wanted to call you earlier, but I couldn't get myself to say the words out loud. So I'm writing this to prove to myself it really happened.

It's horrible.

I was working late, like I always do, and so was Dr. Shineman, which he usually does. It's the only time we're ever alone in the lab, and before tonight I've always liked it—it felt intimate and professional all at once.

But tonight something went terribly wrong. I was alone in the lab, preparing my slides, when suddenly I had this funny feeling that someone else was in the room. Before I could even turn around, Dr. Shineman started shoving himself against me, kissing my neck and grabbing my breasts.

I was so shocked and revolted. Lilly, you know that I've been dreaming about kissing him all summer long, but not like that!

I pushed him away and politely asked him to stop. But he didn't. And then I got scared and angry and shouted NO! Don't do this. Please.

He got furious. He looked right at me and said, "You little bitch. You've been asking for this from the day you started." His eyes were crazy—dilated and intense. He grabbed a beaker that was next to me and slammed it onto the counter so hard it shattered.

Then the creepiest thing of all: his rage dissipated as quickly as it had come over him. He smiled at me in this slimy way and said, "I was only checking your test results." As if he'd just come over to work with me; as if nothing had happened between us; as if I were the crazy one. Then he said, "Good night, Miss Rudman," turned around, and walked back into his office.

I didn't know what to do. I was shaking so hard I dropped the slide I was still holding, and it broke, too. There was glass all over the place. I just grabbed my bag and ran out of there. I didn't even notice I had cut my finger until I was halfway home. And now, hours later, no matter how many showers I take, I can't get this dirty feeling off my skin.

Oh, Lilly, what have I done? Is he right? Was I asking for that? I admit it, I was flirting—sending signals, staring, finding excuses to let our hands touch, going the extra mile to help him—but does that give him the right to attack me? And why did he get so angry when I asked him to stop? Isn't it my right to say no?

I'm so confused and upset. I feel partly responsible and at the same time totally guilty. My head is spinning. Did I not understand the rules of the game? Did I fail to understand that every action has a reaction, especially between men and women? Am I a naïve idiot, or is he just a total pervert? I need a reality check.

I swear, Lilly, I never truly believed anything would really happen between us. But even when I imagined it might, the feelings were always romantic and tender, like in the movies. Not this. Never this.

So now I am in a panic about what I should do. If I show up at work tomorrow, what message does that send? And if I don't, what do I tell Isaac? Shineman is his good friend.

I know you won't get this in time for your answer to do me any good, but writing to you makes me feel less alone, so thanks for listening.

Ugh.

Val

. . . .

JULY 29, 1970

Val,

*God almighty, I've never heard you sound so strung out.
It's good that you called in sick today, and it's good that
you called me.*

*Like I promised, I'm writing this letter so you'll have
something to carry with you at all times, to give you
strength.*

*First, you've made the right decision to go back. You can't
let this guy ruin an otherwise perfect job. And I agree, it's
not just that it's good for your college applications, but
you actually really love the work.*

*So you just have to do what we said before: never be alone
with him, never make eye contact, never stay late, and never
take crap from The Creep.*

*I know how hard this must be for you, maybe more than for
other people, since it's the first time you've let yourself feel
something for a guy. You know what I mean? I really respect
that you let yourself dream about him, even if he didn't turn
out to be who you thought he was. So don't give up on
dreaming.*

*And hey, there is good news here, Val. You obviously have
some natural flirting talent. You just have to stay in the
driver's seat and not let other people take you on their
joyrides.*

*Trust me, flirting should be fun. It only gets dangerous when
signals get crossed. So, you need to learn how to read men.
You need to be clear about what you're saying to them, even
with a touch of your hand.*

And, above all, remember: nobody has a right to grab you the way Dr. Slime-man did.

Keep the faith, Valsky.

Lilly

....

Dear Lilly,

Well, I made it through. Today was my last day of work. What a weird experience this has been.

My fellow lab assistants gave me a little party. They brought in vanilla cupcakes, which we "dissected" into bite-size pieces and served on glass slides. Then we did our last experiment together. We each made a solution of $C_{12}H_2O_{11}$, $C_6H_{12}O_6$, H_2O, and cocoa (better known to you as chocolate syrup), then added lactose (better known to you as milk), and carbon dioxide-infused H_2O (better known to you as seltzer). You know what it was? Egg creams! We drank them out of beakers. (Don't worry, the slides and beakers were brand-new.)

The sweetest part: everyone gave me a toast. They said how helpful I'd been and that they were sad to see me go. It was adorable, and left me feeling good.

On the other hand, Slime-man didn't even say good-bye or anything. I took the high road and wrote him a note of thanks for the opportunity to work there. I slipped it under his door. He saw me, but pretended he didn't.

I'm not upset about what he did anymore, but I couldn't

have gotten through this without you, Lilly. Especially since I kept it a secret from my parents. And Isaac. That was probably the hardest part. Every time your father asked me how it was going, how I liked working with Dr. Shineman, I changed the subject. And it always made me feel so bizarre because I don't even know who I was protecting—me? The Creep? Your father?

The thing that bugs me the most is how unfair the balance of power is. I feel like I can't say anything about what happened, because even though The Creep was the one who did something wrong, he was my boss. Who would ever believe me over him? I mean, here's this prize-winning scientist, and who am I?

I think even Isaac, who knows me well, would probably say I was imagining it.

On the other hand, if I breathed even one word to my parents, they certainly would have believed me—but they also would have yanked me out of there so fast I would have gotten whiplash.

Funny, I knew I'd learn a lot this summer, but I had no idea it would be a crash course in life. I guess in the end it's a good thing. A rude awakening, yes, but eye-opening at the same time.

Okay, now I have five minutes of vacation before school starts. Maybe I'll take a whirlwind trip through Asia, Africa, Europe, and Australia. Or maybe I'll just clean my room and get ready for my senior—did you hear that, SENIOR!!!—year.

Val

P.S. You can do your own experiments with this recipe by adding more or less chocolate, to taste.

....

❦ EXPERIMENTAL EGG CREAM ❧

SERVES 1

2 to 3 tablespoons chocolate syrup (Fox's U-Bet Original Chocolate Flavor Syrup is the best!)	5	ounces whole milk, slightly frozen
	3	ounces seltzer

1. Pour chocolate syrup into a tall glass. Add milk but don't mix.

2. Pour in seltzer to top of glass and mix vigorously, with a long spoon, until frothy.

SEPTEMBER 12, 1970

Dear Val,

The recipe I'm sending has a weird story that goes with it. My mother took me to a farm in Duchess County, where the producer of her play has a house. The two of them disappeared for most of the day. But I found an amazing apple orchard and picked bushels and bushels . . . they were really tart and crunchy, with crazy names like Macouns and Winesap.

I brought some back and made the best apple pie ever. We served it for dessert the night my father came home from his latest book tour. He wanted to celebrate the reviews he got. Everything was going fine until he asked where we'd been all day, and my mother just said, "We took a little drive to the country, to an apple orchard." She didn't say a word about the man we visited. So, in a conspiracy of silence, I didn't tell my father where the apples came from. What was the point? But the thing is, with each bite he took, I felt like I was feeding him my mother's lies.

My parents are truly hopeless. But the pie was great.

Love,

P.S. Did Golden Boy tell you we've been singing together? It's great to harmonize with him. It's as if we've found a whole new level of friendship without talking, just by singing. But don't tell Ben I said that.

....

❧ CONSPIRACY APPLE PIE ❧

MAKES 1 (9-INCH) PIE

FOR THE DOUBLE CRUST:

2½ cups all-purpose flour

½ teaspoon salt

1¼ cups unsalted butter, chilled and cubed

4 to 6 tablespoons ice water

FOR THE FILLING:

6 medium-large apples (use a variety), peeled, cored, and cut into sixteenths

½ cup sugar

⅓ cup all-purpose flour

1 teaspoon ground cinnamon

½ teaspoon salt

¼ teaspoon ground nutmeg

3 tablespoons unsalted butter, cut into pieces

1. To make the crust: in a bowl combine the flour and salt. Using a pastry cutter or fork, add the butter and cut in gently

until the mixture forms coarse crumbs. Add ice water 1 tablespoon at a time as needed, and lightly mix the dough until the mixture just comes together. Form the dough into two equal balls. Wrap tightly with plastic, flatten the balls into discs, and chill for 1 hour.

2. Meanwhile, preheat the oven to 425° F and line a baking sheet with aluminum foil.

3. To make the filling, toss together the apples, sugar, flour, cinnamon, salt, and nutmeg.

4. To assemble the pie: on a floured surface, roll 1 ball of dough out into a 12-inch circle. Transfer the dough to a 9-inch pie plate. Pour the apple filling into the crust. Dot the filling with the butter pieces. Roll out the remaining crust to another 12-inch circle. Place on top of the filling and pinch together the edges of the crusts to seal. Cut several slits in the top of the crust.

5. Transfer the pie to the prepared baking sheet. Bake for 10 minutes, then reduce the heat to 400° F and continue to bake until the pie is golden and bubbling, 40 to 50 minutes more.

OCTOBER 28, 1970

Lilly,

I get butterflies in my stomach every morning before school. I'm working so hard to prove myself. Maybe this whole early-graduation thing is a bad idea.

I hope this is not what college is like. Isaac says not to worry.

He's been very patient with me lately. I think he's really glad

I'm graduating early. The other day he showed me his Harvard yearbook. He looked very young and handsome.

It's hard to imagine our parents before they had us, isn't it? Hard to believe they were ever our age—or, for that matter, that one day we'll be as old as them. Do you think we'll always feel young inside, even when we don't look that way?

By the way, Golden Boy is yet again living up to his name with a new girlfriend, Elena. (We all started calling the girls who really like him "Gold Diggers." He thinks it's funny.) She's from Rio, and he claims she's the inspiration for the song "The Girl from Ipanema." However, after meeting her and hearing her Bronx accent, I think she's really more like the Girl from Pelham Parkway. She really is gorgeous, though. She's so exotic and sexy-looking that next to her, even you would look like a shy and repressed schoolgirl. (In other words, you'd look like me.)

What's new with you? Is your friend Gary still shooting that 8-millimeter film? I still can't believe you're actually considering going topless for it. I think the whole thing is a scam for an NYU film student to get a high school girl to take her clothes off.

So, SillyLilly, write back a long letter and tell me lots of details. In the meantime, here's a Recipe Club recipe for something we used to love to eat together. Remember? (It's also good with sour cream.)

Love,

Val

....

℘ POTATO LATKES WITH ℘
HOMEMADE APPLESAUCE

MAKES ABOUT 3½ DOZEN LATKES

FOR THE APPLESAUCE
(MAKES 1 CUP):

3 apples, peeled and chopped

1 tablespoon honey

1 cinnamon stick

FOR THE LATKES:

½ cup all-purpose flour

1 teaspoon baking powder

2½ teaspoons salt

½ teaspoon ground black pepper

2 eggs, lightly beaten

4 large russet potatoes, peeled and grated

2 large Spanish onions, peeled and grated

Vegetable oil, for frying, as needed

1. To make the applesauce: combine all of the ingredients in a pot with ¼ cup water. Simmer over medium-high heat, stirring occasionally, until the apples break down and form a sauce. Add additional water, if necessary, to reach the desired consistency.

2. To make the latkes: preheat the oven to 250° F. Line a baking sheet with paper towels. In a large bowl, whisk together the flour, baking powder, salt, and pepper. Whisk in the eggs; stir in the potatoes and onions and toss well to combine.

3. Heat ¼-inch oil in a large skillet over medium-high heat and place the prepared baking sheet in the oven. Using your hands, squeeze as much liquid as possible from 1 rounded spoonful of the potato mixture. Place the spoonful into the pan and flatten slightly with a spatula. Cook the potatoes in batches until golden and crisp, 1 to 2 minutes per side. Repeat with the remaining potatoes.

4. Transfer the latkes to the oven to keep warm until all of the potatoes are fried. Serve with a dollop of applesauce.

NOVEMBER 3, 1970

Dahling,

I'm a star!

Gary's film is in the can. And my can is in his can. But I didn't dance the can-can. I just did this fabulous scene on a beach, where I start in the fetal position and unfurl in slow motion like a beautiful flower. It's so amazing and I look so gorgeous. Just watching the rushes gave me a rush. The camera LOVES *me, and I think Gary does too.*

Yes, Val, it WAS *in the nude, but it's* ART. *The way you carry on, it's like I did a remake of* I Am Curious, Yellow. *Relax, it's just a way of expressing my sensuality.*

It's amazing—when you put yourself out there in the world, everything just comes back to you full force. There is a real thrill in exposing yourself—and I don't just mean taking off your clothes. You're giving yourself permission to rock convention, to fly, to be daring, to be free.

But don't mention any of this to a soul.

Love,

Lilly

....

DECEMBER 13, 1970

Miss Valerie Rudman
has the deep honor and pleasure
of cordially inviting
Miss Lilly Stone

TO A GALA
NEW YEAR'S EVE PARTY
AT THE RUDMAN HOME.

FEATURED GUESTS INCLUDE:
Rod McKuen, James Taylor, The Beatles, Bob Dylan,
The Mamas & the Papas, Joan Baez, and more.

There will be a special command performance
by the Stone-Rudman Singers, performing their
personal favorite, "There's a Place for Us."

Please join us in a memorable evening
of WHIIIIIINING *and dining*
and even dancing
under the stars
(or at least under the confetti)
in celebration of the last time
we two
good and great friends
will definitely be living in the same city
on this special holiday.

R.S.V.P. A.S.A.P.

(Oh, Lilly, PLEASE *come. Let's make this a good one, since*
next year I probably won't even be here and before you
know it we'll be old and married and have a hundred
children to take care of. My parents promise they'll leave us
alone all night, and won't even once come into my room.)

Think about it. And here's a good recipe to get you in the
mood.

V.

❦ NEW YEAR'S EVE BLINI ❧
WITH CAVIAR

MAKES ABOUT 5 DOZEN HORS D'OEUVRE-SIZE BLINIS

1	(¼-ounce) package active dry yeast (1¼ teaspoons)	1	cup warm whole milk
1½	tablespoons sugar	6	tablespoons unsalted butter, melted and cooled
½	cup all-purpose flour	2	eggs, lightly beaten
½	cup buckwheat flour		Sour cream, for serving
¼	teaspoon salt		Caviar, for serving

1. Dissolve the yeast and sugar in ¼ cup warm water for 5 minutes. Add the all-purpose flour, buckwheat flour, and salt; stir lightly to combine. Stir in the milk, 3 tablespoons butter, and the eggs. Let rise in a warm place until increased in volume, 1½ to 2 hours. Stir before using.

2. Preheat the oven to 200° F. Heat a large skillet over medium-high heat until hot, and add 1 tablespoon of the remaining butter. Working in batches and adding additional butter as necessary, spoon ½ tablespoon batter into the skillet to make each blini. Cook, turning once, until golden, 1 to 2 minutes per side.

3. Keep warm in the oven until you have finished cooking all the batter.

4. Serve topped with sour cream and caviar.

I'm afraid to say this on the phone, so that's why I'm writing. I can't do New Year's Eve with you. Sorry. Won't you change your mind and come with us, instead? It will be lots of fun at Ben's—singing and playing music and stuff.

Look, Val, I really do want you to be with us, but why do you have to always make such a big deal about you and me being alone together on New Year's Eve? At this point in my life it just feels kind of depressing to be alone with you in your room when the whole world is celebrating.

Val, I'm guessing you're feeling a little bummed out by this, and I can understand if you're pissed. But please don't be, because now's the time I need you on my side. Nobody else is. My father says he's had enough of my "antics" because I stayed out all night. Even my mother got pissed off when she found out I did that nude scene. (Okay, she didn't exactly "find out"—I told her. I thought she'd be proud of me. What a hypocrite! If one of her friends did it she'd know it was art. I bet she's jealous. Not only am I a good actress and totally photogenic, but I have a great body. Sometimes it seems like she thinks she's the only one who's supposed to be admired.)

The question is, why should I stop myself from doing things I want to do? Just to get other people's approval? Just to tiptoe around other people's feelings? I can't be like that. And that's also why I can't say yes to your invite (which was, by the way, very cute.)

I hope you show up at Ben's. I really do.

Love,

Lilly

1971

Hey, Lilly,

It just feels like bad luck to not even say Happy New Year.

So, Happy New Year. I'd say that I had fun at Ben's, but it would be a lie. I doubt you even noticed I left before midnight.

There's nothing like being a third wheel with your own cousin and best friend.

Why is it that whenever you and I get together with other people I end up feeling invisible? It's like everybody's living room becomes your stage. You command attention. You suck up all the air in the room.

I know you're going to say I'm imagining this, so to prove my point let me just give you a hint about what's bothering me: there USED *to be "a place for us" . . . but now there's just a place for* YOU. *Get it?*

Valerie

....

JANUARY 6, 1971

*You know, Val, songs were made to be sung. With anyone. I always love singing "There's a Place for Us" with you—*AND *I loved singing it that night with Ben.*

Why can't you let that be okay? Why do you always try to rein me in and own me? Can't you see it makes me feel trapped?

Look, I really DO love you, and I always will, but we're separate people, and that should be okay. For both of us.

I've been thinking about this since you wrote. Maybe it's hard for you to let go of me because your mother is like she is. What I mean is, you always had to stick close to home and what's safe. So you haven't had as many friends as you could have. And you get kind of scared at parties and in groups, so you pull on me to stick by your side. And when I don't, you feel hurt.

If you ask me (and I know you didn't), you need to fight harder to become more confident. I can't always take care of you when we're with other people. And think about how amazing it would be if you could let the rest of the world see you the way I do when we're alone.

I know that to others you're scared and shy and awkward, but I also know that inside you're fabulous. I can help you. In fact, I have a plan. What are you doing next weekend? We can turn this whole thing around. Trust me.

Love,

Lilly

P.S. Here's a recipe to get your courage up. The secret ingredient is fresh lime juice.

....

❧ GOOD FOR WHAT AILS YOU ❧
GINGER ALE

SERVES 4

FOR THE GINGER WATER:
¾ cup ginger, peeled and finely chopped
2 cups water

FOR THE SIMPLE SYRUP:
1 cup water

¾ cup sugar
Club soda
Juice of one lime
1 lime cut into 4 wedges

1. For the ginger water: bring 2 cups of water to a rolling boil in a saucepan. Add the chopped ginger. Reduce the heat to simmer and cook for 10 minutes. Remove the pan from the heat and cool for 30 minutes. Strain the ginger through a fine mesh strainer. Discard the ginger pieces.

2. For the simple syrup: Bring the water to a boil in a separate saucepan. Dissolve the sugar in the boiling water. Let cool.

3. In 4 tall glasses, mix the ginger water with the simple syrup and club soda to taste. Add a splash of fresh lime juice. Garnish each glass with a lime wedge.

FEBRUARY 8, 1971

Hi Lilly,

THANK YOU, THANK YOU, THANK YOU!

Lilly, that was the best weekend of my life. I've never been "the guest of honor" for anything, let alone a surprise party.

But the biggest surprise was how comfortable I felt. Everybody was nice. Even your friends I had met before and thought didn't like me. Of course, maybe it helped that we all had those rum and Cokes . . . in fact, I can't believe I actually got drunk!!!

When I got home my mother asked how you and I spent the weekend—what we did, where we went, what we ate, who we saw. But instead of telling her every little detail like I usually do, which she loves and needs, I just said, "It was fine. Lilly invited some friends over." Nothing more. She tried to hide it, but I could tell she was very disappointed, as if I were pushing her away. Which maybe I was. But I held on to what you said about needing to become my own person—and I held my tongue. I'm really proud of myself.

I'm in my economics class now and I'd better stop writing because my teacher's giving me a dirty look. Until today I was his best student. God, I'm really going down the drain thanks to you, devil-girl.

Can't you just picture me in college? I'll probably be a pregnant drug addict by the end of my first semester, living in sin with some acidhead dropout in a refrigerator box in the gutter outside my dorm room. Doesn't that sound like fun? I can't wait. Should I see if my unwashed lover has a friend for you? We could double-date.

Speak to you later.

Love,

Me

P.S. Oh, yeah, Recipe Club time. How can I give you a recipe in the middle of my economics class? Hmmm . . . now that I think of it, I already did. Here it is again.

....

RECIPE FOR DISASTER

———————

Take one pure, virginal girl.

Blend well with a wild-woman best friend and a bottle of rum.

Marinate for one hour and stew overnight.

Remove from school using latex gloves and handcuffs.

Chill for two to five years in a state reformatory or minimum-security prison.

APRIL 24, 1971

Dear Lilly,

I can't believe my parents won't let me go to Washington for the march. I hate them so so so so so so much. Once I leave here I will never come back.

WHY DON'T I DEFY THEM?????? I'm practically in college. Why don't I just run out of the house and onto the bus?

I hate the war. I hate my parents. I hate my own spineless nature. I hate myself.

Lilly, like I said on the phone, I pray you will be my eyes and ears. Tell me everything you see and hear and do. I wonder if

the war would end one day sooner if just one more person—
me—would show up in our nation's capital.

Val

....

MAY 1, 1971

Dear Val,

I was in jail. Yes, a real jail.

They put us in this holding pen. It happened because my
mother refused to move when the cops came. There were
thousands of us protesting. We were shouting, "One, two,
three, four! We don't want your fucking war!" And, "Hell
no, we won't go!" There was this huge crowd, but a feeling
of unity, like we were all together and making a difference.
We knew we weren't just protesting Vietnam, but also war
in general.

People came from all over the country. My mother's friend,
Jorgen, got hit hard on the side of his head by a pig who was
trying to "maintain law and order." It was really frightening,
blood all around, people screaming, crying, and running.
Total chaos.

I realized for the first time we aren't just playing around
protesting this war. There really are two sides, with a line
drawn in blood down the middle. And I finally get that
the other side truly hates us—they think we're wrong,
unpatriotic, and dangerous. But it's their hate that feels
dangerous.

You know, Val, we're fragile creatures, us human beings. Not just the poor soldiers who have been fooled into fighting for all the wrong reasons. And not just the poor people at Mai Lai. It's all of us. We could be killed or die at any moment. Being in jail really makes you think about these heavy things. We've really got to live for today.

My mother certainly does. Right now she's obsessed with Jorgen. To tell you the truth, it's not just because he got hurt. It started before that, like the moment we all got on the bus to Washington. She sat next to him instead of me. I was in the seat across from them, next to some way-too-nosy stranger for five hours. Meanwhile, my mother and Jorgen spent the whole ride staring into each other's eyes as if they were the only people on the bus. When everyone started chanting "Make Love, Not War," Jorgen winked at my mother and she giggled, as if it was some inside joke. They were making me more bus sick than the bus.

Later, when we got arrested, she barely turned around to see if I was still with them. It made me realize I've never really had a mom. I've had someone who wanted to be my friend. But she's not even that.

And then there's the whole jail thing. It was terrifying. I mean, I knew we weren't going to be locked up forever, but you're treated like cattle. Herded into a holding pen with a million other protesters. They take everything away from you. (What did they think I was going to do with my house key? Dig an escape tunnel?) And they don't even explain what's happening, when you will be let out, how the system works. They do it to scare you.

My mother couldn't handle it. She started screaming at the top of her lungs, "I demand to be released!" And I saw this look on her face that I've seen before when my father tells her she can't do something she wants to do. It's a combination of rage and sheer panic. I knew then she must feel like she's in jail a lot. And that actually being in a real jail was more than she could take.

Anyway, after hours and hours they let us go. We were hungry, tired, filthy . . . but basically okay. They gave us a court appearance date and we'll have to pay a fine. So, we don't get the electric chair after all. . . .

I did have a little consciousness-raising as a result of this experience: I was thinking a lot about all the things in life that I love. Things I might not ever see again. Things I take for granted. I was thinking about you, Val.

Love,

Lilly

....

JUNE 12, 1971

Dear Val,

My class is going on an overnight camping trip to Bear Mountain the same weekend as your graduation. I just can't miss this trip. Do you mind? I appreciate that you went to a lot of trouble to get extra tickets for me and my parents. My father says he is going to represent our family.

Anyway, thanks for showing me the speech you'll read, you VAL-*edictorian! I was impressed. I don't think I would have been able to say so many wise things. The part I liked the second-best was when you said there's hope for humankind if humans could be kind. I told Tony. He wears peace symbols on his sneakers. And he has a peace symbol earring. He said he could really relate, and I'm sure he could. He says if he gets drafted he's going to Canada. I wish you could meet him, except that I need to break up with him soon because he's annoying me a lot.*

But the part I loved the most was when you talked about me. At least, I hope it was about me when you wrote about "the power of friendship to sustain a life of meaning."

This is a recipe in honor of your big day. (Sour cream and curry powder are the secret, with mango chutney.) Serve it with cut-up carrots and celery. (If you soak the veggies in ice water for a while, they get really crisp.)

Love,

Lilly

....

⊗ DIPLOMA DIP WITH VEGGIES ⊗

MAKES ABOUT 2 CUPS DIP

||||||||||||||||||||||||||||||||||||||||||||||||||||||||||||||||||||||||||||||||||||||||||||||||||||||||||||||||||||||||||||

3	tablespoons unsalted butter	2	tablespoons mango chutney, chopped
6	scallions, thinly sliced		Pinch salt
1	tablespoon curry powder		Raw sliced vegetables, for dipping
1	cup sour cream		
½	cup mayonnaise		

1. In a small skillet over medium heat, melt the butter. Add the scallions and cook until slightly softened, about 2

minutes. Stir in the curry powder and reduce the heat to medium-low. Continue to cook for 4 minutes more.

2. In a bowl, stir together the sour cream, mayonnaise, chutney, and salt. Stir in the curry mixture. Cover and chill at least 30 minutes before serving.

3. Serve with raw sliced vegetables.

JUNE 17, 1971

Lilly,

Listen, I'm not even surprised you aren't coming. I didn't really expect that you would. Well, maybe at first I hoped. But I've come to realize you are the way you are, and I can't change you.

We don't need to talk about this again. I'm okay with it. Really. Especially since I'm starting college and we're traveling down separate paths anyway. I just want to tell you that yes, that reference in my speech to friendship certainly was inspired by you. Who else if not you?

Okay, changing the subject . . . you know my father's invention I mentioned a while ago? The hydraulic lift that was supposed to make us rich? Surprise, surprise, it didn't. (Thank God my parents agreed to let Isaac pay for the expenses not covered by my scholarship, or I never would get out of here.) It turns out that something like this was already developed—by NASA of all places—so the patent office refused to give my father the rights to it.

He's trying hard to be philosophical about the whole thing.

In fact, he was so sweet. He brought home ice cream to cheer us all up, and reminded us that every knock is a boost. But we could see the disappointment in his eyes. My mother told him that if he's doing the same work as NASA, he must be doing something right. On a good day she can be very loving and supportive. I think when she rallies like that, and finds her strength, it means more to my father than actually selling his inventions.

Anyway, in his honor, and to make him feel better, my mother and I invented something to go with the ice cream: a pecan cookie called The Nutty Professor. They were so good we're gonna make them again for my graduation party, but you can have the recipe now since you can't come.

Love,

Val

....

❧ THE NUTTY PROFESSOR ❧
COOKIES

MAKES ABOUT 3 DOZEN COOKIES

- ½ cup light brown sugar
- ½ cup granulated sugar
- ½ cup unsalted butter (1 stick)
- 1 egg
- 1 teaspoon vanilla extract
- 1¾ cups all-purpose flour
- 2 teaspoons baking powder
- ½ teaspoon salt
- ½ cup finely chopped pecans
- Butter or shortening for greasing baking sheets

1. In a large bowl, beat the sugars and butter together until light and creamy. Beat in the egg and vanilla. In a separate bowl, combine the flour, baking powder, and salt. Gradually add the dry ingredients to the wet ingredients and mix to combine. Fold in the chopped pecans.

2. Shape the dough into one log about 2 inches in diameter. Wrap tightly with plastic wrap and refrigerate at least 6 hours or overnight.

3. The next day, or when you are ready to bake the cookies, preheat the oven to 400° F. Grease 3 baking sheets.

4. Slice the dough into ¼-inch-thick rounds. Arrange the rounds 1½ inches apart on the prepared cookie sheets. Bake until just golden, 7 to 10 minutes. Transfer the cookies to a wire rack to cool.

JUNE 18, 1971

Damn it, Lilly, your phone is always busy!!

Listen, I have to go up to Radcliffe in the middle of August for freshman orientation. This leads me to proposing a fantastic idea: you and I go up to Cambridge together! You live with me in the dorm for two weeks or so and then when school starts, you return to New York.

Doesn't it sound perfect? Isaac seems excited about the prospect of us doing this together—he seems to think it will inspire you to want to go to college more. My parents love the idea that I won't be alone. And I think it would be amazing—we'll finally be roommates! I'll have plenty of time to hang out with you, and when I'm busy, you can sightsee or do stuff in Cambridge or Boston. There are millions of great bookstores. Or you could just hang around Harvard Yard and talk to people. Lots of guys sit around playing guitar.

What do you think? Call me the SECOND you get this, even though by the time you do we'll have talked already about a thousand times.

Love,

V.

P.S. To tell you the truth, I'm also a little scared about starting my "real life" all by myself. It would be SO GREAT if you could keep me company a little.

P.P.S. Here's a recipe for brain food. One bite and you're a genius. Two bites and you get into the college of your choice.

....

❧ "REAL LIFE" RED SNAPPER ☙

SERVES 8

8 (8-ounce) red snapper fillets	3 tablespoons fresh chopped dill
Salt	
Ground black pepper	1 teaspoon finely grated lemon zest
½ cup breadcrumbs	
¼ cup unsalted butter, softened	1 garlic clove, finely chopped
3 tablespoons fresh chopped parsley	

1. Preheat the oven to 450° F. Season the fish on both sides with salt and pepper.

2. Combine the breadcrumbs, butter, parsley, dill, lemon zest, and garlic in a bowl. Divide the mixture among the fish fillets, coating each fillet evenly with topping. Transfer the fillets to a baking sheet.

3. Bake for 8 minutes. Reduce the heat to broil and cook, watching carefully, for 1 to 2 minutes more, until just golden.

AUGUST 5, 1971

Dear Val,

I'll be at Penn Station exactly at 8:30, don't worry. Listen, you aren't alone, okay? Just get that through your head! And hey, when your mother says you shouldn't leave her, that's really crazy. You have to be strong. Remember our motto: be your own person!

Okay, enough of the pep talk. Now let's get down to business. Since you asked, this is what I'd bring if I were you:

> *A choker: either beads or Puka shells*
> *Safari dress shirt*
> *An Army jacket*
> *A halter top*
> *Bell-bottom jeans with flower patches (whatever you do, don't bring new ones)*
> *The tie-dyed shirt I gave you for your birthday*
> *A macramé vest (got mine in the Village)*

Crochet hat
Patchouli incense
Strawberry lip gloss

Some singles, like: "Moon Shadow" by Cat Stevens
"Brand New Key" by Melanie
"I Feel the Earth Move" by Carol King

Also, clove cigarettes (I know you don't smoke, but if
you have some it will look good)
Rolling papers for getting high (same as above)

If you want, I can give you my diaphragm box, the old one,
so you can at least have that to put in your drawer if your
new friends are snoops. That way you don't have to be
embarrassed or worry about what they think. Good idea?

And . . . of course, don't forget this: our recipe collection!!!!!!

Hey, are you in mourning like me? Did you hear the news?
They closed Palisades Amusement Park . . . it no longer
"swings all day and after dark"—remember when we used to
sing that together? Remember when we put on that play
about the two crazy women who live underneath a roller
coaster? (Smile!)

I'm actually really honored that you asked me to take you to
school instead of anyone else. It's very cool.

See you next week. Don't be so nervous! Get as excited as
you were a few weeks ago. It will be more than fun—it will
be a blast.

Love,

Lilly

....

SEPTEMBER 22, 1971

Hello again Lilly—

It's 2 a.m. I'm desperately trying to block out what I'm hearing in the dormitory hallway: running feet . . . shrill laughter . . . the sounds of people who AREN'T *miserable, depressed, and lonely.*

My roommate doesn't make things any easier. She smokes so much pot, it's like living in a cloud of smoke. It's a cheap secondhand high, if you like that sort of thing. I've put in for a transfer.

I'm hoping you don't think I am trying to act out a melodrama. It's just hard to describe how everything could be so subdued and yet so intense at the same time. I thought you went to school to learn lofty ideas, to exercise your intellect, to get to the next level of understanding and insight. But apparently the majority of people here think expanding your mind means tripping.

But there are worse things than drugs. I can't stop thinking about a boy in my calc class who tried to commit suicide last week. I only knew him by sight. They say he came here crazy, but I'm beginning to think he was just a quick study. The rest of us will probably be jumping out the windows in about two weeks.

The good news? Sometimes, when I'm not in the world but just in my head or in my books, or in the sound of a smart teacher's voice, I feel transported, at peace. And I feel like I finally know what my brain was meant to do. I wish we could have classes 24 hours a day and skip the living part.

Please write—I really need to hear from a normal person.

(Not that you're that normal, but everything is relative.) I really am pretty damn lonely.

Love and kisses,

Val

....

OCTOBER 1, 1971

Dear Val,

I tried to call your dorm but your roommate is not only a pothead, she's a moron. Did you even get my messages?

It sounds like you're having a hard time. Do you want some company? I could take the train up. Oh, and since you can't cook while you're at school, except on that puny hot plate, I thought I'd give you a recipe for something good to drink.

Love,

Lilly

⤶ WARM AMARETTO MILK ⤷

SERVES 2

1 cup whole milk	Whipped cream
2 shots amaretto	Thinly sliced orange rind

1. Heat the milk in a small pot until simmering. Stir in the amaretto.

2. Pour into 2 mugs. Top with whipped cream and garnish with orange rind.

Hi Lilly,

It's taken almost all semester to get adjusted, but I finally am. What a deep relief.

To be honest, I feel a little nervous about coming home for Thanksgiving, because I'm scared of getting sucked back into my old family dynamics. I hope everyone can accept that I've changed. I don't mean to sound like a pretentious twit, but I feel like I've matured. College has been good for me. Independence agrees with me. And being away from my mother thrills me. (Will lightning strike? I just had to say it.)

Every day at school is made better by the friends I'm making, especially one woman. Her name is Ellen Jacobs. She lives at the other end of the hall, but the dorm is so big and impersonal it's a miracle we ever found each other. She's incredibly intelligent and funny, and I adore her. Next semester we're going to room together.

Ellen's not going home until winter break because it's too expensive to fly back to Chicago. So I invited her to The Beautiful Bronx for Thanksgiving (believe it or not, she's totally psyched—she's never been to New York). I really want her to meet everyone—especially you! She knows all about you, every detail. You're gonna love each other.

Oh, Lilly, you would be really proud of me. I'm starting to understand what it takes to make friends: it's all about connecting with other strong, intelligent, focused women. About abandoning the shell you've been hiding in your whole life. And when you do it right, you're rewarded with love. With people who really get you. Who never judge you. Who admire you for who you are and what you have to offer.

Lilly, there's something I need to ask you before we see each other. It might sound trivial to you, but it's been troubling me: Isaac keeps writing me letters, "encouraging" (read: demanding) me to move away from math, get more into the hard sciences, and prepare for medical school.

But I don't want to. Isn't that my right? Shouldn't I be at a point where I'm choosing my own destiny? Or at least my own major?!

So, here's the problem: how do I tell him it's time for me to make my own decisions? That I can no longer just blindly follow his blueprint for my education? He's going to be so horribly disappointed in me. Angry, too. And maybe that's his right since he's footing a good part of the bill.

Any tips on handling him?

Sigh.

What's going on with you? Let's definitely get together while I'm in New York (I mean, apart from seeing each other on Thanksgiving Day). Ben is bringing a date. (Have you met his new girlfriend? I heard she's from some tiny country in Indonesia that nobody ever heard of, and she speaks about 27 words of English. She's supposed to be yet another exotic beauty, though. So we can all stare at her even if we can't actually talk to her.)

By the way, here's my dorm room special for the Recipe Club. It's great for breakfast or a late-night, study-break snack. See you in a couple of days.

Lots of love,

Valerie

....

❦ DORM ROOM OATMEAL WITH ❧
DRIED FRUIT & NUTS

SERVES 2

1 cup whole milk	¼ cup raisins
1 cup water	¼ cup toasted walnuts, chopped
⅛ teaspoon salt	½ teaspoon ground cinnamon
1 cup rolled oats	2 tablespoons maple syrup

1. In a small saucepan over medium heat, bring the milk, 1 cup water, and salt to a simmer.

2. Add the oats and cook, stirring, until thickened, 6 to 8 minutes.

3. Stir in the raisins, walnuts, cinnamon, and maple syrup. Serve hot.

DECEMBER 5, 1971

Val,

Thanksgiving only just happened and already everyone's Christmas shopping. Why does that bother me? Maybe I'm bummed about something else. I've been feeling so off-kilter ever since you left to go back to school.

Since we spoke last night I've been thinking about how to answer your question. What did I think of Ellen? She's shy. Soft-spoken. Quiet. Polite. Serious. That's one way to put it.

But if you want an honest answer, I'd say she's not very good socially. She doesn't have any sense of humor—maybe she should take a course in irony. And why was everybody hanging on her every word when she was telling that endless story about volunteer work she did in Guatemala? Probably because her voice is so low. The only way you know she's talking is if you watch her lips flap.

But other than that she was nice.

Before you say it, no, I'm not jealous. But the thing is, Val, it's like you're changing. It's cool you're digging college and stuff, but the past few times, when we've gotten together, it's like some stranger has stolen your body! I mean, I was so glad to see you. There you were. Val with the same exact bangs. The same exact blue sweatshirt. But you were acting so weird. So full of yourself. It wasn't you. And I wondered if you were trying to show off. What's up? Why are you putting on such an act?

Anyway, if that's what college does to a person, I don't think I really want to go.

Val, what I'm really wondering is, WHO ARE YOU? My advice: just be your old self. That's the Val I like best.

1972

JANUARY 8, 1972

L—

Once you told me I was the kind of person who always wanted things to stay the same. At the time it hurt my feelings, but then I realized you were probably right.

Now I think YOU'RE *the one who can't handle change. Look, I'm sorry you're so upset with me, Lilly. I wish we could have been together on New Year's Eve, too. And I'm really sorry if I left you in the lurch. But Ellen and I couldn't finalize our Chicago plans until the last minute, and I assumed you would understand. I hope you do.*

Anyway, it was good I went. Ellen's family is fantastic! I loved her parents, and also her brother Jeff is amazing. He's two years older (Ben's age). Jeff's a lot like Ellen—brilliant and kind, and funny and deep. Only he's a lot more handsome! I am sure he and I will stay friends. Right now he's at school at UCLA, *but he's transferring to Harvard next year! So until then we'll be pen pals.*

But you are still—and will always remain—my FAVORITE *pen pal of all time. Happy New Year, my dearest friend.*

Love,

V.

....

☙ PEN PAL PECAN RICE ❧

SERVES 6 TO 8

|||||||||||||||||||||||||||||||||||||||||||||||||||||||||||||||||||||||||||||||||||||||||||||||||||||||||||||||||||||||

2	tablespoons unsalted butter	1	teaspoon salt
¾	onion, finely chopped	⅓	cup chopped, toasted pecans
2	cups long-grain rice	3	tablespoons finely chopped tarragon
2	cups chicken stock		
1¾	cup water		

1. In a medium pot over medium-high heat, melt the butter. Add the onion and cook, stirring, for 5 minutes. Stir in the rice and cook for 3 minutes more.

2. Add the stock, 1¾ cups water, and salt. Bring to a boil, then reduce the heat to a simmer. Cook, covered, for 15 minutes. Let stand, covered, for 5 to 7 minutes more.

3. Fluff the rice with a fork. Stir in the pecans and tarragon, and serve.

MARCH 6, 1972

Lillypad,

Are you okay? Your last postcard sounded strange. Like you were feeling lost or something. Do you want to come here before the semester ends? I'd love you to visit.

You alluded to getting high a lot. I hope you're not tripping—it can't be good for your brain cells. I'm only writing this because I'm worried, not because I'm preaching. Anyway, take it for what it's worth.

Actually, I'm a little confused about a couple of things. Are you or aren't you applying to colleges? What would you do if you don't go? Lilly, don't make decisions based on how crummy you feel right at this second. I promise, the minute you leave home, everything looks different. It looks better. Try to be patient. Soon high school will be over, and all that junk with your parents will go away forever.

Do you ever try talking to Ben about this stuff? Even though he acts flip, he usually has some real insight into family interactions. I know you two hang out sometimes, and I'm sure that he reveals some of himself to you. But the times I've seen you together, he's always very light and breezy. And there's more to him than that. He's more serious than you might think. If you share real problems with him, I know he'll respond sincerely, and be a true friend. He has his own kind of wisdom that comes from all he's been through.

By the way, that guy I told you about—Ellen's brother Jeff? He and I have become really good friends. He writes the most beautiful letters in the world. He's poetic and sensitive as well as being incredibly brilliant and handsome. I can't wait till he transfers here in September. It's funny to miss somebody I barely know as much as I do. (I mean, we only spent a couple of days together.) But I do. I really, really do.

And I miss you too, Lillyface! Come visit. But 'til then, try this to wash away your blues.

Love,

Madam Pen Pal

....

❧ WASH-AWAY-THE-BLUES ❧
BERRY COBBLER

SERVES 6

FOR THE BLUEBERRY
FILLING:

Butter or shortening for
greasing baking dish

3 cups fresh or frozen
blueberries

2 tablespoons granulated
sugar

2 tablespoons brown sugar

1 tablespoon freshly squeezed
lemon juice

1½ teaspoons vanilla extract

1 teaspoon finely grated
lemon zest

½ teaspoon all-purpose flour

1 tablespoon butter, melted

FOR THE TOPPING:

1¾ cups all-purpose flour

5 tablespoons granulated
sugar

4 teaspoons baking powder

5 tablespoons butter, chilled
and cut into cubes

1 cup milk, plus additional,
as needed

2 teaspoons granulated sugar

¼ teaspoon ground cinnamon

1. Preheat the oven to 375° F. Lightly grease an 8-inch square
baking dish.

2. For the filling: combine the blueberries, sugars, lemon
juice, vanilla, and lemon zest in a bowl. Toss with the flour.
Stir in the melted butter. Pour the berry mixture into the
prepared pan.

3. For the topping: whisk together the flour, 5 tablespoons
sugar, and baking powder in a medium bowl. Cut in the
butter using your fingers or a pastry cutter until the mixture
forms coarse crumbs. Make a well in the center, and quickly
stir in the milk. Mix just until moistened. You should
have a very thick batter. If the batter seems too dry, add 1
tablespoon of milk at a time until it comes together. Cover,
and let the batter rest for 10 minutes.

4. Spoon the batter over the blueberries, leaving only a few
small holes for the berries to peek through. Mix together the

JUNE 1, 1972

Dear Val,

Do you know what happened? My father got furious at me and said he won't come to my graduation if I don't change my mind about not going to college. He said that I am "on a slippery slope of ruining my life." But it feels more like he thinks I'm ruining HIS.

What can I say? I don't know words to explain what's been happening in my head. But music says a lot more. I'm listening to Carly Simon's "Anticipation" and thinking about how I can't wait for something to happen in my life . . . but I'm worried I can't really count on anything.

I certainly can't count on my parents. My mother won't see me graduate, either. She just called to say she'll still be on tour. So, it looks like it will just be you and Ben out there rooting for me! (It makes me guilty that I didn't go to yours. You are always such a good friend.)

Did Ben tell you that I broke up with Doug? That lasted about a month. Ben said it was just as well. He didn't like "Douggie the Druggie," as he called him. (Ben never seems to like anyone I go out with. Sometimes he's worse than my father.)

You were right about what you said. He's a good listener and a strong support when it feels like nobody else even gives a damn.

Call me when you know your exact travel plans. And meanwhile, here's my overdue Recipe Club contribution. At least food is something to count on. And especially this . . . because when you anticipate how it tastes, you can COUNT ON IT giving you great pleasure! Especially with that raspberry jam we used to make!

See you soon.

Love,

Lilly

....

༒ COUNT-ON-IT CORNBREAD ༒

MAKES 1 (9-INCH) CORNBREAD CAKE

Butter or shortening for greasing pan

1 cup cornmeal

½ cup whole-wheat flour

½ cup all-purpose flour

¼ cup rolled oats

2 teaspoons baking powder

1 teaspoon salt

½ cup whole milk

½ cup buttermilk

½ cup melted butter

2 eggs

¼ cup honey

2 tablespoons molasses

1. Preheat the oven to 350° F. Grease a 9 x 9-inch baking pan.

2. In a large bowl, combine the cornmeal, the flours, oats, baking powder, and salt.

3. In a separate bowl, whisk together the milk, buttermilk, butter, eggs, honey, and molasses.

4. Add the wet ingredients to the dry ingredients and stir until just combined.

5. Pour the batter into the prepared pan. Bake until golden on top and a toothpick inserted in the center comes out clean, 25 minutes.

JUNE 23, 1972

Dear Val,

Remember when you said that graduating from high school would make me feel liberated and changed?

It didn't.

The truth is, when I walked up on that stage, shook hands with the headmaster, and took my diploma, I felt like crap. Everyone was cheering, and I know I was smiling as I walked down the steps, but inside I felt this crash. Not that I wasn't proud or happy. Just that I realized I was facing my life and am unsure about where I am going and how I will get there. And I felt myself becoming more and more scared, in a way I've never felt before.

Val, the only thing I know for sure is that I desperately want to sing. I want music to be not just a part of my life, but ALL of my life. Period. It's nonnegotiable. And I'm going to make it happen. I've just got to figure out how college does or doesn't fit into this. And I've got to be able to forge ahead no matter what roadblocks my father puts in my way.

And that's why I'm grateful, more than you could ever realize, that you were with me yesterday. I was really touched by you coming. Even if I didn't say what I was feeling, I could tell that you looked into my heart and knew what I was going through.

You are the best.

Love, hugs and kisses,

Lilly

....

JULY 25, 1972

Dear Val,

Well, I've been given an ultimatum. Either I try college for a year, or my father says he will "disown" me. I told him, go ahead! Disown me.

We didn't speak for three days.

But here's the sad and sorry truth . . . I gave in. I'm going to NYU in September. The only good thing: it's down near the Village Gate and all the other clubs. But even so, I don't know how I'll get through a year.

Do you have a recipe for survival?

Speaking of which, you owe me two recipes. I know I should

wait for yours, but I just have to send you this one. It's from Jamaica. I got it from a man I met who sings reggae. We jammed together at this dive in Brooklyn. It was totally cool. Ben came with some friends. I think the recipe is really named for my father.

Love,

Lilly

....

❦ JERK PORK ❧

SERVES 8 TO 10

1 (6- to 9-pound) pork shoulder roast

Salt

FOR THE RUB:

¼ cup ground allspice

3 tablespoons brown sugar

1 tablespoon finely chopped fresh gingerroot

1 tablespoon soy sauce

1 tablespoon finely chopped fresh thyme

1½ teaspoons freshly squeezed lime juice

½ teaspoon ground cinnamon

¼ teaspoon ground nutmeg

1 bunch scallions, finely chopped

2 Scotch bonnet peppers, seeded and finely chopped

3 garlic cloves, finely chopped

1. To make the rub: combine all of the ingredients in a mortar and pestle and grind to a paste.

2. With a sharp knife, score the thick fat on the pork shoulder, but do not cut into the meat. Using gloved hands, rub a thick coating of the jerk sauce on the exterior of the pork so it is completely covered. (Refrigerate any leftover sauce. It will keep for up to 1 month.) Place the pork in a

roasting pan and cover with aluminum foil. Refrigerate to marinate at least 24 hours or up to two days.

3. When you are ready to cook the roast, allow the pork to sit at room temperature at least one hour.

4. Preheat the oven to 450° F. Season the pork generously with salt.

5. Roast, uncovered, for 30 minutes. Then lower the temperature to 300°F and roast for 3 hours more, until very tender. Let the pork rest at least 30 minutes before carving.

SEPTEMBER 2, 1972

Darlingest Lilly,

I'm in love!!

Things with Jeff have taken a turn for the . . . romantic! We're really in love, Lilly! For the first time in my life, I'm in love!

I can't wait for you to meet him. He's everything I've ever looked for. (Can you believe this is me talking?????!!!) Yup, at last I really AM the "wild" girl my mother was afraid I'd become. Thank you, God, thank you.

I know you want details. The best one I can give you is that with Jeff I went, overnight, from cloistered nun to unbridled lover. The intimacy is spiritual and physical at the same time. When I feel his breath on my skin, or his heart beating against mine, I feel connected to the universe. Part of something beautiful and bigger than I am. And every time it just gets better. I feel seen, heard, known, felt, loved, wanted, adored. I only hope I am giving him those gifts as well.

Or, to put it in Lillytalk . . . what a difference a boyfriend makes! Okay, okay, I'm a slow learner. But I'm finally here!

I gotta run to class now—sorry, sorry, sorry. But now that you're in college, you know how intense it can be.

Sent from me to you, with love from my full, full heart. . . .

Valerie

....

⟨⟨ WILD GIRL ⟩⟩
WILD MUSHROOM SALAD

SERVES 4

1 pound mixed wild mushrooms	Ground black pepper
¼ cup extra-virgin olive oil	6 cups washed salad greens
¾ teaspoon salt, plus additional, if necessary	1½ teaspoons cider vinegar
	1 teaspoon soy sauce

1. Preheat the oven to 450° F.

2. Toss the mushrooms with 2 tablespoons of the olive oil, ¾ teaspoon salt, and pepper to taste. Spread out the mushrooms on a baking sheet. Roast, tossing once halfway through, until crisp and golden, 20 to 25 minutes.

3. In a bowl, combine the mushrooms with the salad greens, the remaining 2 tablespoons of olive oil, the vinegar, and soy sauce. Salt and pepper to taste. Toss well.

Dear Val,

If I lie on my bed and reach my arms out I can touch the walls on either side of this sardine can they call a dorm. It's dress rehearsal for a coffin.

That was the good news. The bad news is that I'm already falling behind in my classes—might help if I went to them—and school's only been in session for twenty minutes. Being here makes me feel like I sold my soul.

I went to meet my mother for lunch yesterday, hoping to find an ally. She wouldn't come downtown—said if I wanted to see her, she'd squeeze me in for a lunchtime break. So I had to go all the way up to the theater district, to Sardi's. We sat at "her" table—the one underneath the Hirschfeld caricature of her.

As usual, it was like star central—every stage celeb came over to bow at the feet of the magnificent Katherine Stone. Just as I was about to tell her why I needed to see her, I was interrupted by Ben Vereen and Bob Fosse, who stopped to fawn over her latest fabulous set. When they finally left, I managed to tell her I wanted to leave school. Instead of responding to me, she flirted for ten minutes with Cliff Gorman, who she knew from that production she helped mount in Westport a few years ago.

After he split, I finally got to the point: that college right now is a huge mistake. And that I need her help in convincing my father of this. And that supporting me as an artist would be the most loving gesture my parents could ever make.

*But by then dessert had arrived, and so had Mike Nichols,
who pulled up a chair and polished off half my rice pudding.*

*When my mother asked for the check, Bob the Maître d' did
a little bow and said, "Miss Katherine, the honor is ours."
She feigned surprise, protested, and pretended to reach for
her wallet (which undoubtedly was empty). Then she blew a
kiss to the entire restaurant, and made a hasty retreat before
he could change his mind. It's their usual routine.*

*Standing outside on 44th Street, while hailing a cab, she
finally let me know she'd been listening. She said she could
see I'm unhappy and knows how hard it is to be doing
something I don't like. For a minute I felt hopeful—like she'd
really heard me. I even got all teary.*

*Then the other shoe dropped. She said, "You can't just think
about yourself, Lilly. There are three of us in this family. And
it's in everyone's interest for you to do exactly as your father
wishes."*

*Translation: if my father feels like he's controlling me, he's
less likely to try to control her. And that keeps the peace
between them.*

More translation: I'm screwed.

Ain't life grand?

*So Val, maybe you can come for a visit? I know your course
load is heavy, but in between our yakking sessions you could
do work at the NYU library. (I've heard they actually do have
a library. . . .)*

Love,

Lilly

P.S. *Jeff is one hell of a lucky guy. Does he know that? And it sounds like you lucked out, too. Are you guys getting serious? Will I meet him soon? I really am very psyched for you, Val. I mean it. You've needed and wanted this for such a long time. One word of advice: don't mistake great sex for great love.*

P.P.S. *I got a recipe for vegetarian samosas from an Indian student down the hall. She's homesick a lot so she talks about the food her family makes. They are so loving of one another, it gives you hope for the world. Or, at least, for families. Maybe the recipe will give us some of their good karma.*

P.P.P.S. *Serve the samosas with a pineapple chutney dipping sauce. And any leftover potato filling makes a yummy Indian-spiced potato salad!*

....

GOOD KARMA VEGGIE SAMOSAS

MAKES 24 SAMOSAS

FOR THE PINEAPPLE CHUTNEY DIPPING SAUCE:

⅔ cup mayonnaise

½ cup pineapple chutney, chopped

¼ cup fresh chopped cilantro

FOR THE DOUGH:

1½ cups all-purpose flour, plus additional for flouring surface

Large pinch salt

¼ cup (½ stick) unsalted butter, softened

4 to 5 tablespoons warm water

FOR THE FILLING:

¼ cup vegetable oil

1 large red onion, diced

Salt

1¾ pound potatoes (about 3 large), peeled and cut into ¼-inch cubes

1 tablespoon fresh minced gingerroot

1 jalapeño, seeded and minced

1 tablespoon curry powder

½ cup water

2 tablespoons freshly squeezed lemon juice

1 cup frozen peas

3 tablespoons chopped fresh cilantro

Vegetable oil, for frying

1. For the dipping sauce: whisk together the mayonnaise, chutney, and cilantro. Cover with plastic and refrigerate until ready to use.

2. For the dough: combine the flour and salt in a bowl. Cut in the butter until it forms pea-size pieces. Add 4 to 5 tablespooons warm water, 1 tablespoon at a time, until the mixture just comes together to form a ball. Transfer the dough to a floured surface and knead for 10 minutes. Wrap in plastic and transfer to the refrigerator for 1 hour.

3. Meanwhile, make the filling. Heat the oil in a large skillet over medium-high heat. Add the onion and a pinch of salt; cook, stirring, for 10 minutes. Stir in the potatoes, 1 teaspoon salt, the ginger, and the jalapeño. Cook until the potatoes are slightly softened, about 10 minutes. Add the curry powder and cook for 1 minute. Add ½ cup water and the lemon juice.

Cover the pan and cook over medium heat until tender, about 25 minutes. Stir in the peas and cook, covered, for 5 minutes more. Stir in the cilantro. Taste and adjust the seasoning if necessary. Let cool.

4. To assemble the samosas, divide the dough into 25 equal balls. On a floured surface, roll each ball into a 4-inch circle. Cut each circle in half. Put a heaping spoonful of filling in the middle of a half-circle. Brush the edges of each samosa lightly with water and fold the dough over the filling; press the edges with a fork to seal. Transfer to a baking sheet and cover with a damp towel until all the samosas are filled. Repeat with the remaining dough and filling.

5. Fill a medium pot ⅔ full with oil. Heat the oil to 375° F. Fry the samosas in batches, taking care not to overcrowd the pot, until the samosas are golden all over, about 3 minutes per side. Remove with a slotted spoon to a paper-towel-lined plate to drain. Serve with the pineapple chutney dipping sauce.

OCTOBER 29, 1972

Lilly—

I'm terrified, and I don't know what to do. Jeff is as freaked out as I am.

I know you said you'd do everything in the world to help me, but what does that actually mean? It's not like you know this person. Are you sure he's a real doctor? What if he's just some maniac? Do you realize I could bleed to death from some filthy coat hanger? I keep picturing myself dying on some stained mattress on a tenement floor. And all because I had sex. Which, by the way, I obviously couldn't even do correctly—I mean, who gets pregnant after the first time?

I feel like this is divine retribution for defying my mother.

Sometimes I feel I should just have the baby. Marry Jeff and just have it. But then I think, oh, God, no, I can't. I just can't. It would ruin everything—my life, his life, our relationship, everything.

Lilly, why is this happening? Why? Is there something I'm supposed to learn from it? Please help me understand. I'm dying inside.

V.

....

NOVEMBER 4, 1972

Dear Val,

There's nothing to understand. You just got unlucky. It happens. Don't blame yourself or you'll never enjoy sex again. It's really just one of those shitty things.

Who knows why one person gets knocked up the minute she takes her clothes off, and other people can't get pregnant no matter how hard they try.

So let's stay focused on solving the problem. This is all you need to know: your train gets in at 11:30 a.m. I'll be there at the gate to the track. We'll go straight to meet my friend, Cloud. She's the one who set everything up. (Don't worry, she's not as spacey as her name suggests. In fact, she's very sweet and smart and understanding. I've been wanting the two of you to meet—of course, under better circumstances.)

Cloud will take us to the doctor. She had the same procedure done by him two years ago when she was still dating men (long story . . .). She said he is extremely gentle. He has an office in Chinatown. He doesn't speak lots of English, but Cloud knows some Mandarin. It costs $250. If you want, I can loan it to you.

Oh, sweetie, I'm so sorry you have to go through this. But I'll be right by your side. Call and tell me if Jeff will be coming, too. I've booked a room for both of you at the Gramercy Hotel—my treat. (Actually, my father's treat. Wouldn't he freak if he knew how I'm spending the pocket money he gives me every month?) But if Jeff can't make it, you and I can crash there because you shouldn't be alone. Anyway, I couldn't possibly bring you back to my matchbox of a dorm room.

I love you always. Kisses and hugs. Bring the bear I gave you. He'll keep you company.

Love,

Lilly

P.S. You can stop apologizing about calling in the middle of the night. You know I'm up then, anyway. And the main thing is, I'm always there for you, so PLEASE don't worry! I've taken care of everything.

P.P.S. When this is over, and well behind you, we damn well better march on Washington about women's rights. Cloud is hopeful there will soon be an enlightened Congress and we'll see some legislation. I doubt it. . . .

P.P.P.S. I promise I won't tell Ben. So no one in your family will ever know, I swear!!!!

Dearest Darlingest Lilly,

Just a fast note to tell you we got back to Boston uneventfully. I'm feeling okay.

Jeff and I talked the whole way home, and we decided to just put this whole episode behind us and move on. Chapter closed, nightmare over.

Well, almost over. I confess I am haunted . . . more than a little . . . by thoughts of the child I almost had. What did I just lose? Who would he have been? What might she have given to the world? What kind of mother would I have been? What kind of love might I have offered that child . . . and what would I have received in return?

I know there's no sense in asking these questions, but it's impossible to entirely let them go. So I have to constantly remind myself that neither Jeff nor I is in a place to get married or have a family—though this experience got us both thinking about what it all means, and whether or not it's something we want.

Lilly, you know how much I used to dream about getting married—but now, I realize, it was in such a little-girl way. If I ever do get married, I want so much more than the white dress or the wedding cake. For me it won't be about upholding convention, but about honoring the right to make choices with another human being who shares my ideals. It's about daring to hold hands and, together, take an amazing leap of faith.

Maybe one day Jeff will be that man for me, and I will be that woman for him. Right now, neither of us is ready to take the journey.

Lilly, my sweet SillyLilly, I don't know how to begin to thank you. In the last week you've helped me more than I've ever been helped. I'm speechless with gratitude. Not only did you make all the horrible arrangements (which must have been so difficult for you), but you somehow, miraculously, made the whole terrible thing feel okay. Not that it was exactly fun . . . but you know what I mean. Because you always know what I mean. You know me and care for me in a way nobody ever has.

I couldn't survive without your friendship, Lilly. I love you so much for loving me the way you do. Thank you, thank you, thank you forever.

And love and thanks from Jeff, too. Please tell Cloud how grateful to her I am (we are) for helping make the arrangements.

A zillion kisses from your not-so-secret admirer, foolish with adoration,

ValPal

P.S. Is it tacky to include a recipe in a love letter? Maybe. Here's one anyway. The friendship part is in honor of you—the fool part is in honor of me!

....

⚬ APPLE AND PEAR ⚭
FRIENDSHIP FOOL

SERVES 4

|||||||||||||||||||||||||||||||||||||||||||||||||||||||||||||||||||||||||||||||||||||||||||||||||||||||||||||||

2	medium apples, peeled, cored, and cubed
2	pears, peeled, cored, and cubed
2	tablespoons granulated sugar

1	cup heavy cream
2	tablespoons confectioners' sugar
2	teaspoons vanilla extract

1. In a medium pan over medium heat, combine the apples, pears, and granulated sugar. Cook, covered, until the fruit is tender and almost falling apart, about 15 minutes. Pass the fruit through a food mill and let the puree cool.

2. Just before serving, whip the cream until soft peaks form. Add the confectioners' sugar and vanilla and continue to beat until stiff peaks form. Fold in the chilled fruit puree, leaving some streaks of cream in the mixture. Serve cold.

NOVEMBER 12, 1972

Dear Val,

Let me just explain what I meant on the phone, okay?

The situation that day was obviously difficult for you and Jeff, and highly emotional. So it's hard for me to know exactly what I would think of him under normal circumstances. All I meant was that he just seemed slightly distant at a time when you should have been covered in hugs.

I'm not saying you're being starry-eyed about him, and yes, it was good he came to be with you for the whole ordeal. But then again, why shouldn't he? Why should we always be so grateful to men for doing things they SHOULD *do? I mean, he was half the reason you got pregnant!*

Anyway, I'm glad things are going well with you two.

I was touched that you shared with me all your thoughts of what might have been had you gone through with it. It's a little like grieving, especially since you're someone who definitely wants children.

It's funny what I've taken away from your experience. Now I am clearer than ever that I don't want to be a mother. I believe it's impossible to be a good mother if you've never had one yourself. Plus, to be totally honest, there's too much of Katherine Stone in me. I can't imagine giving myself over to someone else. Caring that much about letting someone else's needs come first. Not to mention getting so wrapped up with a guy that I want him around my life day after day, year after year. No way.

Cloud says hello. We are going to a Joan Baez concert next week. And then, off to a women's retreat in Massachusetts for the weekend. Cloud's really opening my eyes to lots of stuff. I've joined her consciousness-raising group. It's one of the few things I'm enjoying at school.

Here's a totally fab dish from Cloud. Stuffed pepper with kasha. One bite and you're on cloud nine!

Lillypad

....

❧ CLOUD NINE STUFFED PEPPERS ❧

MAKES 4 STUFFED PEPPERS

|||||||||||||||||||||||||||||||||||||||||||||||||||||||||||||||||||||||||||||||||||||||||||||||||||||||||||||||||||||||||||||

2 cups raw bulgur wheat

3¾ cups water

2 teaspoons salt, plus additional for sprinkling

4 green peppers

¼ cup oil

1 cup finely diced celery

¼ cup finely diced carrot

1 bunch green onions, trimmed and sliced

1 garlic clove, minced

½ cup finely chopped spinach

½ cup finely diced green beans

Pinch cayenne

1 tomato, sliced

---

1. Preheat the oven to 350° F.

2. In a large pot over medium-high heat, combine the bulgur with 3¾ cups water and 1 teaspoon salt. Simmer, covered, until grains are tender and most of the water is evaporated, about 15 minutes. Drain any remaining water.

3. Meanwhile, with a knife, remove the tops from the peppers; finely chop peppers and set aside. Discard the cores and seeds. Place the peppers in a steamer basket set over a pot of simmering water and cook, covered, until just tender, 5 to 7 minutes.

4. Heat 2 tablespoons oil in a medium pan over medium-high heat. Add the celery, carrot, green onions, chopped green pepper, and garlic. Cook, stirring until softened, about 5 minutes. Add the spinach, green beans, ¼ cup water, and cayenne. Cover and cook over medium heat for 5 minutes.

5. Combine the vegetables and the grains. Add the remaining 2 tablespoons oil and 1 teaspoon salt. Divide the filling among the four peppers. Top each pepper with a tomato slice and sprinkle the tomato lightly with salt. Bake for 15 minutes.

DECEMBER 8, 1972

Hey Silly,

Wanna make believe we're 11?

I do.

So here's my idea. Let's have New Year's Eve together like we used to do. Just the two of us—you and me, and a stack of records. Let's spare no expense and do it up right: ice cream sodas, pretzels, confetti, the works. Even Vienna finger cookies AND *chocolate-covered grahams. My treat. Let me know you can do it and I'll start shopping for our outfits: how about a couple of ball gowns, mink stoles, and tiaras?*

Actually, we could wear aprons instead and cook a great dinner together—wouldn't that be fun? Do you want to try making that pastitsio we talked about? Or go classic with a coq au vin? Let me know. Jeff is going home for the holiday, but I'm not going with him.

Are you free? If you are, my place or yours? You choose. Anywhere you pick is fine with me.

Love,

Me

....

DECEMBER 11, 1972

Yes! Yes! Yes!

I can't wait. I mean, I'm sorry Jeff is going home and you don't feel ready to do the hang-with-his-parents thing, but

I'm totally into the you-and-me thing. I'll come up to Boston—it will be great to get away.

So, ValPal, let's ring in 1973 together and wash away whatever we want to forget about from 1972 with a good bottle of Moët I just lifted from my father's wine rack. (Don't worry, he won't even notice. Besides, if he knew it was for you, he would say, take two!)

Catch ya later,

Lilly

....

❧ COQ AU VIN ☙

SERVES 4

½ pound pearl onions, peeled

6 tablespoons unsalted butter

½ pound white mushrooms, quartered

½ pound bacon, diced

3 pounds skinned chicken thighs and legs

Salt

Ground black pepper

2 medium carrots, peeled and roughly chopped

2 celery stalks, roughly chopped

1 medium onion, chopped

2 garlic cloves, finely chopped

¼ cup all-purpose flour

3 cups red wine

1 cups chicken stock

5 sprigs thyme

5 sprigs parsley

1 bay leaf

Boiled potatoes, for serving

1. Cook the pearl onions in large pot of boiling water for 2 minutes. Drain and cool. Peel. Melt 3 tablespoons butter in a large, heavy skillet over medium-high heat. Add the pearl onions and mushrooms and sauté until the mushrooms are

tender and the onions are golden, about 10 minutes. Transfer to a bowl.

2. Cook the bacon in the same skillet until brown and crisp, about 7 minutes. Transfer the bacon to a bowl, and remove all but 2 tablespoons fat from the skillet.

3. Season the chicken with salt and pepper. Add the chicken to the skillet and cook, turning occasionally and working in batches if necessary, until the chicken is brown all over, 10 to 15 minutes. Transfer the chicken to a plate.

4. Melt the remaining 3 tablespoons butter in the skillet over medium heat. Add the carrots, celery, onion, and garlic and cook over medium heat until softened, about 10 minutes. Add the flour and brown for 5 minutes.

5. Pour in the wine and stock; add the thyme, parsley, and bay leaf (if desired, tie the herbs together with kitchen string). Bring to a boil and cook, scraping up the browned bits at the bottom of the pan, until the sauce has thickened, about 5 minutes. Return the chicken and half the bacon to the skillet. Simmer for 25 minutes, then turn the chicken pieces and simmer for 15 minutes more.

6. Transfer the chicken to a platter and strain the sauce. Combine the chicken, strained sauce, remaining bacon, mushrooms, and pearl onions in the skillet and cook for 5 minutes, until the sauce is slightly reduced. Season with salt and pepper, if necessary, and serve accompanied by boiled potatoes.

❧ NEW YEAR'S EVE PASTITSIO ❧

SERVES 8

FOR THE PASTA:

1 pound ziti pasta

⅓ cup grated Parmesan cheese

2 tablespoons unsalted butter, melted

½ teaspoon salt

¼ teaspoon ground nutmeg

Ground black pepper

3 eggs, lightly beaten

FOR THE MEAT SAUCE:

2 tablespoons unsalted butter

1 onion, finely chopped

1 garlic clove, finely chopped

1½ pounds ground beef

¼ cup tomato sauce

½ cup chicken stock

½ teaspoon ground cinnamon

Pinch sugar

Pinch salt

Ground black pepper

FOR THE CREAM SAUCE:

¾ cup unsalted butter

¾ cup all-purpose flour

3 cups whole milk

½ teaspoon ground nutmeg

Salt

Ground black pepper

1 egg, lightly beaten

Butter or shortening for greasing pan

¼ cup grated Parmesan, for sprinkling

1. Preheat the oven to 350° F. Grease a 9 x 13-inch baking pan.

2. Cook the pasta according to package directions. Drain. Toss the pasta with the cheese, butter, salt, nutmeg, and pepper. Let the mixture cool slightly, then stir in the eggs.

3. For the meat sauce, melt the butter in a large skillet over medium-high heat. Cook the onion and garlic until soft, about 5 minutes. Add the meat and cook, stirring, until well browned. Add the tomato sauce, stock, cinnamon, sugar, salt, and pepper to taste. Cover and simmer gently for 15 minutes.

4. For the cream sauce, melt the butter in a medium pot over medium-high heat. Add the flour and cook for 2 minutes, stirring frequently. Pour in the milk and bring to a boil; cook

for 1 minute. Stir in the nutmeg, salt, and pepper. Let cool slightly, then whisk in the egg.

5. To assemble, spread half the ziti in the prepared pan. Top with the meat sauce, then the remaining ziti. Pour the cream sauce over the ziti and sprinkle with the cheese. Bake until golden-brown, about 50 minutes. Let cool 10 minutes before slicing.

1973

Hi Val,

I told my father dorm life was killing me and that if he made me stay there one more night I'd quit school. Of course, that freaked him out.

But it worked! So, now I've moved out of that vile dorm. Got my own pad. It's on 10th Street off Second Avenue, in a hellhole tenement that the landlord rents to students (and, if I'm any indication, to potential dropouts). New phone number, too. It's all on the enclosed card, which, you'll notice, is also an announcement for my next gig at Dizzy's. (Can you come? Probably not, I know how crazed you are, but I just had to ask. . . .)

Just so you know, my father doesn't have a clue that I'm still performing. I had to promise I would stop in exchange for his continued financial support. I know, I know . . . a lie. But it's a white lie and it isn't hurting anyone. So, let him think I've got a book in my face at all times . . . never a microphone! Please don't say a word, okay? I mean, if you happen to speak to him anytime soon.

Today I hung up the blue and white batik bedspread you gave me last year. I put it on the bedroom wall to cover the cracks in the paint. It helped cheer the place up a lot.

Love,

Lilly

....

❧ HOME-OF-MY-OWN HAMBURGERS ❧

SERVES 4

1½ pounds ground beef	4 ounces blue cheese, crumbled
2 garlic cloves, finely chopped	1 medium ripe tomato, sliced, for serving
2 tablespoons Dijon mustard	
1 teaspoon salt	Lettuce, for serving
Ground black pepper	
4 hamburger buns	

1. In a bowl, combine the beef, garlic, mustard, salt, and pepper. Form the beef into 4 patties.

2. Heat a medium pan over medium-high heat. Add the patties and cook, turning once, 3 to 4 minutes per side for medium-rare.

3. Transfer the patties to the hamburger buns. Top each burger with 1 ounce cheese, a tomato slice, and some lettuce. Serve.

FEBRUARY 14, 1973

Happy VAL-*entines, Val!*

Hope you and Jeff are doing something romantic and fun.

My love-life news: zip. I'm starting to think I should consider other options. Celibacy crossed my mind for about half a second. Cloud says I should learn to express my sexual being the same way I sing: reaching into my soul to find the melody in my heart. She loves my voice. She's incredibly supportive.

I can't tell you how much that means to me right now. I feel like I'm at an important but scary crossroads in my life where I really have to make some huge decisions.

Cloud is coming over tonight. I'm putting together my first home-cooked meal for her. Only one burner on the stove works, and to light it you have to strike a match, say a prayer, then blow three times and hope the flames don't singe your eyebrows. Life is full of adventures these days.

Did I tell you that Katherine the Great returned from her latest tour? Apparently, when the show ended, so did her relationship with that choreographer. (My father and she seem to be getting along okay again. Especially since they only spend five minutes together before one or the other travels. Now he's gone away on another cross-country book promotion for The Fear Impulse. *Can you believe how famous this book is making him?)*

Anyway, my mother called and asked me to meet her for dinner. She said she wanted us to catch up and have some "one-to-one girl time." Of course it led to yet another Memorable Meal Moment (you'll love this one).

KATHERINE: *Lillian, darling, pass the wine, I have something vitally important to tell you. . . .*

ME: *Let me guess . . . a new "friend?"*

KATHERINE: *How obnoxious! You sound just like your father. And besides, I have no friends. I'm too old. Terribly, terribly old. In fact, I'm sick . . . to death. Lilly, there's no choice for me now. I need surgery before time runs out.*

ME *(genuinely frightened):* *Mom, what's wrong?*

KATHERINE: *I need a face-lift.*

So, what began as an evening of making up for lost time with me ended with her in tears, about her. And about me telling her how beautiful she is, and trying to console her.

Salt to the wound: when the check came she said she'd forgotten her wallet and . . . could I handle it?

All of this leaves me a little sad on this day that's supposed to be about love.

Write or call soon. We're way behind on our recipes.

The Lone Lilly

....

FEBRUARY 15, 1973

Dear Val,

Last night's dinner with Cloud was a huge success! So, I decided to send you the dessert recipe—a sumptuous and sexy chocolate cake dusted with cocoa. Like Cupid's arrow, it put love back into my life.

Look, sweetie, it's time for me to tell you what I have been circling around in my own head for months: I love Cloud. And she loves me. I can hear your startled question, and the answer is, YES. That way. The way you love Jeff. Or, as Cloud says, "completely, consummately, consumingly."

Are you shocked?

I have to admit, it took even me by surprise. I always thought of myself as being irresistible to men. I didn't realize I was that way for women, too.

It's not like I'm done with men. It's just a relief to be with someone who finds her way around my body without me having to give her a road map. And there's a closeness that isn't even about the sex. Strange for me to say, but that might be the most appealing part.

Val, what do you think of all this? Please let me know. Call. Write. I want to hear from you.

Love,

P.S. *Try the cake with a scoop of the Recipe Club's Cinnamon Ice Cream.*

....

❧ CUPID'S CHOCOLATE CAKE ❧

SERVES 8

FOR THE CHOCOLATE CAKE:

Butter or shortening for greasing pan and rack

⅓ cup unsweetened cocoa

⅔ cup boiling water

2 egg yolks

1 whole egg

2 teaspoons vanilla

1½ cups plus 1 tablespoon cake flour

1 cup sugar

2 teaspoons baking powder

½ teaspoon salt

½ cup (1 stick) unsalted butter, melted

FOR THE CHOCOLATE GLAZE:

7½ ounces bittersweet chocolate

---

1. Preheat the oven to 350° F. Grease a 9-inch cake pan and line with parchment paper.

2. In a medium bowl, whisk together the cocoa and ⅔ cup boiling water until smooth. Cool.

3. In another bowl, whisk together the egg yolks and egg, ¼ cup of the cocoa mixture, and the vanilla. Whisk together the flour, sugar, baking powder, and salt. Add the butter and remaining cocoa mixture, and beat with an electric mixer on low speed until just combined. Increase the speed to medium and beat for 2 minutes. Scrape down the sides of the bowl and add the egg mixture slowly, beating until fully incorporated (about 1½ minutes total).

4. Scrape the batter into the prepared pan and smooth with a spatula. Bake just until a toothpick inserted in the center comes out clean, 30 to 40 minutes. Do not overbake. Let the cake cool for 10 minutes, then invert onto a greased wire rack set over a rimmed baking sheet, and cool completely before glazing.

5. For the glaze: place the chocolate in a medium bowl. In a small pot, bring the cream to a simmer. Pour the cream over the chocolate and let sit for 2 minutes. Gently whisk the mixture until fully combined. Let cool until just warm to the touch.

6. Pour the glaze directly over the center of the cake, allowing the glaze to pour down over the sides. Use an offset spatula to smooth the glaze evenly over the sides of the cake. Let set for 1 hour before serving.

FEBRUARY 20, 1973

Dear Lilly,

Holy cow!

Okay, I admit it, I'm confused. And blown away. And unsure what's appropriate for me to say in response.

On the one hand, I believe you have a right to love anyone.

On the other, to be completely honest, I don't like the idea of you being with Cloud. Given my propensity for analysis, it surprises me not just that I have these feelings, but that I can't figure out why I have them. There's just something about her that bothers me.

Boy oh boy, Lilly, I'm ashamed. I'm a bad friend, a hypocrite, a parlor liberal. But there you have it: the mixed bag of my gut reactions.

Maybe your feelings for Cloud shouldn't be such a surprise. In retrospect, it's obvious that you two had strong feelings for each other. It's just that when I was in New York, I was so consumed by my own problems that I didn't pay much attention to what was going on.

Now I hear you saying your feelings for her are different than any you've ever had before—for anyone. So if it's love, as you contend, then I wish you all the happiness in the world.

Lilly, I'm sorry if I'm not sounding 100 percent enthusiastic. And of course, I support you in this. I'm only telling you these things because you asked, and to honor our promise to always be honest.

So don't hate me.

I love you and want you to be happy.

Val

....

Dear Val,

I won't pretend I'm not hurt. For some reason, when it's a boyfriend you don't like, I let that roll off my back. But with Cloud, it's different.

I really hoped you would groove with her, and see all the beauty in her that I do. I wanted the two of you to be great friends. I imagined that you'd think I'd done a smart thing by letting myself be with someone who is so caring, devoted, and evolved.

But don't worry, I don't hate you. In fact, Cloud urges me to honor your honesty. She says you must see my love for her as an unexpected change, and I should give you time to adjust.

Cloud suggests that you eat brown rice and cashews on a daily basis, and consider a total macrobiotic diet to cure yourself of ill feelings. She says if you do this for a few months, cleansing your body of toxins will steer you toward a sense of inner peace and allow you to accept growth in others you love.

Cloud also thinks I should consider taking on a new name. One that's neither matriarchal nor patriarchal. One that reflects my true spiritual self. We went to a healer who gave me a personal mantra and a new way to identify myself. I'm trying it out here for the first time.

Peace,

Luna

....

❧ INNER-PEACE BROWN RICE ❧ AND CASHEWS

SERVES 4

⅓⅓⅓

¼ cup extra-virgin olive oil	½ pound white mushrooms, sliced
¼ cup scallions, thinly sliced	6 cups spinach leaves (about 5 ounces)
1 garlic clove, finely chopped	
1 cup short-grain brown rice	¾ teaspoon soy sauce
2 cups vegetable stock	Ground black pepper
¼ teaspoon salt	
¾ cup unsalted, roasted cashews	

1. Heat 2 tablespoons oil in a medium pot over medium-high heat. Add the scallions and garlic and cook for 3 minutes. Add the rice and cook, stirring, for 2 minutes more. Add the stock and salt and bring to a boil. Cover and let simmer for 40 minutes. Remove from the heat and let sit for 10 minutes more.

2. Meanwhile, heat the remaining 2 tablespoons oil in a medium skillet over medium-high heat. Add coarsely-chopped cashews with the mushrooms and cook, tossing until the mushrooms are softened and the cashews are golden, about five minutes. Add the spinach and soy sauce

> and cook until wilted, 3 to 4 minutes more. Season with pepper. Stir the vegetables into the cooked rice. Taste and adjust the seasoning, if necessary.

MARCH 14, 1973

*Dear Luna-*TIC,

Sounds like Cloud wants to kill me, not cure me. In which case, I will end up needing antibiotics more than macrobiotics.

Lilly-Luna, there are thousands of ways I would prove my undying loyalty and friendship to you, but a steady diet of brown rice and cashews is not one of them.

My road to enlightenment will be paved with peanut brittle.

I honestly, truly, really, seriously hope you and Cloud are having fun.

Kisses.

Love,

Val

. . . .

⟨ ENLIGHTENED PEANUT BRITTLE ⟩

MAKES ABOUT 6 CUPS BRITTLE

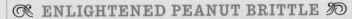

Butter or shortening for greasing equipment
1½ cups granulated sugar
1 cup water
¾ cup light corn syrup

2 cups chopped peanuts
2 tablespoons unsalted butter
1 tablespoon baking soda

1. Grease a large baking sheet. Line the sheet with parchment paper, and grease the parchment.

2. In a medium pot set over medium-high heat, combine the sugar, 1 cup water, and corn syrup. Cook until the mixture reads 260° F on a candy thermometer, about 30 minutes.

3. Stir in the peanuts and butter, and continue cooking until the mixture reaches a temperature of 295° F, about 15 minutes more. Stir in the baking soda until just combined (the mixture will be foaming).

4. Immediately pour the mixture out onto the prepared baking sheet. Use a greased rubber spatula to smooth the mixture to ¼-inch thickness. Let cool completely. Break into pieces and store in an airtight container.

Val!

Look!!! Look!!! Look!!!

A review in the Village Voice! *"Lovely Lilly," it said. (Guess I'll ditch Luna.)*

The "tremulous" voice the reviewer "adored" was really just me being nervous. It's very flattering, don't you think? He totally dug my sound. I can't tell you what an ego boost it's been, not to mention that I got booked for another month at the club—AND an agent called me!

One potential drag: if my father sees the write-ups he's going to put two and two together, and he'll bust me. Actually, what am I worrying about? He'll never see it—reading the arts section gives him indigestion. Every time he looks at it he sees my mother's name linked up with some new show— and some new guy.

And it's not like I got something published in a scientific journal, like you did. (Do you know he framed your article and hung it on the wall near his desk?)

Anyway, I know you'll be proud of me, so I wanted to make sure you got a copy.

Cloud says all these good things are happening because I finally stopped counting the negatives in my life and started appreciating the positives. (I know you're still a little critical of her, but really, she does good things for my head.)

And Val, I saved the best for last: I'm one of ten singers invited to perform at a special showcase for "up-and-coming cabaret artists" at Issy's Keynote. Save the date: September 21.

Lots of producers and A&R people will be there, and it's THE place to be discovered these days. I know this will be my big break.

Soon you'll be able to say you knew me when!

I'm celebrating by having Cloud over for a totally indulgent dinner. Fresh ricotta cheese is the trick with this dish. Wish you were here to have some!

Love,

"Lovely Lilly"

P.S. Don't forget:

Lilly's Big Break!

September 21, 1973

8:30 PM

BE THERE . . . OR BE SQUARE!

(Oh, wait, you already are. Just joking! You know I love you.)

....

⊗ RAVE-REVIEWS RAVIOLI ⊗

SERVES 6

⁞⁞⁞

FOR THE PASTA DOUGH:

- 3 cups all-purpose flour, plus more for rolling out
- 4 eggs
- 1 teaspoon extra-virgin olive oil
- ½ teaspoon salt

FOR THE TOMATO SAUCE:

- ¼ cup extra-virgin olive oil
- 1 medium onion
- 2 garlic cloves
- Pinch red pepper flakes
- 2 (28-ounce) cans whole, peeled tomatoes, broken up with a fork

- ¾ teaspoon salt
- Ground black pepper
- ¼ cup fresh chopped basil

FOR THE FILLING:

- 2 cups ricotta cheese
- 1 egg
- ½ teaspoon salt
- ⅛ teaspoon ground nutmeg
- Ground black pepper
- Grated Parmesan cheese, for serving

1. For the pasta dough: place the flour in a bowl and make a well in the center. In a separate bowl, whisk together the eggs, the oil, and salt. Pour the egg mixture into the flour well, and whisk together until a dough forms. Turn the dough out onto a lightly floured surface and knead until smooth and elastic, about 10 minutes. Cover and let rest in the refrigerator for 1 hour.

2. Meanwhile, make the sauce. Heat the oil in a large pot over medium-high heat. Add the onion, garlic, and red pepper flakes and cook, stirring, for 5 minutes. Add the tomatoes, salt, and pepper. Bring to a boil, then reduce the heat and simmer gently, uncovered, for 1 hour. Stir in the basil. Cover and keep warm over very low heat.

3. Combine all the filling ingredients in a bowl; mix well.

4. To prepare the ravioli, bring a large pot of salted water to a boil. Divide the dough into 4 equal parts. On a floured surface,

roll one portion of dough into an 8 x 16-inch rectangle (cover the remaining portions of dough with a damp towel). The dough should be as thin as possible.

5. Using a sharp knife, slice the dough lengthwise into 4 equal strips. Then slice the dough again crosswise into 4 equal strips (you should have sixteen 2 x 4-inch rectangles). Spoon 1 teaspoon ricotta filling on one half of each rectangle. Brush the edges of the rectangle lightly with water, and fold the dough over the filling, pressing the edges with a fork to seal. Transfer the finished ravioli to a baking sheet and cover with a damp towel until all of the ravioli have been filled. Repeat the rolling process with the remaining dough.

6. Cook the ravioli in the boiling water until al dente, about 4 minutes. Drain. Transfer the pasta to a platter and serve topped with tomato sauce and a sprinkle of Parmesan cheese.

JUNE 12, 1973

Dear Lillyface,

Isn't this photo hilarious? I'm sending it to you because I thought it would make you laugh. Jeff took it at Walden Pond a couple of weeks ago. It was a perfect day—warm with a light breeze, the leaves a luscious brand-new green. Glorious.

Anyway, one thing led to another, and Jeff dared me to take my shirt off and hug a tree to prove I was really a transcendental pantheist. And—as this picture proves—I did! I am! Can you believe it? Repressed little me, running around naked in the woods? I keep laughing every time I think about how surprised you will be. And how happy for me, too.

Lilly, I love him so much. He makes my world feel bigger and better. And because he acts happy when I assert myself, I feel more confident than ever. The only scary thing about being with him is that he always seems to know exactly what he wants. For example, he's absolutely certain he'll go to medical school. So everything he does academically is about that. Sometimes I feel like he expects me to be just like him. (He kind of resembles Isaac in this respect. Hmmm . . . let's forget I said that.)

Write to me, okay? Here's a fabulous pound cake recipe. We ate it on the picnic. It's as light as my heart.

Love,

The Naked Wood Sprite

....

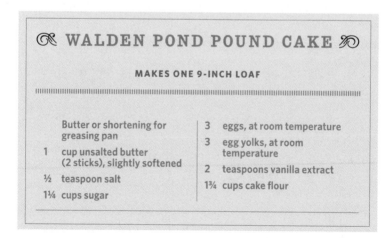

⌘ WALDEN POND POUND CAKE ⌀

MAKES ONE 9-INCH LOAF

Butter or shortening for greasing pan	3 eggs, at room temperature
1 cup unsalted butter (2 sticks), slightly softened	3 egg yolks, at room temperature
½ teaspoon salt	2 teaspoons vanilla extract
1¼ cups sugar	1¾ cups cake flour

1. Preheat the oven to 325° F. Grease a 9 x 5 x 3-inch loaf pan.

2. Using an electric mixer, beat the butter and salt until creamy, about 2 minutes. Scrape the bowl and beat 1 minute more. With the mixer running, gradually add the sugar. Beat until light and fluffy, 3 to 4 minutes. Scrape down the bowl.

3. In a separate bowl, whisk together the eggs, yolks, and vanilla extract. With the mixer running, pour the egg mixture slowly into the butter mixture. Beat 3 minutes more.

4. Fold the flour into the egg mixture a little at a time.

5. Pour the batter into the prepared pan. Bake until golden-brown and a toothpick inserted into the center comes out clean, 50 to 60 minutes.

AUGUST 15, 1973

Val,

I know you can't come to my Big Night because of school, but I wanted to send you and Jeff the showcase invitation anyway. Obviously, cleavage is my middle name.

I've been singing my ass off every single day, and feel more ready than ever. I know I can't miss.

Remember I told you we're only allowed to present one song? Well, FINALLY, *after going through every songbook and piece of sheet music ever published, I've made my choice: "Everything's Coming Up Roses." The title says it all—it's exactly how I feel.*

Val, I'm at the brink of something bigger than anyone could imagine. Have you ever had this feeling that the earth is shifting under your feet, and that all the planets are aligned in your favor? I've never been more certain of myself. And when the reviews come pouring in, that's when I will finally PROVE *to my father that he was wrong about me. I can and will be so much more than he thinks.*

If you can change your plans, just show up, even at the last minute. I'm on at about 8:30.

Curtain up! Light the lights! I've got nothing to hit but the heights!

Love,

Lilly

....

SEPTEMBER 21, 1973

Loveliest,

HOW DID IT GO???? *I called for hours tonight, but you must have been out on the town being feted by all your new fans.*

Jeff and I invited a bunch of friends over and toasted you as we listened to the cast album of Gypsy *at exactly 8:30. We even made a special cocktail in your honor: Everything's Coming Up Rose's Lime Gimlet.*

I'm so proud of you! I bragged about you all night. I told everyone I was your first accompanist, and always your biggest admirer. Now it's time to share you with the millions of lucky people soon to discover what I've always known: Lillian Stone is a star!

Brava!

V.

....

❦ EVERYTHING'S COMING ❧ UP ROSE'S LIME GIMLET

SERVES 2

|||||||||||||||||||||||||||||||||||||||||||||||||||||||||||||||||||||||||||||||||||||||||||||||||||||||||||||||||

4 ounces London dry gin	Cracked ice
1⅓ ounces Rose's lime juice	Lime slices

1. Combine the first two ingredients in a cocktail shaker.
2. Add cracked ice and shake well.
3. Strain into chilled cocktail glasses.
4. Garnish the rim of each glass with a lime slice.

SEPTEMBER 29, 1973

Lilly—

What's going on? I haven't heard one word from you since the show. Why aren't you answering your phone? What's keeping you so busy?

Write, call, send a smoke signal, something. Just let me know you're okay.

Love,
Val

. . . .

OCTOBER 5, 1973

Dear Lilly,

Hello? Anyone there? Have you secretly joined the Weathermen? Joined a cult? Run off to Hollywood?

I'm getting worried. Ben says you're not answering his calls, either. And that he never sees you at the clubs. He said he thought you might be pissed that he didn't make it to your showcase, but I said you had disappeared off the face of the planet. He told me to relax, you're probably just doing your own thing.

But I can't relax.

Do me a favor and respond. Even a postcard will do. And you know how I feel about postcards.

Love,
Val

. . . .

OCTOBER 11, 1973

Dear Val,

Please stop worrying. And please don't bother calling—I've unplugged the phone.

It's not you. It's not us. It's me. I just need some space, and can't answer questions right now.

Trust me, okay? I'll be in touch . . . when I'm ready.

Love,

Lilly

....

OCTOBER 15, 1973

Dear Lilly,

I can't imagine what's so bad in your life that you can't share it with me. This is so unlike you. I AM worried, even though you told me not to be. I'm sending you this fabulous, comforting recipe in the hopes that it will entice you to resurface. Remember: I love you.

Val

....

❦ MISSING YOU WARMLY ❧
LENTIL SALAD

SERVES 4 TO 6

1	tablespoon extra-virgin olive oil	1	teaspoon salt
1	cup finely diced carrot	½	teaspoon ground black pepper
1	cup finely diced celery		FOR THE DRESSING:
1	cup finely diced onion	2 to 3	tablespoons red wine vinegar, to taste
1	garlic clove, finely chopped	1½	tablespoons Dijon mustard
6	cups vegetable stock or water	½	cup extra virgin olive oil
2	cups lentils		Salt
3	thyme branches		Ground black pepper
1	bay leaf	¼	cup fresh chopped parsley

1. Heat the oil in a medium pot over medium-high heat. Sauté the carrot, the celery, and onion until softened, about 5 minutes. Add the garlic and sauté 1 minute more. Stir in the stock, lentils, thyme branches, and bay leaf. Bring to a boil; reduce to a simmer and cook until almost tender, 15 to 20 minutes. Add salt and pepper and simmer until tender, but not falling apart, 5 to 10 minutes more (this may take more time, depending on the age of the lentils). Drain, if necessary. Discard the thyme and bay leaf; transfer the lentils to a bowl.

2. For the dressing: whisk together the vinegar and mustard. Slowly whisk in the oil. Season to taste with salt and pepper. Pour the dressing over the lentils and toss to combine. Stir in the parsley. Serve warm or at room temperature.

OCTOBER 30, 1973

Lilly,

This is insane!

We haven't talked for almost two months! Your phone still just rings and rings. Are you even living in your apartment?

At this point, I'm way more than worried—I'm mad.

I called your parents. Your mother said you're checking in once a week, as always. She told me you said you have a new "friend." (Is she referring to Cloud? Did you change your mind and decide to tell them about her?) And that school's keeping you busy. (Since when? Last I heard, you thought you'd get mono if you woke up before noon.) That's when it dawned on me they aren't the people I should be asking about you.

So I tried calling Cloud. Some girl answered and said she was out. I left my number, but Cloud never called me back. I felt awkward calling again. Did she even tell you I called?

Lilly, haven't you had enough "space" by now? Enough time to figure out whatever it is that's bothering you? What IS bothering you? You can tell me. You can tell me anything! What gives? I've never seen you like this, ever.

It's getting impossible to not take this personally.

Lillyface, I miss you. Terribly.

If I don't hear from you soon I'm getting on a train to New York. I'll just camp on your doorstep until you appear.

PLEASE call. Any time, day or night. I'm begging you.

Val

NOVEMBER 5, 1973

Dear Lilly,

I hope you get this before I arrive on Friday.

Damn it, why don't you just answer your phone? There's a solution to whatever is wrong. Let me help you find it.

I'm coming down the minute my classes are over. I'm heading straight from Penn Station to your apartment. Assuming the train gets in on time, I'll get to you by about 1:15.

Be there. Please.

Val

....

NOVEMBER 15, 1973

For Christ's sake, Val, I thought you were on my side. I thought you would keep my secrets. I thought you were my best friend.

Wrong.

Thanks to you, my world has exploded. My father disowned me. Cut me off completely, like he's always threatened to. Even worse—far worse—he's so furious I doubt he'll ever forgive me.

Didn't it EVER occur to you the reason I wasn't answering the door, or your calls, or your letters, was that I didn't want to see you or speak to you? I just couldn't. I was humiliated.

Heartbroken. Why am I even telling you this? You certainly don't deserve an explanation.

But you sure as hell do deserve to understand just how wrong you were to interfere.

The day before the showcase, Cloud dumped me for another woman—a stringy-haired bitch who lies about singing backup for Springsteen and Stevie Wonder. Cloud has been cheating with her for months. Now they're living together and I hope they rot in hell.

I was devastated. Crushed. A complete wreck. It's the first time anyone's ever walked out on me, and I couldn't handle it. I could barely scrape myself off the floor to get to the showcase, and once I got there, I flopped beyond imagination.

Can you even understand what this means? I didn't just blow it, I was a total joke. A clown. A loser. I started in the wrong key. Forgot half the words to the song. Lost pace with my accompanist. And when I went for the high note—and missed—there was such horrible feedback from the amp, people covered their ears and cringed. By the time I finished, the place was dead silent except for one embarrassed couple who were kind enough to clap out of pity.

To their credit, the critics didn't destroy me. Instead, every single one of them simply left me out of their reviews. As if I didn't even exist.

Four days later, I bucked myself up enough to call the producer of the showcase, hoping to explain what happened and beg for a second chance. He wouldn't come to the phone. Finally, after my fifth try, he answered. He said, "I'm only taking your call to put future audiences out of their misery. Please limit your singing to the shower." Then he slammed down the phone.

So I needed to be still, alone, without having to put up a front. To you or anyone. I just didn't want your pity. I didn't want your words of condolence. Or encouragement. I just wanted to recover, on my own. To put myself back together.

And I needed to figure out my next step. To show everyone how wrong they've been about me—and how wrongly they've treated me. And I mean every single one of those fucking sonofabitches: Cloud and her hideous lying girlfriend . . . that arrogant, condescending producer . . . my selfish mother and her absolute indifference to me . . . and not the least, my father. My goddamn—unloving, critical, holier-than-thou father.

Especially him.

He's never approved of my singing or performing. In fact, my whole life, he's tried to stop me from expressing myself. He views every effort I've made to realize my hopes and dreams as a rebellion, a deliberate contradiction of his marching orders. The only way he'll ever genuinely value me is if I give up everything I love to become an extension of him. To become the good girl who lives to fulfill his every expectation.

Funny, who does that remind me of? Oh yeah, you. Perfect Valerie. The Savior, the Good Fairy, the Diplomat. That's how you want to come off—but I've got your number. You slither around people, like the snake in the grass you are.

What the hell did you think you were doing, Val? Playing private eye, digging up the dirty details of my life?

What were you thinking? Calling Cloud, tracking down my

landlord, snooping around the registrar's office to see if I was still enrolled?

And worst of all—reporting EVERYTHING you learned to my father . . . in detail! Telling him I dropped out! Telling him I've been deceiving him for months! Are you fucking insane?

No, there's a better word for you: traitor.

Don't even try to deny it—my father told me everything you did. He sent me a letter. He began by saying he was glad I wasn't accepting visitors, because he was too disgusted by my behavior to even look at me. Then he wrote, "Valerie has opened my eyes to the truth."

He explained in detail how you nosed around, meddled, pried, and otherwise interfered in my life. Of course, his take was that you were providing "the diligent, compassionate, investigative work of a concerned and devoted friend." Then he went on a manic psychobabble rant, including this gem: "Sadly, what you've done to me should come as no surprise, Lillian. As Sigmund Freud reminds us, children are completely egoistic; they feel their needs intensely and strive ruthlessly to satisfy them."

He signed off with a parting shot: "Lillian, your deceit shows total disrespect. I am utterly ashamed of you. How unfortunate that you have chosen to emulate the worst qualities of your mother. I never expected my own daughter to betray me in this way. I am enclosing one final check; after this you are on your own. I have paid my last dime to a thankless child."

Val, you of all people should understand the power that man has! Wasn't it obvious that telling him everything would ruin my life? Why was it more important for you to inform on me than to be my friend? Why did you do it?

Don't give me crap about being worried. I sent you a letter. You knew I wasn't dead. I told you I needed space. Why couldn't you just respect that? Why couldn't you just trust me, like I asked?

Was I offending your moralistic, Saint Val standards? I'm sure you think I'm at fault for what happened. Okay, I'll suck up my share of the blame for lying to him and taking his money under false pretenses. (Just for the record, I had every intention of telling him the truth—but on my own terms.)

And I'm sure you'll chalk this whole thing up to me being unbearably spoiled. Maybe I am. But it's so much more complicated—and you know that. YOU'RE *the smart one who once said my father's money is "the currency of his affection." So how can you blame me for being afraid to cut those strings? For holding on desperately to the one thing—the only thing—he's ever given me?*

Well, now there's nothing left to hang on to. Including our friendship.

. . . .

NOVEMBER 19, 1973

Lilly,

How can I make you understand if you hang up on me every time I call? You've got to listen!

God, Lilly, you make me feel like I'm confessing a terrible crime. But I'm not! I NEVER *meant to hurt you.*

I'm begging you to believe me—I wasn't trying to meddle, to embarrass you in any way, to find out what you were hiding—I just wanted to find YOU.

The only reason I went to your father was because I believed you were in desperate pain, and needed help. Lilly, I'd been sick with worry about you. My anxiety had gotten so overwhelming. Night after night I was imagining every terrible scenario: you, too deep into drugs to get out; you, too depressed to function. Or even worse, you, suicidal. (Of course, knowing what I know now, I hear how overreactive that all sounds.)

I imagined that together Isaac and I could reach you. I started by telling him it had been months since you and I had spoken. I explained that the last I'd heard was a brief note saying you needed "space."

He asked why I thought you would say such a thing, and when I had no clear answer—only vague anxieties—he let loose with an inquisition, a barrage of questions: what has Lilly been doing? What's her state of mind? Who has she been spending time with?

I told him everything I knew, believing that was in your best interest. I said things seemed to have been going extremely well for you. He pressed for specifics. So I gave the example of how euphoric you'd been over your upcoming showcase.

He tilted his head back and closed his eyes, the way he always does when he's thinking hard. Then, in his calmest, most commanding voice, he said, "Valerie, there is a reason you have chosen to come here today. I believe it is time for you to divulge all that you have been withholding. Tell me everything. We need to help Lilly."

I was so relieved to hear these words—to know I had an ally, to know we would find you, that you would be safe—that I started to cry. In my huge rush of relief, I put aside any worries about betraying your confidences. I told him everything I knew and had just discovered: about you performing, about you missing classes, falling behind, and then dropping out. (At least I had the presence of mind not to mention Cloud.)

Lilly, knowing what I know now, I would do anything to take it all back.

By the time I finished giving him my "report," I could tell by the look on his face that he was way more angry than concerned. I knew I needed to backpedal fast. So I gave an impassioned speech, saying you were doing what you absolutely needed to do. That your actions were not capricious. That you weren't trying to disobey him, or to be disrespectful.

I explained that right now, school, for you, was counter-productive. That his alternative to anger was pride in your accomplishments. That you've been working tirelessly on your singing. And that the showcase you'd been accepted to was extremely prestigious. It reflected your passion, talent, and commitment.

I told him I admired you, and so should he. I begged him to see you as an autonomous person, not just as his child.

He smiled and nodded in agreement. He said, "How lucky Lilly is to have you as her friend." I took that to mean he understood you needed his love and support, perhaps now more than ever.

Then he said, "Valerie, your job here is done. You did the right thing by coming to me. And you should stop your worrying. It's out of your hands now. I will handle the situation."

We ate lunch together. Afterward he put me in a cab to Penn Station, promising everything would be fine.

By the time I got back to Boston, I'd given myself permission to stop worrying.

Lilly, I swear to you, I had no idea he was planning to cut you off. I had no idea that he'd use ME to punish YOU.

I feel like I've fallen into the depths of a Greek tragedy, where the only possible resolution is inexorable grief.

I can only beg your forgiveness. Please forgive me, Lilly. Please.

Valerie

....

NOVEMBER 23, 1973

I can't forgive you. I just can't.

Lilly

....

DECEMBER 12, 1973

Lilly,

I'm desperate to see you in person. We have to straighten this out.

Please talk to me.

I'll come down whenever you say. I'll meet you anyplace you want. Just tell me when and where.

I know we can fix this. I know we can.

....

DECEMBER 20, 1973

Don't come near me.

I never want to see you again.

Lilly

....

DECEMBER 31, 1973

Dear Lilly,

Happy New Year. You know I'm thinking about you tonight.

I've given up on hearing from you, but I can't, I won't, let you go.

To send you more words feels meaningless and hollow. So I'm sending you a recipe instead. It's something I know you'll love. It uses olives—an ancient symbol of faithfulness, patience, and peace.

Lilly, I love you and I always will. And I will wait a million seasons for you to find your way back home to me.

Until then, no matter what else happens in our lives, we'll always share the delicious secrets of the Recipe Club.

Valerie

....

❧ FORGIVENESS TAPENADE ❧
WITH TOAST POINTS

MAKES 1 CUP

1 cup pitted black olives, finely chopped	3 garlic cloves, finely chopped
3 tablespoons extra-virgin olive oil	5 anchovy fillets
1 tablespoon capers	Ground black pepper
Freshly squeezed juice of ½ lemon	Toast points, for serving

1. Combine all of the tapenade ingredients in a blender and whir until smooth.

2. Serve with toast points.

Part Three: 2002

Isaac Stone, 83, Psychiatrist, Author, Expert on Phobias

Dr. Isaac Stone died of heart failure yesterday, at his home in Manhattan. He was 83 years old.

A noted psychiatrist and author of 20 books and countless scholarly articles, Dr. Stone was known chiefly for his best-selling book, The Fear Impulse, a controversial look at the etiology and treatment of phobias.

Dr. Stone was widely praised for his pioneering work, which advanced the medical awareness of phobias. But he was equally criticized by some factions of the mental health community who questioned the efficacy of his methodology.

Dr. Stone is survived by his wife, stage designer and director Katherine Stone, and their daughter, Lillian.

Funeral services will be private. A memorial tribute will be held at the New York Institute for Psychodynamic Interrelations, **March 7**, 2002, at 2 p.m.

Val looked up at Jeff, sitting across from her at the kitchen table. She put down her mug and pushed the newspaper toward him. The color had drained from her face. "Isaac's dead."

Jeff scanned the obituary and shrugged. "Well, he lived a good, long life. Long enough to screw up everyone around him."

"Don't say that, Jeff. Even if it's true. You have no right."

Jeff raised an eyebrow. He didn't need to do anything else to remind Val that he'd been the one she'd turned to every time she and Lilly had a fight about Isaac. In fact, Isaac had deeply affected his life, too.

"Okay, okay," Val agreed, "you do have a right. I'm sorry."

"Don't be, I get it." He walked around the table to give her a hug. Val let herself be wrapped in his arms and closed her eyes. She needed a minute to collect herself, to somehow absorb the unwelcome news. Slowing her breathing, she turned her attention to the familiar sounds of her early-morning world: the determined tapping of a red-headed finch at the feeder just outside the window; the hiss of steam forcing its way through sixty-year-old pipes; Jeff's heart beating steadily against her ear, pressed to his chest.

"Isaac was a big part of your world for a really long time," he whispered. "This has to hurt."

Valerie could tell Jeff wanted to protect her. He looked into her eyes as if waiting for tears, but there weren't any. In truth she felt strangely empty. Glancing at the clock above the sink, she gently withdrew from his embrace. She stood up, smoothing the wrinkles from her black woolen trousers. "I've got to go to work." Her voice was tight and controlled.

"Valerie, honey, don't do that thing," Jeff said. "It's okay to have feelings about him. Even about her."

Val sighed. For two years she and Jeff had avoided talking about Lilly, at Val's request. Which didn't mean Val had ever stopped thinking about Lilly—or had ever stopped struggling with the decision that their last good-bye was good-bye for good.

Though it was barely snowing outside, the slate path leading from the house to the driveway was slippery. Val secured the top button of her shearling coat, and clutched a brown cashmere scarf tightly around her neck. It occurred to her that the chill she felt was as much about Isaac as it was about the weather.

She figured the half-hour drive to work would calm her down. No music, no news, just the sense of moving forward. Instead, her anxiety increased along with the speedometer.

By 80 miles per hour, long-buried feelings began to surface.

Isaac, she thought, *now what? We'll never have a chance to get things right, to fix what went wrong.*

The heat in the car was blasting, so Val was surprised when she unexpectedly shivered. She had the eerie sensation she was no longer alone. She checked to be sure the doors were locked. She glanced at the empty passenger seat, and nervously eyed the back of the car through the rearview mirror. She couldn't shake the feeling Isaac was right there with her.

Superstitious me.

But rational thinking didn't help. Val needed to speak to Isaac—and she knew, against reason, he needed to hear from her.

Oh, Isaac, no more anger. We had enough of that.

She paused, biting her lower lip, only to remember how Isaac would always tell her to stop. "It's unbecoming," he would say, reproachful words softened by an affectionate tone.

You see? Every little thing reminds me of you. You're part of me, whether I like it or not.

In frustration, Val smacked her fist against the steering wheel. The horn hit a strident note, but Val didn't notice.

You died thinking I hate you! But it's so much more complicated than that. I love you. Despite your faults, despite the many ways you are . . . were . . . so imperfectly human.

Fat, wet snowflakes melted against the windshield of Val's car. The repetitive rhythm of the wipers was soothing. She slowed down and tried to focus on her driving. It was dangerous out there.

Be here, be now, she told herself. *Breathe.*

But nothing could stop the flurry of memories and emotions. In her mind she was no longer behind the wheel, but once again sitting beside her father in the front row of the funeral parlor, staring at her mother's simple pine casket. Beside them was Isaac, old and frail, his familiar hands—fingers still long and strangely youthful—gripping the carved handle of his cane. She felt his eyes on her, but she could barely look at him. Forget making amends. She'd had no sympathy, just a bottomless well of anger. It didn't sink in that time was slipping away.

I guess I never really believed you would die.

Death was a sad but inevitable part of Val's professional landscape; as a doctor she had learned to cope. But in her private life all bets were off. Even now, several years after her mother's death, Val still expected to hear Kitty's concerned voice on the phone every Sunday night. When Val visited her father's house, she still looked for her mother at the kitchen table.

And then there was Lilly. Lilly. Always Lilly in the shadows of Val's unspoken thoughts and dreams. As if Lilly, too, were a ghost.

I should call her.

The thought of contacting Lilly made Val's heart race. She pressed harder on the gas pedal. Eighty-five miles an hour and counting. The snowy fields became a blur.

More than anything Val wanted to break through her self-imposed wall of silence . . . more than anything she feared doing just that. She began composing a letter to Lilly in her mind. She wanted to say something kind and generous. And real.

Lilly, I'm so sad for you. But I know even in your grief you must see the gift you and Isaac ultimately gave each other: you allowed your love to bring you together, rather than letting your anger keep you apart. At the end, your father knew he had a caring, loyal, beautiful daughter. He knew you loved him.

That felt right. At least so far. But Valerie worried about what to say next. How to reach out and keep her distance at the same time.

I hope these thoughts bring you peace.

Lilly, I also hope you'll receive this in the manner in which it is intended: not as an overture to renew our friendship, but simply to say how truly sorry I am for your loss.

Deep in her reverie, Val didn't hear the siren or see the flashing lights. It wasn't until the trooper had pulled up beside her car that she realized he was signaling for her to stop. As she slowed, her car skidded onto the icy shoulder.

The trooper stood beside her door, motioning for her to roll down the window. It took Val a moment to shake off the fog. To realize he was asking for her license and registration.

"What's your hurry, ma'am? There's black ice on the road. Do you realize you were going almost 90 miles an hour?" He stared coolly into her eyes.

"I'm sorry . . . really, so sorry. . . ." Valerie looked down, surprised to see herself clutching the steering wheel so hard her hands were shaking. "I just. . . ."

There were no more words. No explanations. Nothing to hold back the torrent of uncontrollable tears.

The wind was whipping snow into the car. But the trooper wasn't done with his scolding.

"Sorry doesn't cut it, ma'am," he said sternly, handing her a ticket. "You could have killed someone. Then what good would sorry do you?"

Arthur hung up the phone on the wall next to his workbench. Though he was grateful Valerie had called with the news, it worried him that she sounded so disturbed. He had tried to be stoic for his daughter, but in truth he, too, needed some solace. Good-byes of every kind were always hard for him. Each ordinary farewell was an uncomfortable reminder of friends and family who were gone for good. Now, sadly, he could add Isaac to that list.

Reaching across the circuit board he'd been working on, Arthur flicked off the power. There was a small pop. "Oh, not again," he sighed. "Damn wires." He would fix it later—not a bad thing to have an afternoon project. Especially these days. He closed the door of Val's former bedroom—now his laboratory and refuge—and walked the length of his apartment toward the newspaper he knew would be waiting for him at the front door.

In the foyer a tarnished oval mirror grabbed his attention. An old face with two days' worth of gray stubble gazed back at him. But the eyes were still blue, bright, clear, and curious. In a single glance he could see who he once was, who he had become, and who he would soon be. "Time to shave, pal," he told his reflection.

The newspaper was on the doormat, wrapped in blue plastic, as usual. He took it inside, locking the door behind him. Arthur spread the paper open on the dining room table. He knew exactly where to look, of course; at his age, one did.

The obituary's handful of paragraphs neatly—and imperfectly—summed up the life of a man. A man, Arthur noted, who spent as much time at this table as anybody. Who made everybody's lives simultaneously easier and more complicated. Who drove people to their best and their worst—and who, ultimately, drove people away.

"Guess I'm the last man standing," he mumbled. It was more of an observation than a complaint.

———•———

"Yoo-hoo! Honey, I'm home!"

Lilly rolled her eyes and laughed out loud. Her mother obviously had never bothered relinquishing the keys to Isaac's apartment after she'd pulled her great disappearing act.

"I'm in the kitchen," Lilly shouted. "Come on in."

Katherine swooped into the room as if she were coming back on stage for her third encore. Draped in fur—a silver fox coat with matching hat and muff—she looked to Lilly like a delusional escapee from Czarist Russia as she leaned against the doorframe, deliberately striking a femme fatale pose. Her mouth was pouty, perfectly lined, and neatly stained a pomegranate red. Her eyes, dramatically circled with black kohl, sparkled with the joy of having a receptive audience.

It was all an obvious attempt to keep Lilly smiling, and it worked.

Katherine appraised the scene before her. Lilly was in sweatpants, T-shirt, and a soiled apron, her long auburn hair a messy tangle of waves. A pyramid of finely chopped onions was piled on a blue plastic cutting board, waiting to be sautéed; pots of water filled with lasagna noodles were boiling furiously; empty cans of tomatoes had left messy rings on the worn butcher-block counter.

"What . . . a . . . dump!" Katherine did her best Bette Davis imitation. It was one of her favorite lines and always got the laugh.

"Hi to you, too," Lilly said, returning her mother's air kiss as Katherine threw her coat and accessories on a kitchen chair and breezed past. She made a beeline to the dining room bar cabinet. Lilly coughed, a little overwhelmed by the strong smell of her mother's gardenia perfume.

"What's for dinner?" Katherine called out. "Should I open red or white? Or bubbly?"

"Ummm . . . I think, given the circumstances, Champagne doesn't exactly strike the right tone . . ." Lilly said, hard-pressed to disguise her impatience.

"Oh, right. Your father's dead," Katherine mused, contemplating the selection of Italian wines Isaac had carefully arranged by age and region. It took just a moment for her to pluck an expensive Barolo from the rack. "Okay, then, better red than dead."

She carried the wine bottle like a trophy into the kitchen. "Isaac's favorite!" she announced triumphantly. "He would die all over again if he knew I were here opening this up."

Katherine reached into the drawer beneath the counter and fished around. "What a pack rat your father was," she said, holding up a rusted tea infuser. "Where's the damn corkscrew? And why can't Isaac ever put anything back where it goes?"

"The tea thing is mine," Lilly answered softly. "I've been living here for two years. Remember?"

With a wave of her hand, Katherine dismissed her daughter's assertion of belonging, her reminder that she, too, had a claim to this space.

"Dad's corkscrew is on the table by the wine rack," Lilly continued, her irritation increasing. "It's exactly where it should be."

"*Someone's* in a bad mood. Someone should lighten up. Would someone like a glass of wine?" Katherine reached out to tuck a strand of Lilly's hair behind her ear. An old gesture of apology.

Lilly smiled, "Someone would. Thanks."

Katherine retrieved the elegant silver corkscrew. She admired its delicately rendered handle. A nearly imperceptible nostalgia shadowed her face, but just for an instant. "The Cecils gave this to us as a wedding gift. It must be a million years old."

"Careful, you're dating yourself," Lilly teased. Of course, in Lilly's mind, her mother would always be young, beautiful, and alluring—even with the deep lines that ringed her neck and the age spots on her hands that could no longer be passed off as freckles. Plastic surgery could only do so much.

Katherine didn't respond. Instead, she overfilled two glasses and handed one to her daughter.

"Let's toast," Katherine said, raising her glass toward the ceiling. "I'll start." She closed her eyes, as if thinking long and hard about how to honor the memory of Isaac, how to sum up all their years of war and peace. Lilly waited expectantly, wondering what her mother would say.

At last Katherine opened her eyes. Her face was somber, her gaze reflective.

"Okay, I've got it," she said. "'I'd rather have a bottle in front of me than a frontal lobotomy.'"

Lilly cracked up, despite herself. "Come on . . . I thought you meant, let's toast Dad. Let's talk about the things we loved about him. Or the things he loved."

"Okay. Let me think . . . well, what did he love beyond the sound of his own long-winded monologues?"

"Katherine, be serious," Lilly said. She needed to eulogize her father properly and she wanted her mother to join her in the effort. "He loved a lot of things, and passionately. You know that. His orchids, for instance . . . "

"Brilliant! Let's toast Isaac's precious orchids. How about this one—it's a classic: 'You can lead a horticulture, but you can't make her think.'"

This time Lilly laughed so hard wine sprayed from her mouth. "Thanks a lot, Mom."

Katherine was on a roll. She tossed back the last of her drink and poured herself another one. "All right, you'll appreciate this. It pays tribute to your father's favorite obsession: psychoanalysis. Ready? 'Anyone who sees a psychiatrist . . . ought to have his head examined.'"

"And anyone who marries one ought to . . . ?" Lilly's sardonic voice trailed off.

"Anyone who marries one ought to . . . *leave*." Katherine set down her glass defiantly. "Which I did. Magnificently, I might add."

"Here we go," Lilly sighed, girding herself for yet another evening of ego-to-ego, no-punches-pulled combat. If things continued this way, she knew she was facing a long night of sparring against the ropes.

As if on cue, the kitchen timer's shrill bell signaled the end of the round. The players returned to their corners. Lilly went back to the stove, where she unceremoniously dumped the cooked lasagna noodles into a colander, relieved to be engulfed in a warm cloud of steam. Katherine took a seat on a counter stool, busying herself with a stained recipe card she found leaning against a bottle of olive oil.

"Lovelorn Lasagna? What's that? If I eat it will I get heartbreak—or heartburn?"

"Very funny." Lilly scowled. Although she knew her mother was joking, she still felt insulted.

"Oh, honey, lighten up. I'm sure it will be delicious. In any case, it's a charming name."

"Dad gets the credit for that." Lilly smiled.

"Oh, I get it now . . . Lovelorn Lasagna . . . it's about me!" She was obviously flattered. "He was always pining for me—even when I was only in the next room."

"It had nothing to do with you!" Lilly snapped, irritated. "It was about me. He named it for me."

"Why you?" Katherine was mildly petulant. She put the recipe card down, but couldn't let it go. Lilly saw her mother was torn between disappointment and curiosity. Curiosity won out. "So give me the dirt. Who broke your heart?"

"Just some guy."

Lilly thought back to an afternoon, decades ago, when she and her father were standing in this exact spot. Until now, her memory had always been about her adolescent longing for Luke and the painful humiliation she'd felt after he'd rejected her. But all these years later—and now that Isaac was gone—she could only recall the feeling of closeness she and her father shared that day. It was one of the few times both of them had let down their guard. One of the few times Isaac had behaved like the father she'd always wished for.

"So . . . boy trouble, was it? You certainly were a tempestuous little thing," Katherine said admiringly. "In love with love. Just like me."

"Am I just like you?"

"Why . . . is that so horrible?"

"No! That's not what I meant. . . ." It took Lilly a moment to try to figure out what she did mean. "Katherine," she stammered, "do you know . . . do you believe . . . I love you?"

"What kind of absurd question is that? Of course you love me, darling. Everybody loves me!"

"I'm serious."

"Oh dear, you're getting sentimental. Maudlin. Is it the wine?"

Lilly shot her mother a dark look.

"Okay, I see the writing on the wall. What we need here is a real Mother-Daughter-Moment. Fine. We can do that." Katherine poured the remains of the wine into her empty glass and took a big gulp. "Here's the thing. Death upsets people. I understand. Believe it or not, I'm upset, too. I'm actually quite sorry we lost Isaac." Katherine's voice thickened. "Who else will I argue with?"

She took a moment to compose herself. "Apparently you'd like me to put your mind at rest, in case I drop dead on the way home tonight. So yes, my darling daughter, I know you love me. I also know at times you hate me. And both of those things are okay with me."

Lilly choked back the need to cry. "And what about Dad? Did he know I loved him?"

"Oh, Lilly, have I taught you nothing? Don't you realize postmortem recriminations never do anyone any good?"

"Can't you just answer the question? Please? I really need to know."

Katherine paused as if she were trying to figure out how to phrase her answer. "Your father was a complicated man. Love wasn't what made him tick. He craved devotion. Canine fidelity. Utter and total dependence. I couldn't give any of that to him. And frankly, neither could you."

None of this was news to Lilly. And yet hearing these harsh words in this apartment—where her father's very absence made him all the more present—felt somehow hurtful and confusing.

But Katherine refused to notice her daughter's distress. "Unfortunately, you seem to suffer from the stupidity of your generation. You all want 'closure.' Take my word for it, the only closure is that your father is dead. So what was the question, my darling? Can I confirm that your father knew you loved him? Yes, Lilly, I believe he did. In fact, I'm sure he did. Why else would he have allowed you to redeem yourself by playing his nursemaid these past few years?"

The impatient tapping of Katherine's manicured fingernails on the countertop signaled she was just about done. "At this point, my lovelorn lamb, the only question you should really be asking yourself is this: was getting him to love you worth it?"

Lilly reached into her apron pocket and wrapped her fingers

around the letter she'd just received that morning. A letter that had simultaneously lifted her heart, comforted her . . . and opened an old wound. It was from Val. Just a few sentences filled with kindness, wisdom—and unbridgeable distance. In her mind she could hear Val's voice: *"At the end, your father knew he had a caring, loyal, beautiful daughter. He knew you loved him."*

"Yes," Lilly said to her mother. "It was worth it."

———————

"No," Jeff cried, putting his head under the pillow. "Why did you set the alarm? It's Saturday."

Val rolled over and pulled him closer. "I didn't hear anything. Go back to sleep."

But the insistent ringing was not the clock. It was the doorbell.

"Who could it be at this hour?" Val complained.

"Go find out."

"No, you get it. Be my knight in shining pajamas."

"You get it. Be my mother."

"You get it. I need my beauty rest."

"You get it. I'm older and more tired. And once you're down there, could you make the coffee?"

Before Val could think of a witty comeback the doorbell rang again . . . and again.

This time, whoever was ringing meant business.

"Okay, you win. Go back to sleep." Jeff threw his feet over the side of the bed. The old pine floor planks groaned. Lulu, the black and white cat, appeared out of nowhere. Meowing loudly, she demanded her morning meal.

"Don't forget to feed her," Val murmured as Jeff headed downstairs. "And then feed me."

The doorbell rang again.

"I'll wake you up when breakfast is ready."

Grateful for another half-hour of rest, Val pulled the covers around herself tightly, and tried to find her way back to the odd dream she'd been having. All she could remember was the image of a woman weaving purposefully through a crowd on a busy city street, and the feeling that this stranger was leading her to someplace important.

But it was impossible to return to the dream; the spell had been broken. *All smoke and mirrors*, Val thought.

A fragment of some poetry memorized decades ago came back to her, as it often did at unexpected moments. *Our joys as winged dreams do fly/Why then should sorrow last?* She could never remember the third line, or even who wrote it. But she knew the ending: *Grieve not for what is past.*

Now fully awake, Val stretched with a noisy sigh. She was hungry. If she got out of bed she could make French toast instead of settling for Jeff's burned toast.

"Hey," she called down to Jeff. "I'm up."

"Don't shout, I'm right here," Jeff said, coming back into the bedroom, an official-looking package in his hands. "This is for you. I had to sign for it. Who's Harry Julian?"

"Harry Who-lian? I don't know who you're talking about. Gimme."

Valerie took in the "Esquire" attached to Harry Julian's name and the fancy Madison Avenue address. She opened the package carefully, pulling out two separate documents: one a single sheet of expensive embossed stationery; the other an envelope secured by a heavy, old-fashioned wax seal. Embedded in the red wax were the initials "I.S.," intertwined in a familiar grapevine-pattern embrace.

"I'd know that anywhere," she whispered.

Valerie read the unsealed letter first. Her eyes got big. "Here," she said, handing it to Jeff. "You're never going to believe this."

HARRY JULIAN, ESQ.

ESTATE LAW

598 MADISON AVENUE, NEW YORK, NY 10022

February 20, 2002

Dr. Valerie Rudman
23 Sutter Street
Boston, MA 02110

Dear Dr. Rudman,

I am an attorney for the estate of Dr. Isaac Stone.

Dr. Stone asked me to provide you with the enclosed letter upon his death.

I am sending this to you via a private courier service to ensure safe delivery. Please be assured the document given to me by my client has remained in my possession in its original, sealed condition; further, it has remained sealed since the time of Dr. Stone's death.

If I may be of additional assistance to you in this or any other matter, please do not hesitate to contact me.

My condolences for your loss.

Sincerely,

Harry Julian

Harry Julian

"Whoa, voices from the Other Side," Jeff said, reading the letter. "I thought stuff like this only happened in B movies."

As soon as he saw Valerie's face he realized she was not amused. Jeff sat down next to her on the edge of the bed and put a reassuring arm around her shoulder. Together they pondered the mysterious, still-unopened missive resting in her lap. It was clear Val was afraid to touch it. But over and over she read the handwritten words on the face of the envelope:

In the event of my death, deliver this, sealed, to Miss Valerie Rudman.

It was a familiar scrawl. One that used to put the fear of God into Val when Isaac wrote letters of rebuke, one that she treasured when he commended her on something she'd done well. Her shelves were heavy with books inscribed with this very script.

"Go on, open it," Jeff said. "You can handle whatever he had to say."

"Isn't this silly . . . I'm scared."

"Do you want me to read it to you?"

"No. I just need some time alone." Val touched Jeff's arm. "Is that okay?"

He grazed her lips with a kiss. "I'll go make that coffee. Come down when you're ready."

The curtains were still drawn in the bedroom, but as the winter sun peeked in and out from behind a cloud, the room darkened or brightened in a random way, dappling the walls with patches of shadow. Val leaned back against the pillows, did some of the deep breathing she'd learned could quiet her anxiety, and centered herself.

Okay, Isaac, I'm ready.

She picked up the envelope and turned it over, running her fingers across the letters of the seal. As it broke, tiny pieces of wax splintered, landing on the bright white sheets. They looked to her like droplets of blood.

It took just a minute to read the letter, handwritten in the same black ink Isaac had used on the front of the envelope.

Isaac Stone, M.D., Ph.D.

145 RIVERSIDE DRIVE, NEW YORK, NY 10024

My Dearest Valerie,

The very fact that you are reading this means I have crossed the great divide. Perhaps now I am learning firsthand whether or not the remark you used to make, as a precocious but awkward child, holds up to scientific scrutiny: "The only good thing about being dead is no school dances."

But humor aside, let me get straight to the point of the matter—a point you may well feel I should have gotten to by now. Valerie, despite what you may have come to believe, I am a man who has lived a life very full of feeling. I have known great passion. I have also known the pain of loss. But these two emotions reached their apex—colliding with devastating impact—when your mother and I fell in love.

While the realities of life and family obligations kept Kitty and me from living fully together, what we always shared entirely was an infinite love for you. You see, what I am in essence saying is this:

Valerie, I am your father.

Your mother and I promised each other that only upon our deaths would I reveal this to you. Now that you know the truth, you will understand why you have been so important to me. And why I've always hovered around you like a guardian angel. As the esteemed Dr. Freud said, "I cannot think of any need in childhood as strong as the need for a father's protection."

I've kept this secret forever with immeasurable difficulty, as did your mother. Now, the burden of it is yours and yours alone. I have not told another living soul. Do with it what you wish. Apart from the gifts I've left you in my will, my greatest legacy to you is this truth.

I hope you will find it in your heart to understand why we kept silent on this matter and to remember me as the man who loved you and who gave you life.

Valerie felt incapable of moving. She lay propped up on her pillows for what seemed like an eternity.

When the bedroom door creaked open it was followed by a sudden cold draft. The room slowly came back into focus: the pale white walls, the wooden blanket chest at the foot of the bed, the mantle covered with half-burned candles.

Val had the sensation something or someone was there on the bed with her. Touching her. Talking to her. It was only Lulu the cat, who had jumped up for her morning nap. The cat mewed softly.

"Lulu's a good girl," Val murmured in a whisper, her usual love song to her sweet kitty. Val peered into Lulu's green, blinking eyes. Touching her cat suffused Val with sudden warmth; it was like standing in sunlight after a long convalescence.

I need to tell Lilly.

She untangled the sheets and stood up abruptly. Isaac's letter fluttered from her lap to the floor. As she reached down to pick it up, the sheet of paper hitched itself to another sudden breeze and flew under the bed, as if acting out a willfully perverse disinclination to be retrieved. Val's mouth tightened at the corners. She was inclined to let the letter stay there forever, to pretend it never existed.

But her rational mind took the lead. Lifting the neatly pleated taupe linen bedskirt, Val could see the letter, a patch of pure white light in the dark underbelly of the box spring. She reached way under the bed and managed to retrieve it.

Lulu, watching Val on the floor and thinking a game was in progress, jumped down to join her. She butted her head on Valerie's thigh, purred loudly, and yawned with languid, feline ostentation. When she meowed again it was with the reproachful air of an underfed child.

TO: **LSTONE**@dotnet.com
FROM: **VRUDMAN**@webworld.com
DATE: **FEBRUARY 25, 2002**
SUBJECT: **URGENT—PLEASE READ AT ONCE!**

Lilly,

I understand how strange and difficult it must be to hear from me again, especially in your time of grief. I hope you know I wouldn't be contacting you unless it were essential.

It's so hard to write this . . . I'm shaking.

Something unbelievable just happened: your father's estate lawyer sent me a letter written by Isaac.

I'm overnighting a copy to you. Find someplace private to read it. And as you do, please keep in mind: *this is not my fault.*

I desperately wish I hadn't been forced into the role of unwelcome messenger. But Lilly, the letter explains everything.

And Lilly, I'm begging you to keep this between us. So many people would be devastated if they knew—especially my father and your mother.

Val

....

———•———

This is nothing more than emotional terrorism, Lilly thought. She threw Isaac's letter across her desk and pushed her chair back roughly, as if distancing herself from what she had just read.

He wants the world to continue revolving around him even after he's dead. And what does she want? For me to hate him? For me to admit he loved her more? They can both go to hell.

Lilly walked over to the full-length mirror on the back of the closet door. What she saw was a good-looking woman who still had the ability to turn heads.

Except, that is, for the incipient white stripe in her otherwise perfect auburn hair. Except for the extra ten pounds that sat where she sat. Except for the half-circles that cupped her teasing brown eyes.

Well, it's a look, she thought wryly. *A look that's gotta go. Now.*

Lilly headed into the bathroom attached to Isaac's bedroom. She rummaged around beneath the sink, knowing from previous snooping expeditions exactly what was still under there: all the lotions, potions, and beauty creams that once had belonged to her mother. All the things Isaac had refused to throw away.

Pay dirt: an unopened box of hair dye. It was "Ruby Vixen," left over from what Katherine always called her Red Period.

That's the ticket!

Lilly ripped open the box and dared herself to continue. In less than an hour all traces of her gray hair—and her brown hair, for that matter—had vanished. She was transformed.

She looked approvingly at her image.

Ooh, sizzling, baby. If you're not Ruby Vixen, no one is.

But by the time Lilly finished cleaning up the dye-stained bathroom, her momentary elation had subsided. She inspected herself more closely under the bathroom's strong lights, and realized her forehead was dotted with crimson smudges.

Damn, now what? I look like a leper.

But it was more than the botched hair job that was disturbing her. It was having to face the one thing she'd been avoiding: her speech for Isaac's memorial service. Lilly returned to her desk. She called up the computer file "Dad's Eulogy," and read through the loving tribute she had written spontaneously on the night Isaac died. She lingered on the last paragraph:

It took me a long time to accept that I had to share my father with the world. But I came to realize he had a noble purpose.

Noble, my ass, Lilly muttered.

A higher calling. A gift for healing that meant he couldn't always be a father first.

Because he was too busy being a father to Val. And who knows who the hell else . . .

And for that I admire him more than I ever admired anyone. He willingly made sacrifices in order to fulfill his lifelong mission: helping others to heal.

And helping himself to anything that furthered his personal, selfish needs . . .

I loved my father. And I always will.

Lilly held down the Delete button on the keyboard. She watched with grim satisfaction as the words vanished into the ether.

<hr/>

TO: **LSTONE**@dotnet.com
FROM: **VRUDMAN**@webworld.com
DATE: **MARCH 1, 2002**
SUBJECT: **DID YOU GET WHAT I SENT?**

Lilly,

I can only imagine that your silence is an indication of how flabbergasted and upset you must be. I understand—I'm in the same state.

Or perhaps—and maybe more likely—you've been respecting the distance I asked for two years ago, after our last (failed) attempt to reconnect.

If this is the reason you haven't responded to me, I hope you'll understand I've changed my mind. Because the truth is, we need to talk. Isaac's letter doesn't just explain everything—it changes everything. It's given me such insight into the ways you and I have always related to each other . . . or failed to relate to each other.

We have so much to unravel.

I haven't called in case you're not ready to hear from me in person. But we do need to meet, hopefully face-to-face. And soon. My father and I are thinking of coming to Isaac's memorial service. It will be kind of scary . . . surreal . . .

strange (I'm not sure how to even characterize it) for you and me to be together again after all these decades. But I guess this is as good a time as any to break the ice.

Lilly, sorry to harp on this, but I must ask you again not to say anything about Isaac's letter in my father's presence. For all the obvious reasons.

Can you and I find some time either before or after the service to talk? Tell me what works for you.

Val

....

* * *

Why Lilly should choose to seek refuge in her father's greenhouse, the room he so often used as a retreat, was a question she would ask herself much later. For now she accepted it as a desperately needed sanctuary—a place where well-practiced routine could supplant runaway emotions.

She tossed Isaac's letter on the mosaic table beside the bag of wood chips. She breathed in deeply. The air smelled like a moist rain forest. An overhead fan quietly circulated a fresh breeze, cooling her flushed cheeks. Lilly scanned the more than 300 orchids that Isaac referred to as a hobby, though some would have called it an obsession. The plants were everywhere, their fragile, waxy blossoms a riot of color. The smaller orchids claimed every inch of window space. The larger specimens thrived under Isaac's complex network of balanced-spectrum lights—thousand-watt intensity.

That's the kind of light that could make a person confess to a crime, Lilly thought. *Not that it worked on you, Dad.*

She needed to keep busy and was glad for the familiar routine. First thing: prepare for tomorrow's morning sun. She reached for the cord of the venetian blinds. With each subtle twist of the slats she could hear her father's stern lecture: "Lillian, light is probably the single most crucial factor in determining whether or not your plant will bear blossoms. It's necessary for proper growth and nutrient storage. Too little light, it won't bloom. Too much light, it can get sunburned or scorched."

Lilly felt burned herself—scorched from the inside out. She railed silently against Isaac. *Why did you send that letter to her? Why didn't you tell me? All that ever matters to you is Val. She must have loved learning the truth. What were the words she used? "The letter explains everything." Well, I don't think so.*

A copper watering can was waiting for Lilly, heavy and overfilled. She picked it up roughly, ignoring the cool slosh on her bare feet, and began making her rounds. She trickled water on the dry black stones that filled the saucers of the pulsating red Pansy orchids, the delicate pale pink Slippers, the Golden Dancing Ladies.

In the short time since Isaac's death, Lilly had taken on his greenhouse as her filial responsibility. But even before he died, caring for the plants had become part of Lilly's daily life. Each evening her father would beckon her to the orchid room with an insistence she always thought far too dramatic. *They are waiting!* he would announce, demanding she drop whatever she was doing to join him. *You can't keep them waiting!*

In reality, it was her father who could never be kept waiting, growing ever more dependent on others for help, becoming ever more impatient. In part, Isaac needed Lilly by his side because his eyesight was failing; in part, he craved company. So nurturing the orchids, together, became a much-appreciated common ground. It satisfied both Isaac's need to be honored and Lilly's need to be recognized.

But in the light of Isaac's disclosure, it all just felt like another of his arrogant manipulations.

By the time Lilly reached her father's favorite orchid, Darwin's Star, she was seething. How many evenings had she watched him admiring the Star's ray of petals, its cometlike tail, its irresistible nocturnal fragrance?

"So elegant. So beautiful. So like her," she recalled Isaac whispering to himself, his fingers stroking the flower's petals. Lilly always had presumed he was referring to her mother.

But now she knew he had been longing for Kitty.

"This enchantress played a big role in Darwin's theory of natural selection," Lilly remembered Isaac saying as he worshipped the orchid night after night. "He proved that cross-pollination enabled the plant to survive."

And you should know all about cross-pollination, Dad.

A little humor felt good. Lilly could keep things under control that way. She could deal with this.

Everything was going to be okay.

She had a plan.

Analyze This

By LAURA OTTO

If you weren't there, you probably heard about it. The august New York Institute for Psychodynamic Interrelations experienced a kind of nervous breakdown yesterday, as three hundred mourners—family members, colleagues, admirers, and friends—gathered to honor the memory of the Institute's founding father, Dr. Isaac Stone.

GROUP THERAPY

There was standing room only as the international intelligentsia of the psychoanalytic community gathered to remember Dr. Stone. A psychiatrist, author, and one of the most highly paid speakers on the global lecture circuit, he was most celebrated for his groundbreaking book, The Fear Impulse.

The controversy surrounding Dr. Stone's book has been linked to his assertion that phobias, particularly agoraphobia, are fully curable through a method involving visualization and therapeutic compassion. In his book, he wrote about developing his treatment by working over a ten-year period with 53 agoraphobic men and women. He claimed to have cured each one.

Because of laws related to patient confidentiality, Dr. Stone had always refused to reveal any of his patients' identities, and none ever went public. As a result, professional rivals asserted that Dr. Stone's research was unscientific and without substantive proof, and that his claims of success were largely fabricated.

But supporters—among them other therapists as well as thousands of patients worldwide—were adamant that Dr. Stone provided an invaluable breakthrough in treatment. Many of these same supporters waited on line for hours in the chilly rain and wind to get a seat at yesterday's memorial service.

The mood was somber and reverential. That is, until a very personal and dangerous family secret was exposed by Dr. Stone's daughter, Ms. Lillian Stone.

I'M AFRAID YOUR TIME IS UP

Everyone expected a long afternoon. Listed in the program were ten speakers—a mix of family members and highly esteemed psychiatrists, psychologists, and therapists. But just as the first tribute was about to be given by the head of the New York Institute for Psychodynamic Interrelations, Ms. Stone rushed to the podium. Although she was scheduled to give the closing remarks, she clearly had other plans.

Ms. Stone grabbed hold of the microphone, flashed a toothy smile, and tossed back a long mane of wavy red hair. She dropped to the ground an ankle-length brocade cape, revealing a low-cut, black sequined halter top and tight velvet skirt with a slit that ran the length of her thigh. Fishnet stockings and mile-high slingbacks completed the picture.

In sultry tones, Ms. Stone introduced herself as a cabaret singer, rather than as Dr. Stone's daughter. Onlookers bristled with confused and disapproving whispers, which Ms. Stone brazenly ignored. She began singing a tender and wrenching rendition of "Amazing Grace." Despite the crowd's initial irritation with Ms. Stone, everyone was soon enraptured; there was not a dry eye in the house.

But things quickly devolved. Ms. Stone made it clear that she had no intention of ceding the microphone to the next scheduled speaker. Sitting on the edge of the stage—like the legendary Judy Garland at Carnegie Hall—Ms. Stone ("Call me Lilly") began a meandering, intimate, and self-aggrandizing reminiscence of her life as Dr. Stone's only child. Her memories were punctuated by songs, each increasingly inappropriate to the occasion: "My Heart Belongs to Daddy" and "Can't Help Lovin' Dat Man" were delivered with eye-rolling sarcasm. "Fame (I Want to Live Forever)" and "Everything's Coming Up Roses" were sung with unrestrained glee.

Throughout her performance, Ms. Stone became ever more giddy and flirtatious, even exhorting the confused audience to clap and sing along with a spirited rendition of "Oh, Happy Days." For her grand finale, she performed Gershwin's "Things Are Looking Up" with sly and wicked intent: "Bitter was my cup/ But no more will I be the mourner/For I've certainly turned the corner/ Oh things are looking up."

She was finally coaxed off the stage by her mother, Ms. Katherine Stone, the estranged widow of Dr. Stone and a prominent figure in the Broadway theater community. The elder Ms. Stone, well known for her own flamboyance, seemed oddly pleased by her daughter's errant behavior.

After a few minutes of offstage whispering, Katherine Stone returned alone to take control of the situation. Under the evident weight of her peacock-hued turban, flowing white robe, and heavily bejeweled fingers, she proceeded to act as the event's master of ceremonies. A more appropriate mood ensued.

Various friends and colleagues shared their personal stories of Dr. Stone, portraying him as a "strong force of nature," a "brilliant mind," and an "honest, compassionate, and generous" man. The audience was hushed and reverential. Once again it seemed all was going as planned, until. . . .

RECOVERED MEMORIES

Lillian Stone returned to give her scheduled closing remarks. This time she was fully covered by her dark cape. Her demeanor had changed. No more the seductive entertainer, she appeared to be appropriately serious and reflective. And much to the relief of all present, Ms. Stone refrained from singing. But within minutes, she stunned the mourners once more—this time with shocking allegations.

Abruptly departing from prepared remarks she had begun to read—the usual paean to a deceased parent—Ms. Stone announced she had news to share that would "shake the psychoanalytic community to its gullible, pretentious, stupid, useless, insincere, narcissistic core." She explained that despite her father's assertion that *The Fear Impulse* was based upon numerous patients, in truth it was entirely predicated on the life of just one patient, a Ms. Kitty Rudman.

The audience gasped audibly. But the trouble had just begun. Ms. Stone waited until everyone was quiet again before she spoke. With a challenging stare directed at the sea of faces before her, she announced that the aforementioned Ms. Rudman, now deceased, was also her father's longtime lover and mother of his secret love-child.

Ms. Stone went on to publicly condemn her father for his breach of professional ethics, and then astonished the audience with yet another accusation: "What my father called 'the greatest success of his career and the greatest breakthrough in the treatment of phobias,'" she said, "was in truth his greatest failure. Kitty Rudman was never cured. Never. She died a pathetic shut-in in her home in the Bronx, which she had not left for decades. My father lied," she continued, "not only to my family, but to the entire mental-health community. He lied to you. He was a traitor."

A single voice broke through the disconcerted silence. It came from a tall woman, pale and visibly shaking. Standing up from her seat in the back row, she bellowed, "You're the traitor, Lilly!" With that, she took the arm of an elderly man at her side and together they left the room.

It was then, and only then, that Lillian Stone seemed to be truly grieving.

PROZAC, ANYONE?

Following the ceremony, Lillian and Katherine Stone refused to comment on the identity of the angry woman who left the service so abruptly. More than a dozen of Dr. Stone's colleagues were interviewed, but all attempts to determine the woman's name proved fruitless.

There was widespread conjecture that the mystery woman may have been one of Dr. Stone's patients. Several psychiatrists, all of whom wished to remain anonymous, agreed that she showed the classic symptoms of frequently recurring absentia neurosis, which commonly occurs when a patient fails to cope with the loss of a therapist. Other mourners speculated that she was the "love child" referenced by Ms. Stone. To date, the question of the woman's identity remains unanswered.

What is clear is that the New York Institute for Psychodynamic Interrelations will have to do some serious damage control to recover from this day of accusations, gossip, and macabre entertainment. Face it: the fact that the reputation of its founding father was tarnished by his own daughter is enough to give anybody a daddy complex.

On the hour-long subway ride back from the memorial, neither Val nor her father spoke a word. Valerie sat stiffly, hands folded in her lap. She kept her eyes fixed on the subway ads as though she were deciphering deep, hidden significance in the shallow come-ons of laser-wielding doctors and shady bankruptcy lawyers. Arthur, following her cues to keep silent, quietly finished his newspaper crossword puzzle.

Only after the front door of Arthur's apartment was locked behind them did Valerie combust.

"Damn it all to hell, I hate her!"

Arthur didn't respond. He shrugged off his coat and disappeared into the kitchen. Valerie continued to rant as she slumped down on the same blue couch where her mother used to languish.

"How could Lilly have done this to me? To us?" Val shouted.

Her father didn't answer. But as if echoing her feelings, the teakettle let out a shrill scream.

At last Arthur returned to the living room holding a tray weighed down with steaming mugs and a plate of cookies. He placed it on the coffee table and took a seat on the upholstered club chair across from Val. "Graham crackers with jelly," he offered, as if this were the solution to everything.

His implacable demeanor just about did Val in.

"You don't get it, do you?" Val lashed out. She grabbed Isaac's letter from her purse and pushed it into her father's hands. "I didn't want to do this to you, Daddy, but I have no choice now. And you can blame Lilly for that."

Val held her breath as Arthur scanned the letter impassively. She anxiously watched his eyes for signs of emotion—or confirmation.

Instead, he returned it with a dismissive shrug. "Ludicrous!" he exclaimed, handing it back to her.

"I don't think so," Val responded, folding the letter neatly and putting it on the table between them. "I believe everything he says."

Arthur winced. "Valerie, you are my child. No matter what Isaac wrote, you are and always will be my baby girl."

On any other occasion, Arthur's sentimental words would have filled Valerie's eyes with tears. But today, she was blinded with frustration and fury. A lifetime of repressed anger bubbled to the surface.

What Val did next would later engulf her with shame. Waving

the letter in her father's face, she shouted, "You've spent your whole life putting your head in the sand, looking the other way while your wife loved another man in your own house! While you raised another man's child! How could you delude yourself? And how can you continue to turn away from the truth? What's wrong with you?"

Her aggression surprised both of them. She had never spoken to her father like that.

But before she could apologize, Arthur replied defiantly.

"What I'm about to tell you is none of your business," he stated with firm parental authority. "None. But Isaac's fabrications leave me no choice. For your information, I never put my 'head in the sand,' Valerie. Your mother told me everything there was to know, from the beginning. And in turn, I'm telling you only because you need to understand *my* truth, not Isaac's."

He took a deep breath.

"Well before you were born, Kitty and Isaac had a brief affair. It was spontaneous and short-lived. Your mother was remorseful, and confessed it to me immediately. She realized she'd made a terrible mistake. I forgave her. She swore it would never happen again. And as far as I'm concerned, it didn't."

Val was speechless. She wanted so badly to believe her father—but couldn't.

"Valerie," he said, recognizing her skeptical look, "you know your mother never lied."

"She didn't have to," Val exploded, "You're lying to *yourself*!"

Arthur furiously slapped his hand on the coffee table. Hot tea splashed onto the cookies. Val had never seen her father so enraged.

"This letter is not evidence—it's nonsense!" he cried out. "Isaac was possessive. Temperamental. An arrogant fool! He should have taken his romantic ramblings to the grave."

The more volatile her father became the more Val withdrew. She felt herself grow distant and clinical. "Well," she said in a clipped voice, "it doesn't have to be a matter of conjecture. A single DNA test is all we need to know if I'm Isaac's daughter."

She meant this as a practical solution, but Arthur heard it as a cruel rejection. He left the room wordlessly. She heard him stride down the hallway, closing the door of his workshop behind him.

Val found herself alone in a room more cluttered with memories than she would have liked. Nothing had changed since her mother first decorated more than forty years ago: the heavy teal drapes, the credenza with the tarnished silver fruit bowl, the upright piano cluttered with countless framed photos. Her eyes were drawn instinctively to a picture that had always made her slightly uncomfortable, for no reason she could fathom . . . until now. It was a fading color shot of Valerie wedged on the living room couch between her mother and Isaac.

She couldn't remember much about why or when the picture was taken, although Val could see she looked to be about 14 years old and was proudly holding a report card. Her mother and Isaac were smiling at her with obvious pleasure.

Val studied the photo, searching each face for signs that these three people shared something fundamental and profound. She'd always been told she looked just like her mother, although Val was significantly taller and thinner. Still, they both had the same fine, straight hair, the same pale complexion. And what of Isaac? Val compared her own long, narrow face to his. Both had arching eyebrows. Aquiline noses. Generous lips. Never before had she noticed the resemblance. On a primitive level she felt relieved to see Isaac's eyes were brown, while hers were blue like Arthur's—though as a geneticist she knew that meant nothing.

If I were a stranger looking at this photo, Val wondered, *would I assume this girl was that man's daughter?*

Valerie was unsure of the answer—but just acknowledging the similarities between herself and Isaac felt like a certain betrayal of her father. And that seemed sad beyond measure.

Who took this picture? Was it Dad? She wished she could remember. Val sighed audibly. *Of course it was . . . he was always the invisible man. But did he choose that role? Or did he just give in . . . and give up?*

Valerie returned the photo to its place, setting it down precisely on the outline it had left on top of the dusty piano. Suddenly depleted, she threw herself on the couch, wrapped herself in a mohair blanket, and tried to nap. But she couldn't. Her mind kept replaying the awful things she'd said to her father, the hurtful way she'd spoken to him. Val struggled to understand what had brought them to emotional blows. Theirs wasn't an ordinary fight—it was a fight with truth itself, which Arthur was fending off with whatever strength he could still muster.

Why did he do it? Valerie wondered, pondering Arthur's choice to live his whole life turning the other cheek, turning a blind eye, turning himself inside out to keep everyone else happy. *And why wouldn't he believe Isaac?*

It dawned on her, at that moment, that her father had made peace with himself. There was nothing to be gained by forcing him to look unflinchingly at the past. Instead, it was clear what she needed to do: protect him. Preserve his dignity by leaving his fantasies intact.

He has the right to remember his life however it suits him, she thought.

Exhausted, Val drifted into a deep slumber. Daylight was fading when she felt her father's hand on her shoulder. "Dinner's ready, honey."

Arthur had set the dining room table with her mother's good china and silver—and laden it with unopened cartons of Chinese food. The contrast between the fine place settings and the takeout containers was a Rudman family tradition that always made Val smile.

They sat together companionably, eating, drinking, talking— upholding their tacit agreement not to mention Lilly, Isaac, or the letter. Instead, Arthur reminisced. "When I met your mother, one of our first dates was at a Chinese restaurant near the Grand Concourse. We had a wonderful time. . . ."

"And you knew that night she was the girl you wanted to marry," Val interrupted, laughing. The story was part of her childhood mythology.

Arthur's eyes welled with fond memory. "Yes, but I never told you this part: when it was time for dessert, the waiter brought over some lychee nuts and fortune cookies. To our surprise, when we opened them, both our cookies were empty! I felt terrible. I was about to call over the waiter, but Kitty stopped me with a kiss. She said, 'Artie, you're all the good fortune I'll ever need.'"

Arthur reached for his daughter's hand across the table. "Sweetheart, nobody can ever understand another person's marriage. And nobody has the right to sit in judgment."

Val looked down at her father's hands cupping her own, and felt overcome with tenderness. She knew these were the hands that had held her in infancy, steadied her in childhood . . . and opened, exactly when she needed them to, to let her fly freely into a life of her own making, the life she now lived.

"Thank you, Daddy," she whispered.

———•———

The doorbell chimed, but nobody answered.

It was hard to know who was in a deeper slumber: Jeff's breath was slow and rhythmic, Val's eyelids twitched in a flurry of dreams. But sleeping late this Saturday morning wasn't in the cards. By the second ring, Valerie stirred.

"Oh, please, go away," Val moaned sleepily.

"Answer it," Jeff said.

"Not a chance. You know what happened last time. . . ."

"Exactly." Jeff pulled the covers over his head and pretended to snore loudly.

The doorbell rang again.

Resigned, Val rolled out of bed and fought her way into the uncooperative sleeves of her plaid flannel robe. "If there's any justice, it'll be a letter from *your* dead father," she said.

"Hang on!" she shouted as she flew down the stairs, hoping her voice was loud enough to reach whoever was insistently ringing the bell. Her bare feet were cold, and she wished she'd taken the time to find her slippers.

The front door of their old farmhouse was stuck, as usual. "I'm here!" Val called out to the person on the other side as she tugged the knob with two hands. At last the stubborn door gave way. Val was rewarded with a blast of frigid air—and a cold shock of recognition.

It was Lilly.

Standing on the icy porch, she was bundled against the searing chill of the winter morning: a black quilted coat, its hood pulled up over her head, a red wool scarf shielding mouth and nose. All that Val could see of her face were the eyes—staring, intense, demanding. They were undeniably Lilly's.

For what seemed like forever, neither of them could move or say a word.

To Lilly, Val seemed more pale and delicate than ever before. Her sleep-tossed hair was knotted and rebellious. Her features, well-defined and symmetrical, had been made softer by time. Lilly was glad to see Val's expression still had the naïve quality of a trusting child. This suffused Lilly with unexpected, sentimental affection. But what was it that made her heart race? Was it the excitement of seeing her old friend, or the jittery anticipation of what they might say to each other? She wasn't sure.

The rush of adrenaline made her want to bolt, though she knew she hadn't driven 200 miles just to run away. No matter what, she was going to push past this barrage of uncomfortable feelings. She'd come here to take responsibility, not just for all she'd wrongly said, but for all she'd left unsaid.

"If it helps," Lilly blurted, "I hate myself more than you probably hate me."

As if suspended by the glacial air, Lilly's stark confession hung between them. In that instant Val realized how unbearably cold she'd become. How little sensation she had left in her bare feet.

How her teeth chattered. How painful it was to be standing in ten-degree weather wearing nothing more than pajamas and a robe.

Silently motioning Lilly to come inside, Val shut the door behind them. They stood awkwardly in the entry, closer than either one intended, unsure of what to say or do next. Lilly pushed off her hood and unwound the red scarf to reveal trembling lips. The vulnerable, expectant look on her face broke through all of Val's defenses.

"I don't hate you," Val said calmly, realizing the truth of her words only as she spoke them. "I pity you."

Lilly blanched. "Don't bother," she replied. "I do enough of that for myself these days—I don't really need your help."

Suddenly self-conscious about how little she was wearing, Val tightened the belt of her robe. "Lilly, why are you here?" she asked guardedly, crossing her arms over her chest.

She took a seat on the bottom step of the hallway stairs, hugging her knees close to her body.

The question brought Lilly up short. It was so direct. So Val. Lilly fidgeted with the zipper on her jacket. Her answer should have come easily—it was all she had thought about on the four-hour drive from New York to Boston. But now, in the sober clarity of their encounter, everything she'd rehearsed seemed wrong. She looked around, as if to find the right words in the clean, wide floor planks, the carved banister railing, or the framed botanical prints adorning the white walls. She stalled for time by inspecting one of the pictures: a Darwin Star orchid. "How perfect that you should have this here. . . ." Her voice trailed off.

Observing her visitor from her stairway perch, Val sat quietly. She had no intention of easing Lilly's discomfort. She thought how typically audacious it was of Lilly to show up uninvited, how obnoxious of her to arrive unannounced . . . and yet, how brave she was to confront what she'd done.

Although she'd just seen Lilly two days earlier at Isaac's memorial, Val noticed that today she looked different. Her face seemed puffy, rounder. Maybe she was just tired. She certainly seemed subdued.

"I thought about calling," Lilly finally said. Her voice was uncharacteristically meek and deferential. "But that seemed cowardly. I had to *face* you, Val." She looked at Val beseechingly. "My father's letter undid me. Even dead, he still knows how to hurt me." Lilly paused and laughed bitterly. "God, I'm so enraged. The only way I knew how to let it out was to sing at the top of my lungs at his memorial. To let the world know exactly who Isaac Stone really was." Her voice grew stronger as her anger flared. "I needed to stomp on my father's grave. But I never meant to bury you and everyone else in the process."

"Well you damn well near did," Valerie sniped, determined to hold Lilly accountable.

Lilly wiped away the beads of sweat on her forehead as they began trickling down her cheek. She knew the heavy coat and woolen scarf were not the only things making her unbearably hot; it was the emotional energy required to stay in this conversation. She opened her coat, but only halfway, as if to signal she knew she hadn't been invited to stay.

Val didn't say another word. She waited for Lilly's next move.

Lilly took a deep breath and steadied herself. It was time for her to finish, time for her to leave. But she had to make one final offering. "I don't know if this will even matter to you, Val. But I'm sorry. I'm just really very sorry."

The apology was deeply sincere—different from all the gratuitous "I'm sorry"s Lilly had so breezily tossed off over the decades. It left Val stunned. She struggled to maintain a neutral demeanor, conscious of her own emotional transparency. She knew Lilly had always been a master at reading the many ways her face betrayed her: the rise of color that signaled humiliation, the deliberate squint that meant certain anger, the curled lip that conveyed disdain. And now the furrowed brow and downcast eyes that most certainly revealed hurt and confusion.

The last thing Val wanted was to open herself up to Lilly again. Before this morning, Val had convinced herself that what Lilly had done at Isaac's memorial was not only contemptible, but unforgivable. But now, face-to-face with her adversary, Val felt as though the very ground on which she stood was moving slowly, inevitably, like the shifting of tectonic plates. The steely disdain with which she'd armored herself gave way to an uncomfortable feeling of sympathy.

How was it possible, Val wondered, to simultaneously love and hate someone as much as she loved and hated Lilly? Marveling at how complicated their friendship was, Val shook her head—a gesture Lilly interpreted to be a clear message of rejection. She turned to go, wanting nothing more than a dignified exit. But the sticking door refused to open. After three futile tugs on the handle, she was forced to turn to Val for help.

Val smiled tentatively. "Looks like you'll have to stay awhile."

In the awkward moments that followed, every move was charged with meaning and potential misunderstanding. Val politely excused herself to get dressed . . . Lilly insisted she take her time. Val returned, offering to make breakfast . . . Lilly cordially accepted. Val graciously pulled out a chair for Lilly to sit . . . Lilly courteously thanked her.

When Jeff came downstairs he offered Lilly a cautious greeting—and Val a reassuring kiss—before beating a hasty retreat out the front door. It banged behind him, a reminder to both Lilly and Val that they were now truly alone together.

The kitchen quickly took on the homey smells of bacon frying, coffee brewing, and bread toasting. If Val stayed busy at the stove, she knew she could keep a safe distance from Lilly, who had strategically stationed herself at the table across the room. The strain between them was palpable; they ate in silence. By the time they'd finished their meal, Lilly couldn't take it anymore.

"Excuse me," she asked, "but do you want to talk, Val? I mean, really talk?"

"I'm not sure where to begin," Val answered hesitantly. She wiped some invisible crumbs into her napkin. "I'm afraid we'll just wind up where we always wind up. . . ."

"I know," Lilly nodded. "Unable to forgive, unable to forget."

"Well, maybe we're not meant to forget. But I guess we're old enough to learn to forgive."

Lilly let a moment go by before raising her hand in the air, the way a kid does when she wants to be called on in class. "Me first."

Before Val could respond, Lilly launched into a spontaneous monologue. "Okay. Here goes: I forgive you for having a happy life . . . for being better at math. For getting married and for having a good man who loves you." She took a deep breath. "Oh, and for always being the nice one, the smart one, the perfect one. For graduating from high school early . . . and going to college before me, even though I'm older." Her voice grew louder and more manic. "I forgive you for always knowing what you wanted and who you wanted to be. I forgive you for having a career that matters, that makes a difference in people's lives. I forgive you for being a goddamn genius!" she sputtered, her unplanned litany of compliments and complaints reaching breakneck speed. "I forgive you for always being tall and thin and never having to worry about what you eat. For making better macaroni and cheese than I do. For being so damn beautiful and never knowing it."

Val didn't know whether to be flattered or insulted. Strangely enough, none of Lilly's grandstanding surprised her. But what Lilly said next did.

"Val . . . I forgive you for being you. And—hard as it is—I forgive you for being my father's favorite daughter." Lilly lowered her gaze, catching herself in her own lie. "At least I'm trying to."

Lilly sat back, exhausted. But her eyes remained bright, and the expectant look on her face signaled she was ready to accept praise, if not applause.

Val responded by clearing plates from the table and pouring unneeded food into Lulu's bowl. When she ran out of busywork, Val leaned against the sink and turned to Lilly. "You've never really liked me, have you." It was a statement, not a question.

Lilly froze, indignant at having been misunderstood. "That's not true! I do like you, I always have." She closed her eyes, struggling to further explain herself. Flickering images of Isaac rose up before her: the father of her youth, all-knowing, almighty . . . and always unavailable. "I just couldn't stand that he loved you more," she said flatly.

Val couldn't argue with what she knew to be true: she had been the favored child. Still, she felt blamed. "But Lilly, it wasn't my fault," she argued.

"I know that, now. My father's the one to blame." Lilly pushed the hair off her forehead. "God, I could kill him . . . if he wasn't already dead."

The anguish in Lilly's voice pulled Val to her side.

"Oh, Lillypad," Val said, "you're breaking my heart." She placed a tentative hand on Lilly's shoulder. It was the first time in decades they'd touched. Lilly melted, letting herself lean into Val.

"We're in this together," Val whispered. "I mean . . . my mother was just as guilty as Isaac."

"So what are you saying, condemn a dead woman, too?"

Val smiled sadly. "You know, all this crazy drama would have been avoided if they'd just told us the truth from the beginning. What was the point of them keeping their damn secret, anyway?"

"Isn't it obvious? So my control-freak father could make sure nobody lived authentically. So your mother could stay dependent on him. So my mother could take the rap for everything that went wrong in their marriage. So your father could be less of a man than he was. So you could become a nerd. So I could feel worthless."

Valerie laughed hard, grateful for Lilly's irreverence. But in a moment she was serious again, recalling the days when her mother could do no more than recline on a couch in the darkened living room as Isaac tended to her, her father a specter in his own home. "Boy, did their little stew of deceit and repression and shame mess everyone up."

"They're fucked up. They're *all* fucked up." Lilly waved a dismissive hand.

"I appreciate the insight," Val said sardonically. "You're quite the student of human behavior."

"I'm serious, it's a conspiracy of lunatics!" Lilly ranted. "My mother, who claims to know my father better than any of us, says the letter's not about you at all—it's about her! She says it's my father's posthumous revenge for her 'many admirers', and for walking out on their marriage! She called it 'Isaac's last head trip, this time from the grave.'"

Val rolled her eyes. "I'm beginning to have more respect for your eloquent diagnosis. They *are* all fucked up."

"Of course, some more than others," Lilly barreled on, parsing the virtues and sins of their parents. "I mean, your mother may have been as big a liar as my father—but at least she tried to be a good parent to you. And let's not forget your father. Saint Arthur stayed the course, despite everything." With deep regret Lilly remembered her outlandish performance at Isaac's memorial service. "Val, I gotta tell you how ashamed I am for hurting your dad."

"I appreciate that," Val said, "but he's okay. He's a lot stronger than I ever knew."

A shadow of distrust crossed Lilly's face. "You don't have to say that. I know what I did."

"No, really, it's true. What happened at the service was awful, I won't deny that. But ultimately, it was good for us. Especially me. After years of judging my father—looking down on him for being passive and weak—I finally realized he's just loyal to a fault. He's a generous, loving man."

Lilly agreed. "You don't know how lucky you are, Val. Your father's the only one with any natural integrity in this whole bunch, and you've inherited this gift. All I inherited," she added ruefully, "was my father's singular talent for hurting people."

"That's not true," Val countered. "You're a good, good person,

Lilly." She paused, wondering if she dared say what was on her mind . . . and took the leap. "Do you think it's possible that Isaac was a good person, too?"

When Lilly looked confused, Val explained. "I know how hurt you were by his devotion to my mother and me. But maybe he believed he was doing the right thing. Maybe, in his own way, he was being honorable. And maybe, knowing that, you can feel better about him."

"Come on, he's been nothing but *dis*honorable. Especially to me. Don't you realize he wrote to you, and *only* you? Didn't it ever occur to the brilliant shrink that I would have feelings about this, too? No! As always, he treated me as if I didn't exist, as if I . . . " Lilly cut herself off, stamping her foot in frustration. "God, when will I get over this crap? Please tell me, how do I stop?"

It was a simple question . . . with no simple answer.

Lilly and Val both looked out the window, as if seeking a sign from the universe. They gazed past the snow-covered lawn, past the row of spindly white pines, and up toward a cloud-streaked sky.

It was several minutes before Val spoke. Her voice was soft. "I read somewhere that anger is the teacher . . . forgiveness the lesson."

Lilly rolled her eyes. "What five-dollar palm reader told you that?"

Val pointedly ignored her. "I just mean we have to accept our parents for who they are . . . and who they were. Forgive them for their mistakes."

"I can't," Lilly said. "It's impossible for me to forgive him. I'm not that evolved. I'm not that nice. I'm not . . . you."

A black-capped chickadee flitted past the window to the feeder, where a squirrel, greedily hoarding seeds, scolded the bird for invading its cache. The rivalry of the two creatures did not go unobserved by Lilly and Val.

"Look how much time we've lost hating each other because of him," Lilly said. "I'll never forgive him for that."

Val sighed. "I know. But there must be a way to find something good in all this." She paused, hesitant to say the one extraordinary thing neither of them had ever acknowledged . . . afraid to reveal the astonishing gift hidden so long in the darkness of a secret.

Lilly said it for her.

"We're sisters."

There was no parting of the seas, no sun breaking through the gray canopy of sky. But the truth, when it was finally spoken aloud, caressed them like spring's first warm breeze, as though a new world were born.

Postscript: 2003

Hi Sweetie,

I'm so relieved you're coming here this weekend.

I have such mixed feelings about commemorating this anniversary. The one-year mark brings back so many feelings I thought I'd gotten past. And there's a part of me that would rather not deal with this at all.

I've never been good at formal rituals. But I suppose you're right—we should do something to remember my father . . . I mean, your father . . . I mean, our father who art in heaven. Or wherever the hell he wound up. How about if we pop open another one of those expensive bottles he told me never to go near? Tell me what you feel like cooking and we'll make a great meal together.

Speaking of dinner, I have to run now. I'm meeting my mother, who claims to be "suffering greatly in the year since Isaac left me." Apparently, when you're as nuts as she is—and as histrionic—death is the ultimate infidelity. She's probably just mad he died first.

You know, I'll bet her "terrible anguish" is less about her grieving process than what happened the other night: some waitress thought she was her date's grandmother.

Love,

L.

. . . .

TO: **LSTONE**@dotnet.com
FROM: **VRUDMAN**@webworld.com
DATE: **FEBRUARY 12, 2003**
SUBJECT: **RE: HOW DID A YEAR GO BY?**

Given our insane family history, maybe the waitress was right!

But on a serious note, don't you think your mother's been strangely stoic and silent this whole year? She usually thrives on being in the spotlight of every family drama. Yet ever since Isaac's death, it seems like she's been hiding in the wings.

Or maybe I've just been so focused on myself lately that I haven't really thought about her that much. Now that I am, I feel for her. This whole situation could not have been easy.

Hey, Lilly, here's a radical idea: why not invite your mother to join us in memorializing Isaac? Dinner for three?

Val

....

TO: **VRUDMAN**@webworld.com
FROM: **LSTONE**@dotnet.com
DATE: **FEBRUARY 12, 2003**
SUBJECT: **DINNER FOR TWO, THANK YOU!**

Trust me, Katherine the Great will endure. She always finds her way back to center stage.

And you can bet she's planning to memorialize my father in her own special way.

Lilly

KISS
FREUD'S
ASS

A PASSION PLAY

WRITTEN AND DIRECTED
BY KATHERINE STONE

TO: **VRUDMAN@dotnet.com**
FROM: **LSTONE@webworld.com**
DATE: **APRIL 4, 2003**
SUBJECT: **DREAM INTERPRETATION?**

Val,

Put your psychiatric training to the test and interpret this dream, which I had last night, after reading the first reviews of my mother's play:

I was back in the audience for opening night. The curtain went up, and to my amazement, every single role was being played by YOUR *mother! She looked young and healthy and very sexy. The audience was going wild with applause, cheers, and standing ovations. But then I looked around me, and realized every single member of the audience was . . .* ISAAC*!!! I was drowning in a sea of my father.*

I woke up in a full–body sweat.

Lilly

....

TO: **LSTONE**@dotnet.com
FROM: **VRUDMAN**@webworld.com
DATE: **APRIL 5, 2003**
SUBJECT: **TRASH TALK!**

I've interpreted your dream . . . and my expert medical opinion is: you've completely lost your mind. (If it makes you feel any better, I've also recently had dreams about Isaac. But thank God there was just one of him.)

As for dreaming about my mother, I leave that job to my father. Bless his heart, he's valiantly keeping her memory alive. Remember his "secret" invention from a million years ago that I couldn't tell you about? Well, run out THIS MINUTE and get a copy of *Invention News Quarterly*. It'll blow your mind. Call me the second you're done reading.

I am so proud!

Val

....

INVENTION NEWS
QUARTERLY

SPRING 2003

THE SOUNDS OF SILENCE

By LAURA ALEXANDER

"It was my wife's greatest wish," explained inventor and retired high school science teacher Arthur Rudman, whose silent garbage truck has revolutionized the sanitation industry.

Rudman's late wife, Kitty, died two years ago after being housebound for more than 40 years.

Knowing that his wife's sleep was frequently disturbed by the noisy sounds of garbage collection in the early-morning hours, Rudman became determined to do something about it.

An avid inventor, he set his mind to revisiting several of his abandoned designs and expired patents. Over the years, Rudman was awarded more than 300 patents. In 1970 he unsuccessfully competed against NASA for patent rights for a hydraulic lift mechanism. While NASA edged him out of the playing field at that time, Rudman recently revamped his design, resulting in his current, phenomenal success: the world's first quiet garbage truck.

Citizens for a Quiet New York, a quality-of-life watchdog group, is enthusiastic about Rudman's accomplishment. "We believe this goes beyond waste management," the group's statement begins. "Arthur Rudman's contribution to urban life makes him a humanitarian hero."

Rudman is pleased by the attention his creation is attracting. "I've been working on this invention for more than 35 years," he said from his home in the Bronx. "I only wish my darling Kitty had lived to see her dream realized."

TO: VRDUMAN@webworld.com
FROM: LSTONE@dotnet.com
DATE: APRIL 6, 2003
SUBJECT: BETTER LATE THAN NEVER

Finally—your mother can truly rest in peace!!!

Kudos to Arthur. Tell your brilliant, amazing dad his next project should be inventing Mr. Right—for me. (He can start by cloning his own genes for unconditional love and devotion.)

Speaking of unconditional love, am I capable of it? I'd better be, because I just got a heads-up from Children's Dreams, the international adoption agency I told you about. They said they have a little girl for me. A little girl!!!! She's two months old. It's not definite yet, but the hope is I will be able to bring her home before the year is out.

I can't sleep or eat or think straight or work . . . or anything! I'm too excited.

But I'm also worried. I didn't exactly have great parental role models. And I'm practically half a century old.

Holy shit, I'm terrified. (Most of all, I'm terrified of having to stop cursing in front of the baby. . . .)

And, oh, Val, I'm so happy!

So much love,

Lilly

....

Lillypad, this is the best news in the world!! Remember our matching Tammy dolls? This baby will be even better and more adorable. (Oops, I just remembered, you tortured your Tammy doll . . . cut off her hair, drew on her face . . . never mind!)

Seriously, you're going to be a fabulous mother. A funny one, an original one—and yes, an old one! And also a totally perfectly amazing one.

As for your own lack of role models, what's the difference? Look how great you came out! This little girl will be loved by you, and by everybody who loves you, with unmatched clarity and passion. And even if you totally mess her up psychologically, who cares? This little Mini You will be so well dressed by Auntie Val that nobody will notice!

LILLY, I LOVE YOU FOREVER AND EVER!! AND I ALREADY LOVE MY GORGEOUS NIECE!

Val

. . . .

ValPal,

How about a little trip to China the last two weeks of June?

Lilly

P.S. Do you have a recipe for infant formula?

....

Lillypad,

Count me in. I was praying you'd ask for company! I can't wait to go goo-goo-gai pan over the baby!

Love,

Me

P.S. You take care of the bottles for baby, I'll take care of the bottles of bubbly. . . .

....

AN-MAI STONE EST ARRIVÉ!

MY BABY GIRL!

BOLD, ROUND, AND BEAUTIFUL

BORN FEBRUARY 21, 2003
IN ANHUI PROVINCE, CHINA
ADOPTIVE MOTHER LILLY
IS INTOXICATED
WITH JOY!

TO: LSTONE@dotnet.com
FROM: VRUDMAN@webworld.com
DATE: JULY 29, 2003
SUBJECT: AND BABY MAKES FIVE

Silly,

How would you and An-Mai like to come to Boston next weekend? I know it's short notice, but Jeff is desperate to meet our goddaughter, and I miss you both so much!

Plus—surprise!—Ben's flying in from Santa Fe. And he is desperate to meet up with you again! He says it's been way, way, way too long.

So how about it? Our treat, Jeff and I insist. Call us and we can coordinate dates and times. R.S.V. P. A.S.A.P. (but we won't take no for an answer).

Lots of love,

Auntie Val and Uncle Jeff

....

TO: **VRUDMAN**@webworld.com
FROM: **LSTONE**@dotnet.com
DATE: **JULY 30, 2003**
SUBJECT: **BOSTON BOUND**

I discussed it with An-Mai, and she responded to your invitation by drooling. (That's a definite "yes" in Baby Babble.)

I'm a little nervous about seeing Golden Boy—how many decades has it been? Do you think he'll still like me in my new, glorious state of maternal splendor (i.e., bleary-eyed, food-stained, and ravenously addicted to our old Recipe Club Peanut Butter Blondie Bars)?

At least tell me he's got a receding hairline . . . or gained 20 pounds . . . or got dumped by his latest gorgeous-skinny-Viking-or-Brazilian girlfriend . . . or is in some way less perfect than he used to be. . . . Oh, well. It'll be great to see him no matter what. And MORE than great to see you and Jeff.

Mama Lill

....

. . . lullabies and love songs! Val, answer the phone—I need to tell you something BIG!!! Last night, with Ben . . . I popped the question! Of course, the question I asked was, "How'd you like two groovy New York chicks to shack up with you for a month or two?"

A WHOLE MONTH OR TWO!!??? Since when did I get so casual about the commitment thing??? Since when did he??? Talk about getting my act together and taking it on the road! Jesus, Val, I'm so psyched—WHY AREN'T YOU HOME?????!!!! WHOO-HOO! An-Mai and I are moving in with Ben! (It's only temporary, of course—call it a Fall Fling.)

Buzz me pronto.

Lilly-in-Love

....

WERE SHE OLD ENOUGH TO SPEAK,

AN-MAI STONE

WOULD JOYFULLY INVITE YOU TO CELEBRATE

THE WEDDING OF HER MOTHER

LILLY STONE

to

BENJAMIN NATHANIEL GOLD

DATE & TIME: DECEMBER 27, 2003, 4:00 PM

PLACE: OUR HOME

784 CARROLITA STREET

SANTA FE, NEW MEXICO

R.S.V.P.: goldenboy@quicklink.net

TO: **GOLDENBOY@quicklink.net**
FROM: **VRUDMAN@webworld.net**
DATE: **NOVEMBER 16, 2003**
SUBJECT: **TABOO?**

First, the R.S.V.P.: Of course we'll be at your wedding! Wild horses couldn't keep us away. And now let's get this straight:

1. My cousin/fake brother is marrying my best friend/half-sister; which means

2. My cousin/fake brother is becoming my real/half-brother-in-law; which means

3. My most adored/adorable whole-goddaughter/half-niece is now a second cousin, which means

4. My best friend/half-sister is now my cousin-in-law!!!!

Hmmm . . . is this legal in all 50 states?

Kisses,

Val and Jeff

. . . .

TO: **VRUDMAN**@webworld.com
FROM: **LSTONE**@dotnet.com
DATE: **NOVEMBER 17, 2003**
SUBJECT: **BEST FRIEND/HALF-SISTER . . .**

. . . and a full business partner?

Valsky, how about you and I cater the reception together? It'll be a blast. We can cook all our favorite foods.

What do you say?

Love,

Lilly

. . . .

TO: **LSTONE**@dotnet.com
FROM: **VRUDMAN**@webworld.com
DATE: **NOVEMBER 18, 2003**
SUBJECT: **I SAY YES! YES! YES!**

LONG
LIVE
THE
RECIPE
CLUB

Ben & Lilly's

Wedding Dinner

TURKISH "CIGARETTES"
NEW YEAR'S EVE BLINI with CAVIAR
COZY PIGS IN BLANKETS
DIPLOMA DIP with VEGGIES
CHEERFUL SALMON CROQUETTES
GOOD KARMA VEGGIE SAMOSAS
POTATO LATKES with HOMEMADE APPLESAUCE
FORGIVENESS TAPENADE with TOAST POINTS

ITALIAN WEDDING SOUP

"REAL-LIFE" RED SNAPPER
with MISSING YOU WARMLY LENTIL SALAD

WILD DUCK with CHERRY ORCHARD SAUCE

GREEN-EYED GREEN BEANS

PEN-PAL PECAN RICE

CUPID'S CHOCOLATE CAKE

FIRST-KISS CARAMEL ALMOND KISSES

CHOCOLATE-DIPPED HEART COOKIES

CATERED WITH LOVE BY THE RECIPE CLUB

Recipe Index

Acknowledgments

You can't start a recipe club without a kitchen genie. Ours was the talented Melissa Clark, who—along with her able sous-chef, Sarah Huck—turned our ingredient wish lists and flavor profile concepts into approachable, delicious recipes. We thank them both for their sweet dispositions and savory explorations.

While most of our recipes were developed specifically for this book, a few were inspired by food we ate and loved in childhood. For these we thank Laura Garfinkel, Susan Israel, Stella King, Shirley Kraft, the late Grandmas Ella Karas and Lena Garfinkel, and the late Marguerite Joppich.

When we were creating *The Recipe Club*, we looked for a special designer who was as literate as he was imaginative, as pragmatic as he was whimsical and expressive. We found our perfect match in Gary Tooth of Empire Design Studio. Without Gary, our *beautiful* book would be just . . . a book. We thank him profusely for his creative brilliance, calming influence, and kind-hearted patience.

Profound gratitude to the remarkably generous Julie Schaper, who believed in our book and helped bring it into the world. You gave us a gift that changed our lives.

To our agent Carol Mann, you energized this project with your boundless enthusiasm and wise counsel, and we can never thank you enough.

And to Claire Wachtel and her terrific team at HarperCollins, we are so grateful to you for taking our book into the next chapter of its life.

To our Recipe Club groups, thank you for sharing deeply personal stories, original recipes, and unfailing support for our project.

To our many friends . . . what can we say? You are at the heart of this book about friendship. We hope you know how important you are to us. Special thanks to Irwin Epstein and Tom Woodruff, our knights in shining armor.

We want to express our endless gratitude to Laura, Ellen, Steven, and the late Al Garfinkel, and Susan, Bob, and Tony Israel, who cheered us on when we wanted to quit writing and Finally, our infinite loving appreciation to three amazing people and one friendly cat: Pamela Mitchell, Julian Mitchell-Israel, Harry Organek, and Kippy. You made this book possible . . . you make everything possible. We love you.